# Fastest Draw

## Gary Power

A MULESHOE BOOK

First published as an eBook by Muleshoe books 2015

Copyright © 2015 by Gary Power

Paperback first published 2016

A CIP catalogue record for this book is available from the British Library

Designed and Illustrated by Gary Power

Muleshoe Books Galway

ISBN: 978-0-9934079-9-4

*Dedicated to the memory of my mother and my brother*

Misfortunes one can endure—they come from outside, they are accidents. But to suffer for one's own faults—ah!—there is the sting of life.

*Oscar Wilde*

# 1 THE WRITER

GEORGIA, AUGUST 1932. Here I am, bowing up and down like a pick-swinging convict on the stage of the old Savannah theatre house. It's the last day of a lecture tour and hopefully the last lecture I'll ever have to give. I take my final bow, smile, do an about-turn, and walk out through purple curtains. The audience is still clapping as I reach the door of my dressing room, where I meet a sweaty young Scot named Davis. I had sent him away earlier to buy train tickets after deciding not to spend another night at the Desoto Hotel. Panting like a hunting dog, he immediately starts fussing about how I haven't given him time enough for the errands--he'd had to return to the hotel, too. "Yet here you are with tickets and valises clutched in your paws, Davis." I open the door and stand back to let him pass. "Are you a total stranger to spontaneity?" I add, for although competent he's the sort of fellow who requires regular, if not gentle, abuse.

"I'm no stranger to your whims, if that's what you mean, sir." He shuffles by me, shoulder scuffing the doorframe.

I quickly change, and we set off from the dressing room.

In the corridor outside my door I see an admirer I would prefer to avoid waiting for me in the lobby. His questions are complicated and probing, making his company less than desirable. So I make a quick exit by way of a back door. His clipped New England voice grates on me, too. I'm an old Southerner, and despite being known for my put-downs, all I want to do whenever I see him is run. And I can still see him, in my mind, dressed in his white suit and barbershop quartet hat, craning his neck above heads in the lobby, like an egret searching for frogs in a creek.

We leave for the station, through an alley, into the heat of the late afternoon, with Davis insisting we go back to call a cab. I suggest pressing on, saying "We'll hail one on the way."
Soon we come to a crossroads.

Across the street from us is a charity line that trails to the next block, its head snaking around a corner. The waiting men struggle to employ their hands, by folding and unfolding them, sticking them in pockets, or propping up a chin or wall. Crossing the street I spot my admirer again. He seems to be advancing in great strides toward the station by way of a street to my right. At a storefront, near the start of the line, I leave Davis until he can hail a cab, or until the eager devotee is gone.

The store lures me in. A bell alerts a storekeeper with a bulbous forehead and a bad comb over. He gives me a wan smile, then returns to his book. Behind him are poles bearing Confederate flags--a Bonnie Blue and a Stars and Bars. Display cases filled with coins, everything from doubloons to drachmas, are banked to his front. Shafts of sunlight stream through the windows and make motes of dust shine like fireflies. I see a giant butterfly mounted behind glass. A suit of armor stands behind a line of carved walrus tusks, making them look like ghoulish piano keys. Nearby, in a glass bell case, stands a flamingo bleached white by the sun. A sign reads, "Coins and Curios bought and sold." The flamingo has a fixed look of surprise, perhaps owing to the grizzly bear looming nearby.

Beside the armor a double-sided ax stands precariously against the wall. Next to the ax, and likewise threatened, is an antiquated globe set upon a wooden stand. It bears square looking continents and countries, their names written in creeping script. In place of latitude and longitude lines are bizarre sea monsters, as though they were nautical obstacles. I walk down a corridor lined with shelves displaying china and pistols. At the end I turn left. In a dark place, on a shelf, sits a baby orangutan with a scar beneath its left nipple, one hand held submissively behind its head. Beside it, beneath two crossed sabers mounted on the wall, is a rhino skull. My eyes are drawn into a dark socket to the honeycomb labyrinth within. Till a blaring car horn interrupts my gaze. Moments later, the bell over the door chimes and the thudding of unhurried footsteps echoes throughout the store.

"You can't come in here," says the storekeeper.

"I don't know any colored stores to bring it to, sir."

The storekeeper shuts his book. "All right. What is it?" Through the shelves I watch an old Negro hand him something.

"That is a silver dollar, celebrating a hundred years independence, sir. Given to me by the man who designed it."

"Wish I'd friends like that," replies the storekeeper with a trace of sarcasm.

"No sir," the Negro says quickly. "He were no friend of mine. Fact is, I hated him before I ever met him."

Through a magnifier the storekeeper peers at the coin. "There's a spelling mistake," he says with a smile. I can't tell if he's amused or senses a ruse, but what pricks my interest most is not the coin's legitimacy, or even how the old Negro has come to have it in his possession. It's how he could possibly have hated someone before ever meeting him. Davis chooses that moment to knock on the window and beckon me outside. He's flustered. It seems he's been accused of greedily waiting in the charity line for seconds. One man even suggested he had breadcrumbs in his moustache. Still distracted by the curious interaction in the shop, I let Davis lead me onwards, a mistake since he is hopeless at navigation, and we lose valuable time trying to find our way. It has grown dark by the time we see the two towers of Union Station.

A fat gray cloud rolls over us like a slab of stone over a tomb, and a downpour begins. We walk through the entrance and underneath the enormous, rain-hammered, echoing rotunda headed for the train platforms. The admirer is there, eyeing people boarding the trains like a tuberculosis inspector at Ellis Island. I quickly jump into a Jim Crow car on an Atlanta-bound train. "Sir, you're in the wrong coaches," a uniformed porter informs me.

"Sir, I am in the right place. I am part Negro. I would therefore ask you to kindly let me sit amongst my peers." It's a lie, of course--my face, suit, and long hair are all white as cream, unless you believe like Darwin that we all trace back to that ancient race. The colored porter backs off, raising his hat. Looking down the car, I see Davis, gesturing for me to get down. I assume he's telling me that he can't guarantee my safety amongst all the dangerous Negroes. Probably not his exact words, but surely the sentiment he means me to infer. There have been times when I believed the same myself. But I look around, at the old lady, a couple with three young children, and four tired-looking working men, and smile. *Dangerous*? Curious how fatigue makes you see the good in people and luxury inspires fear and a willingness to assume the worst. Well, perhaps I am tired, but to me these folks appear to be the finest ever created, and I am eager to make their acquaintance, or at least become good strangers with the egret. I make my way to Davis. "Don't worry, you can keep my money if anything happens to me."

"That's hardly what I want, sir." He replies with affront.

Davis hands me a Pullman ticket. I take it, but send him away with my valise. I'll find him later. I locate a seat, the whistle sounds, and the train creaks to a gentle roll, into the steamy ether, away from my obligations. As I listen to the clickety-clack of the wheels, the same porter trundles along behind a cart, saying, "Get you some coffee, ma'am, some sandwiches? Some coffee, sir?" With each refusal, the man simply responds with an, "Um-hum." A few seats ahead of me a familiar voice orders a coffee and the speaker, a man, begins to rummage in a pocket. As he pulls out a handkerchief, coins fall to the floor. I go over and pick them up, hoping to encounter a particular dollar coin, for it is the old Negro from the oddity shop, the one who'd been hawking his gift.

I look at the coins with interest as I scoop them into my palm, but they all appear to be of recent issuance. "You going to give them back?" the man asks, though without a trace of impatience in his voice.

"Yes. But would you be so kind as to buy an old man a coffee? I seem to have left my money elsewhere." The man is frowning at me now. I continue. "But what I really want, if you could please tell me, is to know how you've come to own a coin that never was."

Now old Negro's eyes narrow like nervous clams, he slaps a pocket, as if to make sure that his rarity is still contained therein and he appears to reach a decision. "I'll get you coffee ... That coin is real, all right. Weren't ever circulated, that's all." I sit down in the empty seat facing my benefactor. The vendor, his eyes averted, carefully pours us both a cupful. The old Negro pays, counting the change aloud and adding a small tip. The porter flashes lightning white teeth and touches his cap before trundling away.

"May I see it--the coin?" I ask. With exaggerated gravity the old Negro takes out a handkerchief, a different one from another pocket, unfolds it, and pushes it, along with the coin, across the table between us. I have a chance to study him as he does this. He's light-skinned, like the color of a brown paper bag. Aged at least eighty. A worn brown fedora sits on his head at a jaunty angle, the shoulders of his matching suit still darkly patched with rain. The long collars of his faded, yellowing gray shirt curl in like bat wings. His glasses are thick, magnifying brownish-green eyes that almost fill up the lenses; drooping eyelids bisect the tops of both irises in perfect arcs. His clothes are ordinary, dull even, except for his highly shined, tan and white, two-tone shoes. Somehow it all comes together.

Coloreds appear to have a knack for assembling such eccentric mismatches while still looking fashionable. Not that I judge a man by his outward appearance--I say this merely by way of observation, for I know my right eye is the biggest liar I've ever known and my left eye is the second. I pick up the coin and hold it up. "I'm no expert," I say quietly, "but I do know there was never any centenary silver dollar. Wasn't much anything celebratory in 1876, for that matter, after young Custer got his comeuppance. How d'you get it?"

He hooks his right arm to stretch it along the window. "From the man who do the picture for it back in '75." Wrapped around the portrait of George Washington, along the coin's circumference, it reads, *July 4th 1776 – 1876 CELLEBRATING ONE HUNDRED YEARS INDEPENDENCE.*

"And the spelling mistake?"

He shrugs. "His. The Secretary of the Treasury then got to thinking it wasn't such a good idea. I'm Abe Brown, by the way. Pleased to meet you."

He holds out a hand and I shake it while still looking at the coin. "Morton Sweetman. How do you do. I admit, I did hear you in the store ... earlier. I was in the back." Abe sighs with a mix of relief and disappointment. "I don't think it's possible to hate someone before you've ever met him. Though I can't say I've never been wrong." I look at him and smile.

"You wrong as can be," he laughs, "least about that anyhow." The rain has ended and the train wheels' hypnotic rhythm makes the humid car feel womb-like. Abe's eyes, apparently lost in recollection, gaze down at the coin.

I wait quietly, watching drips build before rolling down the window. Finally I can stand it no more. "And how did you meet him, this man who designed the coin?"

He picks up as if we've never paused. "I was back in Texas, looking for my momma, in 1875, she couldn't read and we'd lost touch. I'd sort of run off north, in '63, after my father got himself killed. He was an Irish overseer, you see, and she didn't want me taking up his old job, which the plantation owner wanted me to do. So she told me, 'Go north, son, keep praising the lord, and never look back.' I was never a slave," he says proudly, "because I lived after getting bit by a snake, as a baby child, and got given my freedom. I was free to go with the master's leave, but at that time I were afraid to. Because I had it good, cooking in the big house and getting fed in the finest cotton plantation in Gonzales, Texas. But that same night, after momma said go north, I found a slave stealing in the kitchen. He put a knife to my belly and says if I tell on him I'd end up under the apple tree--that's where all the dead slaves was buried. He just scared and then he calm down. I guess momma knew something I didn't. So after talking with him I go with him.

"First to New Orleans, where I got work on a Union riverboat. Then after Vicksburg fell I got taken all the way up to Camp Defiance, in Cairo, Illinois, where I cooked for the army boys before moving to D.C."

"Why did it take you so long to go back to Texas?"

"Bolinda, my wife, she didn't want me to. Argued about it for years. Of course, looking back, maybe the woman knew how bad it would turn out for me if I did go. Between been lynched and chased I passed through the gates of hell. But I don't tell folks about that no more," Abe says, shifting in his seat and pulling back a purple curtain so it rests fully behind his shoulder. "Wouldn't want them thinking I'm plumb crazy now, would I?" He laughs out loud, as if to offset this remark, though there isn't anything funny that I can see.

"Lynched? You look alive to me," *and with a full set of teeth to boot.* "They did a mighty poor job of it, I am glad to see," I say curiously as I look out the window and settle in for the ride. In the reflection of the glass I see Abe remove his glasses, then polish them using a wine-colored handkerchief before putting them in his front pocket. He draws a slow breath and begins his story.

# 2 ABE

IN 1875, after a month searching Texas, with no luck, I was heading home under an empty blue sky when I came upon trouble. Picture this: I'm sitting on top of a small hill, wearing no shirt as my hands is tied with it, behind my back. In front of me hangs a noose tied from the branch of the only tree around for miles. Just prairie grass, stones, and dust devils as far as the eye can see. Two men on horses are next to me, the Cruikshanks, dressed in black and white, with black hats like Quakers or bible salesmen. They ain't neither, and the only thing they selling is death.

The oldest called Simon. He's got short black hair and a skinny neck. He skinny all over. If he took his shirt off you could count up his ribs like washboard grooves. His eyes are almost black, like a prairie dog's. "You best make your peace with God now, boy."

"If you going to kill me," I say, "how comes you don't shoot me?"

"Sorry, but we got to take you in dead. Only got a few bullets left and there's rogue Injuns near abouts."

I tell them they're making a mistake, that I've done nothing wrong. His brother Peter takes out a poster and reads out, "'Abraham Brown, wanted dead or alive for horse stealing and murder.' Says you got a snakebite on your left wrist." All these years later, that snake is still trying to kill me.

"I don't got no bite mark on my left wrist, it's on my right one."

"That'll do," says Peter.

Then Simon's cheeks ball up in a grin and he tells me the horse I'm on belonged to Roger Symmes, a tax collector, that it has his brand.

"Sure it do, I bought it off him. Got a letter that says so."

"You prolly got it from him before killing him," says Simon, his grin melting off his face like a lump of fat sliding across a hot skillet.

Peter was the younger one, I reckon, friendly-looking, kept on blinking real slow, like a lizard trying to keep his eyeballs wet in the sun. His mouth always seemed open, too, like he'd forgotten to close it after the last time he eat. He can see I'm having a hard time with being hanged, so he holds up the wanted poster to my face.

I tell you, that was one of the angriest moments of my whole life. I'm drawn black as stove polish, as black as the Gold Dust Twins, if you've seen them, only more ugly, with big thick lips.

"That ain't me!" I say, "Why, that's the blackest nigger I ever seen. I'm mulatto--and look, it shows me running with a pig in my arms. Where's the horse?"

"Maybe the artist couldn't fit a horse in the picture." Simon says. "But a thief is a thief--pig or horse, it don't matter."

"Yep, don't matter," says Pete.

"Look how my eyes is done, coming outta my head like that. They ain't half that big," I say, getting desperate.

"You're 'fessing," Peter says, "because you said 'look how *my eyes* is done'."

Simon smiles at his brother's thinking, smiles like a happy skull, because his skin thin as writing paper.

I don't know why I do it, but I lean over and bite that poster with my teeth. Peter pulls it back, leaving a fist-size hole in the poster where my face used to be. They don't like that, but say nothing. They just go to either side of me and ask if I want to pray. I do. I say, "Lord, save these men here from the lake of fire, for killing me, an innocent man."

That ruffles Simon for a second, like a wind blowing on a buzzard raises up the feathers till you see pink skin. But he shakes it off and puts a noose made of new-smelling hemp rope on my neck and tightens it. "Don't you worry where we're headed, boy. We've authority from the state of Texas, and that means God himself." Says Simon, he smiles but looks nervous, too, like maybe I'm telling the truth. For some reason they tarry.

My horse's skin is quiverin', he's got a ginger colored fly biting his neck, right near a vein. He shakes his head, and hair from his mane wafts down over the fly, but the fly, it stays.

My horse snorts then bobs his head up and down and moves a step forward. It's the distance between living and dying for me, because now I can feel the rope gripping my throat and my eyes starting to pop. And while I'm there dying I'm thinking, *Lord, I hate that wanted poster.* Even if my eyes is starting to look like what's drawn on it.

It's the first time I heard of Luke Sprague, the sketch artist, and I hated him for it.

He'd even drawn a little cameo of his face in the bottom corner of that poster, for advertising his business, making him look all fine, and signed beneath it: "Luke Sprague, The Fastest Draw, Austin Texas."

I'm getting dizzy now, knowing I'll soon be dead. Till these two moving shapes appear in the shimmering heat. They were the Johnson brothers, Daryl and Marvin, both with beards, riding horses caked in filth. They come up the hill we on, stopping about twenty feet away. "What you hanging him for?" Marvin says, blowing snot out his nose like that's all I'm worth. He's stocky, with massive forearms and a buffalo-hide waistcoat, with the hair on the outside smoothed flat like wet fur. He wipes his hand on it, like you would before picking up a piece of fruit, and while he doing that he's looking at me. His eyes are small, close together, and pale blue--robin's egg blue, even under the shade of his soiled brown hat. Beneath the dirt on his face his skin could be ivory white.

Simon says, "He's wanted dead or alive. We're decided on dead."

There's nothing to stop my horse moving again, only the boot heels that I'm squeezing tight against his belly. With my hands behind my back the reins was useless. I'm seconds away from hanging and my horse about to move again, I just know it. The rope bites into my neck till my Adam's apple feels like it's turning to juice. The Johnsons come forward a step. I gag from the smell of whiskey and filthy horseflesh coming from them. But my horse moves back, so I get to breathe again. Marvin Johnson looks at the Cruikshanks. "Why don't you shoot him?"

"Because they near out of bullets," I gasp.

Daryl Johnson whips out his guns and says to his brother, "Something's wrong." Then to the Cruikshanks, "We'll take him in alive."

Daryl has a red nose, like a little ball with purple veins in it, but not red from the sun, I think, as the brim of his sweaty brown hat is wide. And though his shoulders are narrower than his brother's, he ain't skinny. For he looks like he's another bigger ball underneath his shirt where his belly is, hanging over his pants like a pregnant woman's. His skin is red and flaky white under his beard, like he only has hair on his chin because he dare not shave.

Daryl's dark blue eyes is sad-looking, too, like on a dog that's got mange.

Simon Cruikshank smiles so big his eyes go to slits. "Wait now, hold on, I think you two are Whistling Bob Johnson's brothers. You stop us earning money here, well, we'll have to go earn it elsewhere, now won't we? But, tell you what, we'll split the money with you. That's fifty dollars four ways, you don't want to make us vexed, that's what this boy here done." Simon quickly moves his horse up beside them, trying to stare them down.

"Sirs," I say to the Johnsons, "the reward for me is five hundred dollars." Simon turns his horse, comes right up to my face, and cusses me. Marvin looks a little concerned about the justice of it all, but Daryl looks like he has no budge in him at all. I keep talking. "Please, sirs," I say, "I got a letter saying I owns this horse, I'm down here looking for my momma, and I--"

Daryl scratches his face. "I don't care nothing about all that shit. Where's this nigger's wanted poster?" Peter hands him the wanted poster. Daryl wants to know why there's a hole in it.

Peter says, "He bit it."

Marvin Johnson reads out, "Abraham Brown." He grabs the poster, balls it up, and stuffs it in my mouth. "He can eat the rest, too. The sheriff will have another."

The Johnsons relieve the Cruikshanks of their guns, take the noose off my neck, and, holding my reins, they start on down the hill.

We've not gone twenty feet when I hear shots. Marvin falls off his horse and lays shivering on the ground like a newborn calf in a storm. Daryl don't move, checking to see if he's all right.

As the Cruikshanks gallop away I see Peter has a derringer in his hand. Seconds later, Marvin gets up. The bullets haven't pierced him. He shakes his arms and body then points a gun at me. "Don't move from where you is at." He mounts up and they ride after the Cruikshanks.

I don't tarry. I spurs my horse and I go. But I've no hat now, my hair is short, the sun is baking my scalp, and my hands is still bound behind me. I look up at the sky, which looks like a crystal blue sea; small black dots cut slowfully along on waves of hot air. I start thinking, *If the bounty hunters don't come after me, I'll just finish up in one of those flying bellies anyhow.*

I ride for I don't know how long till I hear the sound of wheels and hooves.

A stagecoach appears from the shimmering heat waves. It slows down and swerves before me. A picture of a big-eyed-girl having knives thrown at her jostles on its side. It comes to a stop in a cloud of dust. Fancy cream lettering on the side of the coach reads, "The Great Punjabi." From out of the dust steps a man of about forty, wearing a collarless shirt that goes all the way to his feet. He's white, but dark skinned, with brown, surprised looking eyes below large wrinkling eyebrows.

I lean back, swing up a leg, and fall down off my horse. I get on my knees then stand up and spit out the wanted poster.

He sees my hands and takes out a knife. I ask him to loosen my bonds, not cut them, because I still need my shirt.

"Maybe I shouldn't interfere with your destiny," he laughs, with a voice like I've never heard before.

"Destiny!" I say, thinking, *What you talking about? I'm dying out here, what more needs saying?*

He tries to loosen my shirt but fails so he cuts it and ruins it. He goes and gets me a water canteen and, as I drink from it, he picks up the spat-out poster. "Abraham Brown--is this you?" he says in a high-toned English voice, putting his finger through the hole in my face and laughing. Then he must see the little cameo for he says, "Luke Sprague the Fastest Draw," saying it like he don't care for the man.

"You know him?"

"I went round the last town to avoid him." It is strange, because he is sounding Irish now, and I'm thinking, *He's not on the right side of the law either.*

"Which town?" I say.

"Austin, five miles back," he says, his eyebrows arching up like skunk tails. As I'm looking back towards Austin, I'm thinking *I don't want to avoid it,* for I reckon Luke Sprague wouldn't know me, even if he's looking right at me. Maybe I could go to the sheriff in Austin, to see what sort of man he is and get right with the law. Before I go, the man gives me a shirt that kind of looks like a woman's. I frown at it. "It's French," he says, and he throws me a towel for my head, because he sees I've no hat, and he rides away.

20

I go on.

Soon as I reach Austin I ask around for Luke Sprague, but most people don't know who he is. I see the Johnson brothers there, too, talking with an old woman sat on an uncovered wagon wearing a blue dress and a blue bonnet, but they don't see me. Someone told me Luke worked at the telegraph office, so I go there and inside I see a man working. I ask him if he's Luke Sprague, even though I know he ain't. "No." He replies, "I'm replacing him, though, on the telegraphs."

The man staring at me has a forehead that slopes back to a shiny balding head, like on the big end of a boiled egg laying on its side. He's double-chinned, with eyes small and wide spaced, like on a catfish. His moustache, for he has one, is waxed into long points and his lips is pouty, and it seems silly saying this but them lips is fishy looking. He looks at me like a Texan would, like maybe I might be dangerous, but even if I am, it don't matter, because he's dangerous, too. So he won't find me so strange to behold I pull off the towel I'd wrapped around my head and tell him I lost my hat. His face stays the same, just sizing me up, but not pushing me out either.

I look around the office.

On an empty desk lay a *Harper's Weekly* magazine, with a picture of an Irishman, a Negro, and an Anglo on the front page. The Negro looks ugly and the Irishman is drawn the same, only white. The Anglo, now he drawn real handsome, like the way Luke drew himself. Pictures of Luke are there, too, in a folder and spread out along the desk.

In the front window are normal drawings, but on the walls are posters of criminals, killers, and Mexican banditos, all drawn looking ugly and evil. One man called "Chopstick Chinaman Wong," don't know why, maybe he a pickpocket and used sticks to take people's wallets.

And there is a picture of "Gavin O'Neill, The Thieving Irish Bastard," looking like the man who cut my bonds.

Then I see a picture and it's of me.

The desk is worn on top from a man's boots. So he was lazy on top of everything else. On his desk, beside a telegraph machine, sits a phrenology skull that wears a slight grin, like it don't have a care in the world as it stares out onto Austin's streets.

21

I talk a little more to the catfish-man, who tells me Luke is gone off buying a hat, and he don't know when he'll be back. "What do you want of him?" he says, slicking a hand over his sweating head. "You need that towel?" I hand it to him. He pats his head with it. "If you need a drawing done, go to the Negro preacher out in Nineveh." This was a small settlement about ten miles away. He said it politely, and I leave him, thinking, *That's what I'm going to do.*

When I step outside and the door slams the sun hits me.

I remember the towel, but I don't want to go back for it now. So I walk down the shaded side of the street looking through windows.

While later and I'm walking into a drapery store. An old storekeeper is there talking to a man preening himself in a mirror. "Just in from England, sir."

"Where else would it be *just in from*? Your store is called London Gentleman."

It's him.

I go over to him and say, "You Mister Luke Sprague?"

"Yep."

He barely looks at me.

I show him the wanted poster. "You draw this?"

"Draw what? It's a hole."

He removes the hat he trying on and looks at me. To look at, he's not an unhandsome man, but his eyes are dark and odd, like even when they is looking at you they looking past you. When he smiles he only do it with his mouth because his eyes stay the same and, even though he a young man, he has crow's feet round his eyes, but not from the sun. His chin has a dimple on it and his hair is fair, spiky, and neat. He dressed differently to most folks, too, wearing city boots and city clothes.

I say, "But it's you. Ain't it, the 'Fastest Draw'?"

"Already told you I am."

He hands me a coin with a Mexican general on it, then he looks back at the mirror like we done talking. I hold up the coin, wanting to throw it at the mirror to get him to pay me some mind. Something breaks, all right, but it's not me doing the breaking. BANG! A shotgun blast smashes a store window, spraying glass over the floor like a sudden hail shower.

Luke panics, and the storekeeper jumps behind a tailor's dummy. He runs--or limps, I should say, because he has a bad one--outside the store. "He's in there," he says, pointing back towards me. The Johnson brothers are hiding behind barrels across the street, in front of a haberdashery. They fire and duck.

Bullets strike the ground near Luke. He stands there looking stupefied. They could easily kill him, but it's like they afraid of him.

Luke's mouth drops open as he cottons on to the fact they're shooting at him, not me. He runs back into the store and asks the keeper, "You got a gun?" Keeper shakes his head. He confronts me with the same question, and I shakes my head, too. It's said, where the carcass lies vultures will gather. Soon, what with the shooting, the Cruikshanks appear. The Johnsons fire at them, and Luke taps me on the head. "You got a horse?"

"Yeah, out front, where that shooting is at."

Outside at the back of the store there's a horse tied up. Luke jerks his head towards the back. "Can you steal that one, too? You're for hanging anyways."

"I ain't stole nothing," I say. Though pretty soon the men out front would stop shooting at each other ... start thinking about me again. So we run out back, get on the horse, and ride away.

After a few miles I stop when I see a river shaded about by mesquite trees. Seeing no one behind us, I get down and head for the water. As I begin to splash my head, Luke asks, "Why were they shooting at us?" I tell him what happened to me with the Cruikshanks and Johnsons, how I'd seen the Johnsons earlier talking to a woman in a blue dress. "She wearing a tight blue bonnet and a little stooped?"

"Yeah." I say. He tells me she'd come into his office earlier that day, wanting a drawing made from a photo of her dead son, even asked Luke if he'd drawn any pictures of himself because she didn't want her son looking like one of his rogues' gallery. He knew of the Johnson brothers. They were soup bone merchants buying and selling bones and hides around Austin, not real bounty hunters, except on occasion. Her real reason for wanting to see Luke's portraits is something we'd find out later. Women not only have more spite than men, they good at vengeance, too.

I see Luke's reflection rippling in the river.

He's standing behind me, not moving. He suddenly slaps his thighs all angry. At the store he'd been in the middle of breaking fifty dollars he'd got in the bank that morning, now that's where his money is.

"I'll get myself in trouble for this horse, too," I say. "Got to get out of Texas."

"Well, they can't hang you twice. Why are you down here anyway? Haven't they got horses need stealin' where you're from?"

"I'm searching for my family, and yeah, they got horses in Maryland."

His cheeks are balled up like a sneering squirrel's. They drop and his eyes get big as his face goes from mocking to kind.

I say, "How comes you draw me black as the ace of spades?"

He looks at me like he don't understand. "Why does it matter? It's just a map to help people. Anyway, that's not important. What is, is that I got a five hundred dollar prize waiting for me in Washington D.C. If you can get me there, I'll give you a hundred and fifty dollars."

"So how comes you'd need me, if you ain't done nothing wrong? Get the sheriff to help you."

Looking back towards Austin he tells me there's no sheriff. "They're only stringing a useless man along on deputy's wages till he quits or dies." Luke was from near San Antonio. He'd kin there but couldn't go back, not like this, being chased out of Austin, and he pressed for time as it is. He stays quiet a while then he stares at me. "You are quite yellow."

I don't know what to say, so I say, "Yeah."

He keeps staring at me, till it gets under my skin. I shivers and rolls my head, but he keeps staring.

"Well, what are you?"

"How do you mean, what am I?"

"You mulatto, quadroon?"

I scrunches my face up and lowers my head, so that he'll know I ain't comfortable, but his eyes don't move.

"Mulatto."

"The other half Irish?"

"Yeah. How did you know?"

"You're light-skinned, but mostly Negroid."

"That so," I say, and I look around so maybe he'll start fearing about the men we still running from and stop giving me all this attention.

He says, "How do you figure on getting to D.C.?"

"Go south until I hit the road from San Antone to Galveston. Then get a ship to New Orleans. Then get a train on up. The river makes the trains cheaper and there's no Indians on the sea."

Luke squints his eyes and holding out a hand, walks up to me. "All right, it's a deal."

"I'd do better on my own, thank you." I turn and walk towards the horse, leaving his hand nothing but the wind for shaking.

"Slow your boots, my good Negro. I think we got two lots of gunmen after us. I'm sure there's one lot after me and both lots is after you. If we hold together they might shoot each other; they'll surely slow each other down. If we part so will they, and it's a whole pile of money for traveling where you're going anyhow." I think on it, and it makes sense. I walk back, spit in my hand, and we shake on it. I let go his hand and he starts wiping it on his shirt, stopping, with a nervy grin, when he sees me looking.

I say, "How comes you put your picture on my wanted poster? Maybe that ain't wise?"

"Well, that's where you're wrong, my feathered friend. It is clever. That advertising has gotten me picked to do a portrait of George Washington for the centenary silver dollar."

"No. I mean someone might not like how they is drawn. How comes you is called 'Fastest Draw' anyhow? Is you a gunslinger?"

He shakes his head. "Well, no, I'm only an artist. And I could stand here talking, but I think we need to move."

He looks around wary eyed.

"Sure ... I ain't stopping us." I get up on the horse, I help him up, and we go on.

# 3 THE ARTIST

B UZZARDS ARE flying in a circle above us. I'm wondering if they the same ones from earlier, following me all along, and maybe feeling cheated out of a meal now. "Things are changed, birds. I need my flesh after all. You'd be welcome to it otherwise," I say, forgetful that Luke was even there.

When I a boy, about seven, a blind preacher came to dinner one time. Momma told me before he got there, "Abraham, you better not grab no food now, you hear. He the guest and got to be fed first." It was chicken. We hardly ever had chicken. That preacher kept talking on about Jesus, filling his belly, and momma kept listening, forgetting all about me, kept giving him more and more till I started to cry.

"What's the matter, little man? Is you scared of going to hell?" he says, because he'd been talking about it.

I say, "No, I is scared you going eat all that chicken."

The preacher laughed and offered me the last piece, a half-eaten leg with big teeth marks in it. "No," I say. "My momma promised me a whole piece."

I got a spanking after he'd gone, and whenever he came preaching after that, to me he just the man who did me out of some chicken. So I knows how the buzzards is feeling being cheated out of a meal because, to them, I was probably like chicken.

A little bit later I start singing:
"Miss Caroline Gal. Yes ma'am.
Do you see them buzzards? Yes ma'am.
Do you see them flopping? Yes ma'am.
How do you see them? Mighty well.
Miss Caroline Gal. Yes ma'am.
Do you see them buzzards? Yes ma'am."

Luke asked me to stop, because it was upsetting him, so I did. He seemed to be the only white man I ever met who didn't like to hear a colored man sing.

There'd been a breeze, but it died again. It's like the sun still heating up when it ought to be cooling down, as shadows from the trees started getting long. Up ahead something is coming towards us. It's an old Chinaman and a young woman on a laundry wagon. As they come close, Luke gets down and stops them. "Got any water, Mr. Chinaman, sir?" The Chinaman has two silver metal balls in his hand that he keeps rolling about. I see my face in one and Luke's face in the other, and he keeps rolling them in a circle over and over.

The Chinaman looks confused so Luke pretends like he's drinking. He turns back, into his wagon, and gets Luke a water bottle and me a straw hat, a Chinaman hat, because he sees my head is burning. Luke drinks and gives me the bottle then offers them a coin, but the man don't want it. So that the man won't move on, Luke holds up a finger as he takes out a sheet of paper from his jacket, resting it against the wagon, and with a piece of charcoal, in less than a minute, I'd say, he makes a drawing. The picture shows the Chinaman with buckteeth, slanting eyes, and a ponytail, even though he don't got one. He draws his daughter, or whoever she is, the same way, even though she pretty. The drawing is good, but also it's like one of them posters advertising that Chinamen be put on a boat back to China, if you can remembers them Yellow Peril pictures. Luke gives it to the Chinaman, who don't like it and hands it back.

"No, it's for the water," says Luke. The man elbows the woman and she cracks the reins. As the hooves and wheels move we stare after them, watching dust clouds come up and blow over the grassy desert. When the wagon nearly gone, Luke says, "Remember you were singing about buzzards."

"Yeah."

"I hear buzzards will feast on a dead Negro or white man, but won't touch a Mexican."

"What about a Chinaman?"

"That's a good question, Abe, and to be honest, I don't know the answer." We wait till the wagon has disappeared altogether then we get riding again along a dried mud trail. Luke keeps resting his hands on my shoulders, I tell him not to.

"Were you a slave before?"

"No, I just don't want you touchin' me, that's all." So he holds his arms out for balance like he's trying to walk along a snake rail fence. A little further on Luke taps me to stop, so I stop and he gets down to take a piss. Ahead of us the trail forks--one way is used and broad, the other is narrow. I ask him which path we should take.

"I don't know, but let's do it fair, shall we." He points to the trails and says, "Eeny meena mina mo, catch a--"

"Don't say it, don't say nigger. I've heard that enough for one day, thank you."

"I didn't say it."

"No, but you was going to."

"I were going to say, catch a Negro by the toe. I didn't know you're so easily offended." He stares at me then starts looking up at the sun, squinting his eyes, pulling his hat down for a bit then looking up again. He turns to me. "Do you think a Chinaman doesn't like being called a Chinaman then?"

"I don't know, Luke. He a man, he from China, ain't he? How could he mind? Nothing more needs to be said on the matter. Fact is, it probably comes from how bad their English be. They don't say, 'I'm from Ireland' or something like that. It's, 'I man from China, I Chinaman.' It's their own fault they called that so can't be angry about it."

"Maybe you're right. Where do you think 'nigger' comes from?"

"You see, I asks you to not say it and you go right ahead and you do."

"It wasn't right ahead, it only in the natural way of talking I said it. You brought it up in the first place. Hell, what's wrong with 'nigger' anyway?"

"Abolitionists say it just another way to keep the Negro down."

"Abolitionists! You're not slaves anymore. Haven't they got better things to do?" He looks at the sun again with pain in his eyes. "Hell, it's like forbidden fruit now."

"Abe will do fine. I calls you Luke, don't I?"

"I'd prefer Mister Sprague."

"I'd prefer Mister Brown."

"How you are in Texas and alive is a mystery to me."

"I think we need to go."

"Yeah, we do." After about an hour we come upon a rattlesnake, curled up atop a rock, hissing at us. As I pass it slowly the snake's rattle is moving like a hummingbird's wings. Then I see behind us in the distance, like ghosts being called up by it, two distant specs — riders, each one in his own ball of dust.

I spur the horse and we go down a hill.

The area is covered with cottonwoods and we come to a shallow stone-bedded river. I gallop into it and ride with its flow. When it comes time to leave the river, I'm so busy looking back I don't see what's before us. And that's when we stumbles right into them, the Rangers that is.

# 4 RANGERS

THE TRAIN trundles on past a rolling landscape of fields and forests. Abe jumps a little then reaches out for the coin. He pulls it back, folds the handkerchief carefully, and returns it safely to his pocket. "What brings you to Savannah?" he says.

"A speaking engagement."

"Sounds important."

"No. It's a cursed business. If it's not liked on the first day you get recrucified every day of the tour until it's over, with no time really to change it."

"How come you don't quit?"

"Money. My brother got me to invest in several businesses in Florida a few years back. They all folded and dived like pelicans into the big blue ocean." Abe looks perplexed. "The crash ... It nearly bankrupted me, though I'm almost afloat again, thankfully."

"You talk funny."

"I am a writer. Never mind the fact I haven't published anything in years. It's why the lectures. The bank was going to take my house, and my wife won't move to a lesser abode."

Outside my window tiny shotgun shacks stream slowly towards me, ballooning into mansions before vanishing like waves hitting a ship's prow.

"She fussy?"

"No. Old with high standards."

Abe smiles wryly. "When pelicans dive, don't they usually come up with something?"

"Not these ones. I sold 'em."

"Flown south for the winter." Abe laughs swatting a hand. "I'll say no more, them birds is gone."

"As good as."

He squints at me. "You sound white, an' you look white. What you doing here?"

"Not white enough for the white coaches, or black enough for here. I've only a thimble's worth of Negro blood in me."

"That all anyone here has got, a thimbleful. Or their mommas did anyhow. Hee-hee ... Lord forgive me, I shouldn't say that."

"It's all right."

"Where you from?"

"Florida ... Tallahassee ... You ran into Rangers?"

I see him now, as he squats down on the ground--Captain Levi Wilson, that is. Though he's not tall or strong, just a normal size like me, he's the biggest toad in the puddle. His eyes are dark, like looking at a lit match falling down a well till it goes out; they big looking, too, because he has something black rubbed all over the eyelids like crazy war paint. His hat and jacket are as dark as his eyes, and his hair is tangled, greasy, and long. There about a dozen Rangers, all told, and they all point their guns at us, all but him. They tell us to put our arms up and we do. They ask why we're rushing the horse because its mouth's foaming.

"Because we in a river, sirs," I say.

A Ranger asks Luke why his hands were in the air already. "Well, he don't like being touched," he says, meaning me.

"Maybe he was a slave before," says another.

"No way. He was never a slave, he told me so." Says Luke.

"No, I a slave. It just I treated so fine by master, it didn't never really feel like it."

A gun is pointed right in my face by a Ranger named Billy. He's about thirty, ginger haired, with a big round head like a pumpkin, and his chin so big his barber could rightly charge him more than other folks. He has sunken brown eyes and bushy eyebrows that look like desert grass bleached by the sun. The gun cocks. "If you're no Chinaman, what in God's name you wearing a Chinaman hat for?"

I don't need to answer, for I see a man stirring. He's about forty, forty-five. He looks me up and down, stroking his little beard. He stands up, holds his hands out flat, and the Rangers lower their guns. He walks towards us rolling his head, shrugging his shoulders. He's skinny, but all muscle, with shoulders bunched up like a weasel's. His first words to me are, "Maybe master so kind because he fathered you. You're quite light complected. Why don't you want to be touched?"

"Got sunburn, boss."

"Call me Captain."

"Doff your hat, boy, when the captain is speaking to you," Billy says, and I do.

"Settle down, Bill. How d'you get sunburn?"

I lie. "Fell asleep in the sun, Cap'n."

"Where you boys headed?"

Luke says, "Washington D.C."

"A black and a white on one horse going to D.C. The captain turns away, puts his hands on his hips, and laughs. I shwear it, boys, that's the craziest answer ever heard."

The captain spoke with a lisp sometimes because two of his bottom teeth were gone.

Luke says, "We're catching a boat at Galveston."

Even though he has lowered his gun, Billy is still staring at me with his eyebrows spiking up like the hair on an angry dog's neck. He says, "What kind of shirt you got on there?"

I shake my head. "French, I think."

His eyes are full of pain as they look at my shirt, and those eyes is saying, *Something's wrong with these two.* The captain sees his face. "Injun Dave, the fugitive list." A native scout, wearing an old gray officer's coat and three eagle feathers at the back of his head, walks off. He comes back and hands a paper to the captain. The scout stares at us all, proud of himself, as the captain eyes the list. "Nope ... no niggers for one. Don't think you is on it, either of you." I relax, but maybe he's playing with us, so I don't relax too much--in case he'll notice and tighten the drawstrings I can feel around my chest like my heart and lungs are in a bag. Though with the near lynching from before maybe I'm only dreaming things up. The captain rolls up the list and starts slapping his palm with it. "Course this one's old. We're waiting on a new one."

"Well," Luke says, "if you are going to Galveston we can accompany you." He is acting like we free to go. He jumps off the horse, without leave, and starts limping and stretching like the outdoors his very own living quarters. Texas will do that to a man. But as I look around at the other eyes I can see they don't like what he's doing, and amongst those eyes are the darkly colored ones of the captain.

"Galveston--that's on our rounds. What you boys do?"

"I'm an artist, he's a--"

"Cook. I'm a cook," I say.

"A cook! Well, we need one of them ... You may be a talented man, but an artist is as useless to us as a runt sucking on a dead sow's tit. Right then ... You, the gimpy fellow, go brush the horses. If you don't work you don't eat off of us. Less you want us to make you prisoners. Why then we'll feed you for free."

34

He smiles like it's an offer; that our silence says neither of us wants. Then the captain looks our horse over. "You've no provisions, no blankets." He looks closely at the water canteen around Luke's neck. "That's a strange-looking bottle."

"Well, I believe it is from China, sir." The captain purses his lips as if he's saying, *Do tell*, but he don't say it. "We're trusting in providence till we reach Galveston. We'll stock up there."

The captain laughs. "Maybe providence sent you to me."

"Maybe," says Luke. "My name is Gary Johnson, his is Dick Green."

"Don't rightly care what you say your names are, boys, because I think you're lying, both of you. Got anything to show me you're not?" We both say nothing. He closes one eye like he's aiming at us. "Guess you don't. I'm Captain Levi Wilson, of the Texas Rangers, stationed in Corpus Christi. There's a brush by yonder wagon. Sweet potatoes, a calf's heart, and liver there for eating, pots and pans, and so on. We're going for a dip." The Captain looks towards the river. "Be back here inside the hour. You're not Chang and Eng so you don't need to be riding one horse neither. Got us a spare." He nods his head towards a hill beyond the wagon. "Took him off an Injun we was chasing, this morning. Made a good one out of him, didn't we boys?"

Some Rangers laugh at the gallows humor. Luke laughs, too, and says, "Good. My companion here is grateful."

"But--" I say, and that's all I say, because Luke cut over my words.

"Like I said, he's grateful."

"Damn it," the captain says, "let the Negro talk."

"This here's my horse, Cap'n," I say, for I don't want no wild Indian's horse. Just because an Indian can ride it don't mean anyone else can. Luke's eyebrows wrinkle and the centers of his eyes pop open like when you're skipping stones over still water-- he's angry but trying not to show it.

"You," the captain says to Luke, "the gimpy one, take the Injun's horse. It's white with gray spots, saddle blanket ... you won't miss it."

The captain eyes us for a moment then walks off with his band to a place where the river is lazy, bent like a horseshoe into a pool, away from the strong flow.

We walk over to the wagon. Luke picks a sweet potato from it and sniffs it like it's a rotten egg. "Why, were you sunning yourself?"

"I weren't sunning myself. I had no shirt on me when them men was trying to lynch me."

"Can't I go an' be cook, after you lumping me with some crazy horse?" I hear laughing and splashing down at the river.

"No, Luke, I'm the cook."

"But my leg ... Come on, help me out with those horses. Look at them up a hill there and all."

He looks helpless, or maybe he's trying to fool me.

"No, Luke, I'll just do what he says. The captain is kind of scary looking."

"I'm undeceived about that. Think I'd rather have a Portuguese man o' war in my bathtub than get on his wrong side." He was talking about a kind of jellyfish, but at the time, I'm thinking, *He's talking about a sailor*, and it seems odd, like his words fit his eyes. Luke laughs. "Captain Wilson he got quite a lisp on him now, don't he? You hear him say, I shwear? Sounds like a little girl." At the river a few Rangers look back at the sound of laughter.

"Praise the Lord we ran into them. Maybe it the safest place to be." I turn to him. "Luke, maybe it best not to notice how he talking."

He looks at me like I'm stupid, or scared, or something. Then he finds a curry-brush, and he go up the hill to do his chore. I take out sweet potatoes, giving every man two, with three extra for luck, and put them in a cauldron. Soon I hear Luke calling horses like you would to bring chickens along, but I only leave him to it and say nothing. The liver is wrapped inside sackcloth and stuck by dried blood to a cutting board. It and the heart smell fresh, but there's fly eggs on them. I scrape the eggs away with a knife and start cutting the meat in lumps, and as I'm doing that I hear a horse worrying. Up on the hill Luke is trying to take off a saddle. He's kneeling under a white horse's belly, looking like he's trying to milk it. The horse is snorting, stomping, blowing air out through closed lips like it's saying, *Leave me be*.

I'm thinking about what I should do till I hear someone say, "Hey." It's the captain. He's naked and walking towards us. The horse's hooves are making the ground cough up dust.

Luke keeps pulling, trying to loosen the saddle, but it's not right how he doing it. It's not gentle. The horse kicks Luke, cutting one of his brows. He grabs its reins and whips the horse's face till it starts screaming. The captain comes up behind Luke, throws him to the ground, and he rolls down the hill. The captain calms the horse, his chest blowing up and down with hard breathing. He turns to Luke. "What d'you think you're doing?"

"That stupid horse kicked me in the eye."

"There is no stupid horses ... Look! It is cut above the eye here." He gently touches the horse. I see the captain has three big scars on his back, from what I don't know. He walks the horse to a tree and ties it there. Then he turns and stares at Luke with clenched fists resting on his hips and a look on his face, as if Luke is a cow stuck up to its knees in mud and he's wondering out what to do with him. "Hear me now," says the captain. "Stay away from the horses. I'll find other work for you." He taps his lower lip with a finger. "Just need to think what you might be useful for." He scratches his head, shakes his long curly hair to chase away flies, and walks back to the river.

Later on we eat dinner. My cooking is praised even though it's nothing special. Afterwards, as I'm cleaning pots by the river, the captain smiles at me and says, "Night now." He seemed to like me, Morton. Maybe it's because he didn't like Luke and needed to balance his loving with his hating.

Next morning I wake, opening my eyes, to see boots by my face and the sun reflecting off something that's hurting my eyes. "Ever use one of these?" I look up and see the captain standing beside me with a smile on his face and holding a gun in his hands with a pearl handle and silver barrel.

"Not in a time, Cap'n."

"The cook shoots game for us, too. It's yours, for keeping."

"I can't rightly take that from you, Cap'n."

"Shure you can." But he doesn't give me the gun right away, he beckons me to follow him. The air is abuzz with flies. I see my Chinaman hat ain't beside me no more, there's a winter hat there instead. I grab it and follow the captain to down near the gurgling easy river. The captain stops at a fallen tree with six or seven rusty cans on it. "Nice hat. Where's the other one?" he says.

"Don't know. Someone took it, left this one."

"It prolly scaring one of the boys." We are about twenty feet away from the tree. He shuts one eye, bites on his tongue, and aims with his left arm stretched out. He's no shirt on, and the skin on his back looks like melted cheese that's had time to cool off, like maybe a cannonball landed near him one time. He fires and starts laughing when he hits one. "Sometimes, if you hit one in the side, you can knock another over. Love it when I do that. Here." He gives me the gun and I try doing it like him. I shut one eye, aim, and fire, but I miss the cans. I even miss the tree. His face gets disheartened when he sees how bad I is at shooting, then he try to smile. "That's a 37 colt, from Paterson New Jersey, it belonged to a good Ranger. I'll leave you to it." He hands me a box of bullets and walks away, his smile going as he do.

I fire some more, but they all miss. I do hit one, I think, because it falls behind the tree, but when I go to look at it I see an arrow sticking in it. I look around and see Dave, the scout, staring at me. Then he laughs and walks away.

Luke comes walking along. Asking, "Where did your Chinaman hat go to?"

"I don't know, think pumpkin head took it, left me this one." Luke laughs out loud, though I'm not trying to be funny. I tell him how bad my shooting is and how they expecting me to shoot game. He reckons I should shoot trout instead. So we lay down at the river's edge. I see sun shining in Luke's hair, because the water is reflecting like a looking glass. The water is swirling but clear. I see bottom, with stones colored brown, red, and yellow. Small black balls roll along the bottom like tumbleweed, shadows from swirls up above, till the sun shines on them, making them disappear. I think I see sand moving back and forth, but when I look closer the sand is a trout tail. Along the back it has black spots that look like heads on a busy street. The fish shimmers in and out through the shadow balls like it's catching them and by some dark art turning them into spots on its back. I shoot, scattering shadows, stones, and spots, and I'm expecting it to float up, but nothing do.

Luke says, "Lemme try."

I give him the gun and he looks at the water. He shoots and misses, misses bad. I'm thinking, *What! He ain't no better than me at shooting. The Fastest Draw* ... but I say nothing.

I just put out my hand for the gun, but he keeps it. "Give me my gun, PLEASE."

"I hear you. Don't worry. I wouldn't keep a bone belonging to the captain's favorite hunting dog now, would I?" He hands it to me, with his words getting under my skin like mange, because I'm scared maybe they're true.

Finally, I shoot some trout and I cooks them for the Rangers. The captain praises the way I took the bones from the fish without breaking the meat, but also he says, "We got fishing hooks and line. You don't want to go wasting bullets, not on fish."

"I hear it said, Cap'n," I say, and I'm wondering is that his way of telling me that they expecting more of me than fish.

He looks at me. "Your eyelids burned?"

"Yes, Cap'n."

The captain signals to Dave, who walks off.

When he comes back a little while later, he walks real close up to my face. I pull away. The captain says, "Let him, it's gunpowder." Real slow, the scout puts black powder onto my eyelids. "I lost my hat for a while yesterday, too." Which is how come his eyelids looks like the pharaoh's in the picture bible. There's quiet for a while, and I know it is going to be the captain who'll speak next. When he do, he says, "Down the way, near next camp, there's a town. It's got a few taverns. We got to call on someone. You can wait at camp or go to town. You can't come with us."

Luke asks who they are calling on.

Cactus Jack answers. He a slow-talking Ranger with one white eye and pockmarks on his face like a sparrow makes on a pie put out on a ledge for cooling. "A farm down the way got raided a few months back. Two young girls were scalped and done for. It was during the rains. The skirmish is still written in the dried mud."

There is quiet again, till a Ranger starts banging the ground with a stick. He's this Irish boy called Mare, with coal black hair, sad gray-blue eyes, and a scraggly young man's beard that's strangely orange and white on his chin. "We'll get them red bastards, Cactus Jack. Won't we, Captain?"

"Mare, in English now please." The captain says, laughing because the boy's brogue so strong, though I got his words.

39

Billy says, "What are you laughing at, Captain? He speaks English. He said, 'We're going to get those Injuns'." Mare's face goes salmon colored and freckles he have start fading into his skin.

"I consider so, Mare. We've been waiting long enough." Says the Captain.

Luke says, "Pardon, but why you called Cactus Jack?"

"Because I fell onto a cactus," which is easy to figure when you thought on it, though I hadn't of before.

"Is that why your eye is so peculiar?" says Luke, pointing at his own eye and drawing circles there.

"No, I got struck by lightning out on the Pecos. Blinded this eye." He smiles at Luke with his one good eye. There's no life in the other one--it's all glassy, like a dead rabbit's.

Luke nods. Pushing his low lip up over his top one like a trout, he squints. "I see. Why you called Mare then?"

Mare doesn't answer and acts like the question hasn't been asked. He tightens his jaw and pretends like he's looking at something straight ahead. Some Rangers are smalaughing, which is what I calls it when you is smiling and about to laugh, but haven't gotten round to it yet.

Mare knows a laugh is coming. He says, "They don't allow mares in the service ... I turned up to work riding one my first day." A few Rangers laugh, and he tells them to shut up, but he smiling when he says it.

The captain isn't listening. He's caught up trying to loosen fishing line and hooks that are in tangles. He looks confused, puts a line in his mouth and breaks it with his teeth. I guess he don't have the patience to go over all them knots. After eating, as I'm washing up, I see the captain squatting down with a bayonet in his hand, making lines in the dirt. All the Rangers are looking on.

## 5  SLEEPING DOGS

A N HOUR after eating we travel maybe forty miles before
    making camp. Most of the Rangers set out for somewhere
soon after while the captain and a few others stay behind.

Nothing really happened until that evening time, Morton. I
remember the captain, dressed in a white shirt, was sitting under
a tree, looking in a mirror, clipping his goatee. He looks at us, I
mean Luke and me, puts the mirror down, then comes over to us,
stroking his little beard, smiling and looking confused. "What you
waiting on? You can head off to the town, like I told you." Luke
and me start to walk away, but the captain whistles for us to stop.
He and the scout walk over. "Hold up now a minute. In case
either of you is thinking of hightailing, remember we got us Injun
Dave here. He can track you better than any pack of hounds."

At times the captain he sound more Louisiana than Texas. Like
when he says, "here" it sounds like he's saying "hair." The captain
nods at Dave, who grabs my shirt to smell it. He sniffs Luke, too,
then the scout stands back, his proud eyes defying us to run. He
looks the captain in the eye and walks away.

The captain gives us both Ranger badges. "I want you to put these on. Carry guns with you, and remember, boys ... enjoy yourselves." He pronounce "enjoy" as "injoy," sticking his tongue out through the gap in his teeth with his raccoon eyes filling with mirth.

We both put on the badges, as his eyes expecting us to, but there's no ceremony like you'd expect with a Bible or Lone Star flag. Luke gives the captain an obliging smile, "Appreciate it, sir."

The captain stares back at him, then laughs a strange old laugh. He claps me on the shoulder and returns to the tree. Putting his hat on as he takes a seat beneath it, he folds his arms and crosses his boots then bangs the back of his hat against the tree, causing the brim to slip down over his eyes. *What's that all about?* I think to myself. He say carry guns, but Luke don't have one. The captain knows that and he don't give him one neither, and Luke too proud to ask him for one. But I say to myself, *Best stop thinking and just do what he says.*

We ride towards where he pointed us, along a dirt trail, past cotton fields and high sugarcane. After that there is lots of canebrakes and hollyhocks and the ground gets swampy.

I know Luke ain't happy even before he says, "I'd like to hit him across back of his head with a hickory stick."

"You reckon that scout could track us just like a smell hound?"

"I don't know, Abe. I'm somewhat ignorant as to the abilities of the red man."

"Maybe the captain just trying to scare us."

"I think that's where the dog lies."

"What do you mean?"

"It is from a German saying--it means that, 'You are right and this is the reason so.'" A peach tree branch hangs across our path, we duck to pass under it.

"I don't know why he hates me, or why he likes you."

"I don't know, Luke. Maybe you should draw him. It might cheer him some."

"Good idea, but I've no paper."

"It were a joke, Luke. He dangerous. They all is. How comes you don't see that? Don't be asking them no more questions neither. You'll get killed, me along with you. Can't go talking to white folks like that."

"Why'd you say that to me for? I am white folks."

Soon we come to the village it called Branish and it's small. In the center stands a plantation house with these great white pillars. There's a sugar mill nearby.

I guess the plantation has closed down and turned into a village around the house.

Two lines of elms stand in front of the house. Most of them are cut down, but you could tell they there at one time. In the center between the lines of trees is a round brick-lined pond that our horses drink from. Next to the pond lies a fallen tree. Its bark has been taken off and the wood is shiny and coppery from horses rubbing against it. Two roots are sticking in the ground, and more roots, about four or five or six of them, jut into the air, and they all been cut to about two feet from the stump. It looks like a cartwheel with the rim and half the spokes broken away. The tree is a hitching post, we dismount and tie our horses to one of the roots.

I hear banging. At a line of shacks and shops I see a blacksmith working late. His work shed has a front door made out of iron and shaped like a horseshoe.

Inside his boy is squeezing bellows. The man takes a sword out from the furnace. It's the color of the middle of the sun. He bangs it with a hammer, puts it into water, and steam spits up. He takes out another sword, colored purple and red, sticks it back in the fire, and shuts the door. It behooves me to tell you, and I don't know how, but when I see them things it's like someone has stepped on my grave, and I shivers and I know that something terrible will happen that very evening.

I don't drink much, but I want one that night to throw onto the coals of fear glowing deep down in my gut.

We go into this bar, or Luke does and I follow, pocketing my Ranger badge as I do. To my eyes it's full of white folks. And if they don't hold ill will towards me, their bodies is lying. Two men are playing fiddles real fast. One is tall and bald, with long hair that's whipping in front of his eyes as he fiddles, the other is short, with a red face and forearms like a toad. When they done they smile but look surprised, like they wondering, *How come the bar so quiet?* Till they see the reason no one is clapping standing by the door. They wouldn't be playing again till we've gone. I stand there taking their looks on my shoulders. I whisper to Luke, "Let's go to the Negro bar across the way." We'd seen it before.

Luke tries to smile at the people, without his lips moving he says, "No. You're part white, I'm not part Negro, this will do."

"I don't think they seeing that part of me."

Their stares give my words a truth and with no more words we leave.

Outside it's near dark and silent, except for a cricket and our feet crunching on stony ground, and the low sound of women laughing and screaming. We pass the pond, where our horses tied up. Now a rising moon, looking like a Tennessee River pearl, colors the fallen tree a pale green.

We go on and up three wooden steps into the Negro bar. I hear poker chips clicking and smell perfume. Four black Buffalo Soldiers in uniforms are at a table, playing cards, smoking cigars, and drinking whisky. Some whores, white and black, hang about them. One of them sits on a soldier's leg. She's white and pretty, with curly brown locks and hair done up high. But though she smiles her eyes hard and cruel, and her laughing sounds like a cackle.

44

The soldiers are arguing over chips. "That ain't how you split them. You stacks them high and even. Then you splits them."

"Take it easy, Sam, your flint is fixed. I'm not trying to rob you," says another.

"See, you makes two piles and I picks which one of them I wants," says the first one, and he makes two even stacks of red chips. Behind the bar is a big Negro, with tight clipped hair and eyes red from cigar smoke. He's polishing glasses with a raggedy old piece of cloth. His apron is as white and starched as ever you see, but the tables and chairs are turned the same way as in the white bar. For the soldiers are giving us looks now, like the only white thing that should be in that bar is that apron and them whores, and that goes for the bit in me, too. I nod to the soldiers and lowers my head a little, but I still have some pride, not that it shows on the outside. I look at the bartender's cloth twisting inside a glass. The whole bar can hear it squeaking as besides that the noise all quiet and low.

"Saw you the weird sisters," whispers Luke.

"Yeah I seen them," I say. He looks at me then as if he hasn't even spoken.

As I open my mouth to order I hear a man at the table holler, "Two white folks out on the town--what you doing here?"

"Looking for a drink," I say in a low base voice, for that's how I'm being talked to.

"That's a fine weapon you got there, nigger. Yo' master give it to you?" I look down. The gun shines in the candlelight, making trouble for me and me forgetting it's even there. The one giving me sass is this dark nigger by the name of Sam. I know because a level-headed nigger who he playing cards with says:

"Leave them be, Sam. You wouldn't be messing if you was winning."

Another one at the table says, "That's right." So at least two of the four ain't looking for trouble. I turn to order a drink, and what Luke do next makes no sense. I'd forgot about him, and he should of let the colored folk do their talking and kept quiet for a time. But Luke, he stands beside me, and with the cut over his eye, from the hoof, he looks like he's been fighting. He's wearing the Ranger badge, and he sticks out his chest and puts his hand on my shoulder.

"Captain Wilson of the Texas Rangers gave him that gun. You think on your cards and we'll think on our beers. Two beers, barkeep." Luke knuckles the bar as if to say, *Hurry along with them beers, nigger.*

"I don't want a beer," I say. "Mine's a whiskey."

But the barman doesn't hear me because of the noise of cards being slapped down on the table, boots stomping on boards, and Sam banging the bar with a big fist. I see him now. His army cap with the crossed swords is pulled aside, making a shadow on his face the same dark blue color of his cap. Sam has a few white scratches on the left side of his face below his eye, and his neat teeth are ivory white. He has big eyes under his bulging brows. He opens one eye real wide till you can see the red veins, and he shuts the other and tilts his head, so the open eye is up and the shut eye is down. His chest fills up with air. "Nobody ask you nothing. This here's a militar' bar for Negroes. Don't you coming in here telling us to do what we is already doing."

He's right, too, even if he do want trouble.

"Want us to leave?" I say.

Luke steps behind me, trying not to look like what he is. He'd called Sam over, but he don't want to play with him now because Sam looks like a mean dog, and one that might bite. Sam looks at me. He sees that I'm trying to be fair. He put a hand up to his chin like he's thinking. His pink tongue sticks out like a frog's after it's caught a fly. I think his tongue so big it's getting in the way of his words. He licks his lips and his upper lip curls up a bit. I see anger going a bit from his eyes. "You can stay, house-nigger, just can't be armed is all." Real quick Sam grabs the gun from my britches, puts it to the side of his face, holds it there, and shuts his lips tight. Slowly, Sam put the gun inside his coat then he swaggers back to the table, his back to Luke as he do, not seeing him as a danger, though he wrong about that because Luke the sort of man who could call up a mean dog, and one that might bite. The barman gives us beers. I pay and he stares at us.

It's like he's saying, *This ain't the place for you boys, just go.* But the barman, he don't say it. As I'm standing there my belly feels like I've drank a quart of hogwash, all from Sam taking my gun. Because I'm not one for quarrelling.

Luke about to say something to me, but I turn away.

*Sam takes the gun.*

I'm thinking, *You shouldn't have done that, Abe, ignoring him like that. What's he going to do next? Get to feeling lonely and ask those men can we play cards? Then the fool would only start winning and act like he don't know what's happening.* And my mind run away on me, and I laughs at the notion of it.

Luke wants to know what's so funny.

"Nothing," I say.

Sam is looking at me, too, looking at me laugh, his eyes angry again.

This fourth soldier, a pecan colored one, pulls the chips over from the middle of the table to his belly, where there's already a nice pile. So Sam has lost again and he's angry again. This man keeps grinning. It don't look like he'd be the one winning, not with those sleepy eyelids, like two coconut halves about to close.

I remember once on the plantation growing up, we were shooting doves and this one dove looked like it weren't hit. It flies quarter of a mile then drops dead out of the sky, like a feathered hailstone. What Luke say to me next reminds me of that. "Abe," he says, "this is turning ugly. Let's drink and go."

I hear him, but I ignores him.

I walk over to the card table, bold at first then easy, very easy, as if the blue-white cigar smoke circling the table is the gate to a rich man's house. "Excuse me, gentlemen, we is leaving. I'll be having my gun back from you."

Sam stares at his cards. "What gun you talking about?"

I try an' smile. "The gun you minding for me."

"Minding for you? House-nigger, my business is all that I minding." Sam blows a ring of smoke at me. He curls his upper lip and licks it and throws a few chips into the pot. I look around for sense. The two soldiers who trying to calm him before stay quiet now.

A whore, a colored one, says, "Give the boy back his gun." She's smiling at me and wearing this loose red dress that must've belong to a larger woman before. Her eyes are kind, like the color of honey, a dark orange, or maybe the lamp near to her is only making them so.

The whore moves her fingers slow, as rising smoke, up along a soldier's neck and head, leaving them rest there like a crown, and asks me my name.

49

I can tell she thinks I'm a good-looking man. I don't answer, or even really look at her. She only trying to help, but she's making it worse. "My name is Nina. I'm called after a boat. Come on, what's your name?"

"My name is Abe. I'm called after someone ... called Abraham."

Nina laughs.

The white one with the curly hair is stroking a soldier's leg now, and the third woman at the table--though there are others in the bar--is black and heavy, with big dull eyes and a small pouting mouth.

The droopy eyed soldier, has fallen asleep onto his chips. He's no cards in front of him now.

There are other soldiers in the bar, too, maybe eight, nine, or ten of them, who are all looking on, but they ain't going to get involved. I look again at the other two soldiers at the card table, not Sam or droopy eyes. But while Sam stares at his cards they sit there not looking easy. But still, they ain't going to help, not against their friend. I don't know what I'll do. I tell Sam to leave it with the barman. Sam is drunk and mean, sure, but back at camp is the captain, and I can't rightly go back there without that gun.

I walk back over to Luke at the bar and I say to the barman, "I need that gun back. Can you keep it for me? I'll come by and get it in the morning."

He says nothing for a moment. Then he moves his lips around and gives me a nod. "All right." But it feels like what he's really saying is, *I'll try, but I'm promising you nothing. Warned you, din I? But you fools wouldn't listen.*

We leave and ride back to camp under a star-filled sky. After a while I start to calm down, but my stomach tightens when I hears howling and barking.

Coyotes are out, yipping like rebs. One runs across our trail, bringing the fear back over me about not having the gun. Even though later on it saved my life, when I think back about it ... Lord, I wish I'd never seen it again. I was tempted to hightail, but then Luke might've turned me in. I still didn't really trust him enough to say, *Let's run for it.*

After all the ugliness, Luke ain't bothered at all. Why would he be? He's no gun to lose, and he just rides along, looking at the sky, singing something like:

"O Texas, O Texas, your stars are so bright.
If you don't agree with that, mister you've got a fight.
Our Texas cay-oats are the meanest.
Our snakes are the meanest."

He tells me duck when we get to the overhanging peach tree branch, which I do, and he laughs and asks me to sing along with him, which I don't.

When we get back to camp I hear laughing.

The Rangers have a new prisoner, a native, chained up and struggling.

Luke gets off his horse, looks at the Rangers, then he turns and stares over my shoulder into the trees, into the night, his eyes and mouth wide open. He's standing there silent and still for many moments, like he doesn't even know that I'm there.

The captain is walking toward us. Following him is a shadow holding a lamp that's moving side to side like a square butter-churning box, giving the captain's hair a womanly glow. The captain and Billy, who's holding the lamp, stop behind Luke, who's still frozen looking.

The captain says. "GIMPY." Luke jumps. "How your evening go?"

Luke turns then laughs. "Good, Captain, good, except these Buffalo Soldiers took his gun."

Then Luke looks angry, like he trying to hide that he scared. The captain's face goes somber looking and my stomach folds inside of me like a newly ironed shirt.

"He only borrow it, Cap'n. I'll get it back," I say, making little of it.

Billy says to the captain, "We going teach them niggers manners?"

"You speak it, Bill. I'll get your gun back for you." The captain starts walking towards the horses while Billy yells at Rangers to move.

"Wait, Cap'n," I say. He stops and turns back. "If it's my gun, can't you just leave it be?"

"Sorry, son, wouldn't be appreciated." He turns and starts walking again. "Hope you can see that." As he puts his foot in a stirrup and throws his leg over his horse, all I can see is him wanting to pour a bowl of his fury out on that bar.

51

He won't go looking for no tooth for tooth. It'll be more like a mouthful of ivory white teeth, just for a gun. The captain and maybe eight Rangers are up on horses now. He has a white shirt on, which the wind is blowing like a ship's sail. A Ranger brings him his black jacket. He puts it on and pulls his long greasy hair out from under its collar, and they ride away, leaving a few Rangers on guard.

I say to Luke, "What you say that for?"

"He'll get your gun back, don't you worry."

"I don't care about that. He don't neither." Luke's smile slips away. He's looking happy that the captain is gone, but also like he knows I'm scared. I walk towards my horse. "I don't want those men shot over a stupid gun."

Cactus Jack the camp guard. He comes over to see what we're doing, carrying Billy's lantern. It shone up his spooky eye like dew on cotton, like the shining moon surrounded by the big stretching blue blackness of night. As I mount up the wind starts blowing hard, shaking leaves and bending branches that fight and clatter. Cactus looks up. "That's like a Panhandle wind." Luke mounts up, too, and I act like I have reason to be going. He doesn't stop us. We ride off fast, down the dirt trail, past cotton fields, the sugarcane, and the hollyhocks. In among the sound of thundering hooves, as we gallop along, I hear a crash and a loud thump, which is Luke forgetting to duck under the peach tree branch. I rein in and come back. He's on the ground but looks all right.

"This Injun horse is trying to kill me."

"It don't know when to duck, Luke."

I try to get him to hurry along, but he's wanting help, complaining that the fall has dazed him and stolen his wind. He's just sitting there on the ground like a lump of dough. So I've to get down and help him back up, onto his blanket, even though I'm hurrying to save lives. And what's wrong with him? Not a thing, far as I can tell, all because some cracker like him throw a peach stone at the side of the road before I was even born. We get riding again, and my mind is racing with things to say to the captain. I would even have ran into the bar to beg for the gun back, but fate wasn't for it. Before we get to the town we hear low booms of distant guns.

As we come near on a hundred yards from the bar, a colored soldier runs towards us. I hear BANG! And another BANG! He stumbles and falls, face down, into the dirt. Behind him is a man with a pistol in either hand. As I get closer, I see it's the captain. I can do nothing, just watch. A whore runs out in a panic, the one called Nina. The captain shoots her in the heart and she sinks into a heap. I don't think he mean to do it, he just can't stop shooting. Glass smashes in an upstairs window, a colored soldier appears there and fires a few shots, and a Ranger close to the captain crumples like a piece of paper thrown in a fire.

The captain is standing in the middle of it all, like he's thinking, *I shan't be harmed*, and he ain't. He points his pistols at the upper window and shoots three or four times. The soldier's body drapes over the ledge for a moment, then his shirtless corpse falls to the street. Other women rush out and squat crying beside the fallen one. I turn to Luke. He's looking shocked, and I wonder do he blame himself.

I reckon maybe eight colored soldiers died that night, Morton, as well as the woman and that one Ranger. A second Ranger died a few days on. That's the second time Luke Sprague made me angry, just as I was learning to abide him. But it ain't his fault, Captain Wilson being the kind of man he was. I remember seeing the captain with eyes full of lust for power, as he standing there in the still after it all. Though there's not much light and maybe it's just my memory painting the devil's eyes on him.

As he is standing there a whore runs at him in a rage--it's the white one with cruel eyes--and he hits her across the head with his gun. She drops like she's dead, though she ain't.

I don't think he the type to hurt a woman on purpose, I think she just pick a bad time, that's all. The Rangers come out from hiding places, and in a line they walk slowly forward. The wind has died and moonlit mist is coming off them, like it do on horses after they been run. They walk into the bar and there's no more shooting.

Luke and me go to look inside, too.

The bar looks like a twister has been through there. Tables are overturned, Buffalo Soldiers are lying dead in a mess of cards and whisky glasses, one with his guns still in their holsters. The chips all split between them now and no more arguing about it.

Two Negroes who weren't involved get told to drop their guns and leave, which they do. I expect all the card players are dead, but that ain't quite so.

I hear two bangs and see a cloud of black smoke on the ground. Sam, who lies dying by the door, takes half of Mare's bowels out with one shot and hit his leg, too. The boy falls down clutching his belly, crying up to Jesus. The captain points his guns at Sam and shoots till there's nothing but clicks. Sam's eyes close, his cap falls off as his head slumps, and his pink tongue slowly slips out between his lips.

Two Rangers go to help Mare, but I can tell by the captain's face he has Mare for under the clay already. It all sounds awful, the women crying on the street is piteous, but this even worse because he human, not like a bird with a broken wing whose neck you have to break. There's just the waiting till God takes his soul, so we get to hear it all.

"Look here now, Mare," says the captain. "Stop hollering, boy. You're bleeding, but not too bad." Still he don't look at him as he saying it.

Billy says to the captain, "What are you saying, Levi? We've got to get a doctor."

"No, we best go. 'Sides, there's no doctor living in Branish. He's only here every couple weeks." The captain walks behind the bar past the barman and picks up a liquor bottle. "No labels. This moonshine?" The barman says nothing. "You better show me courtesy, nigger. You're working behind a bar, I know you can talk."

"Yessir, it's moonshine."

The captain says to Billy, "Take Mare back to camp." Billy snatches up Mare and walks out of the bar with another Ranger following behind. The captain picks up three more bottles from the bar and holds them in one arm. "You're not supposed to have this, but I need it, for sanitation and the like. I'll even pay you for it." The captain drops coins on the counter--one of them starts spinning, others fall to the floor. "Is that enough?" The bartender don't argue price, only nods. "Sorry about all this," says the captain. He turns to look around, stopping his head suddenly as he sees something by the door. He walks over, squats down, and fumbles in Sam's jacket.

The captain stands up grinning and walks back towards me, holding out the gun. I stand there not thinking, I can't, but it feels like a load around my neck because I'm supposed to act like I'm happy, now I got my gun back. But this is like a gallon more hogwash to swallow and from very filthy pigs. Drips coming off a table from a spilt drink count out the seconds, telling me I got to hurry along and say something, but my lips don't move and the captain is looking at me and he's looking confused.

# 6 PLANS

ALL THE Rangers an' the barman are staring at me now. Luke is, too, staring like he's willing me to take the gun. I guess the captain thinks their moods are low, and he needs cheering for his boys.

So I take the gun and say, "Thank you, Cap'n."

He can see I am hurting about it, about everything. "Look after that gun, and don't go blaming yourself, son, you hear? We've run into these coons before. Wasn't just about the gun." He pats me on the shoulder and starts walking away.

"I figures that myself, Captain."

He turns to me. "What'd you say?"

"I figures that for myself, Cap'n." The barman is staring at me with judging eyes, like I'm the cause of all this, and also like he scared for me, too. The captain looks at me like I'm an ingrate for a second. Then he realizes that I know he used me, that I'm at least a half-smart nigger and no point in him acting like he done me such a favor. For a second I think he's going to rage at me, but he don't, he speaks calm. "Of course you did, son, but sometimes it's nice to hear things you already know inside your head."

I guess it is.

I drifted back to the camp that night in a river of horses, with my head down and my heart with it. I slipped off my horse, turned in and said a prayer for all who died and for myself, to get me through all this. A good leader is supposed to get the best out of his men, and I guess that made the captain a good leader, for if he wanted a fight with them Negro soldiers, me and Luke were the right men to send along and we wouldn't have had to do much of anything. I only think about it now because it's part of the story. Though I think it's best not to think about it anymore, Morton, for the whole clamor made me feel bad within, and I blames myself about it for many years after. But you can fetch water for someone and they can use it to put out a fire or to drown a man, and blaming myself is as much use.

Early next day, the captain woke me. He was down on his knees beside me and wanted to know if I knew any medicine. I said I did and he got me to go help the Irish boy, Mare, who was slipping away. His real name was Cornelius Lambert. He asked me would I remember that. "Sure, Cornelius," I say, "because corn and lamb makes it easy." I give him dog fennel tea, which I have down in my boot, which is good for chills and malaria, and the captain give him corn moonshine before leaving me alone with him, even though Mare told him that he don't drink. There weren't much else I could do. The boy in and out of his thinking and it hard giving him food.

I remember Mare giving me a little bottle with purple liquid inside of it, for keeping away skeeters, he told me, and him asking me to pray for his soul. I guess he knows he'll soon die and he's wondering will he go to hell, purgatory, or heaven. I tell him, "I don't believe in purgatory, Cornelius."

The center of his eyes are perfect circles, black as wet tar, peaceful but flickering like candles, too, like his soul has tidied out its room and about ready to leave. But the gray-blue parts look like they're circling the black centers, gathering like angry storm clouds carrying a big rain. I can't believe my eyes and turn my head away. He gasps, "What if you aren't good enough for heaven or bad enough for hell?"

"I don't know, Mare, I just think God, he got to be fair."

"Fair isn't much use."

He starts to tell me about a house down in Mexico that had two wanted banditos inside of it.

Mare and Billy had crossed the border, chasing them, armed with Winchester 73 rifles. They shot up the house and killed the banditos, but also shot a pregnant Mexican women, leaving her bleeding from the belly like a squeezed leech and her husband with two small children to care for. Mare and Billy had heard the screaming but kept on shooting at the house for near on ten minutes, as they were fired upon and until they no longer were. After that they slung the banditos on their horses and got back, across the border, quick as they could.

I listen till I can't listen any more, and I leave him and walk up to Luke.

He frowns when he sees me. "What's the matter?"

"Don't know what I'm doing with Irish boy."

"Don't worry, a Ranger has gone for a doctor."

"You sure?"

"Course I'm sure. Wouldn't say it otherwise."

"Which one?"

"The teacher."

The teacher was called Joel. He was a little over thirty, and Luke and me had seen him reading a McGuffey Reader the day before. Luke asked him why he was reading it. He told us he wanted to be a teacher. He loved children, but didn't know if he could control a class full of them. Luke told him, "Of course you could, all you need is a hickory stick."

I go back to nurse Mare for a little while, then I walk over to the captain. Before I speak he says, "Leave him, go shoot game. Take Gimpy along."

I didn't want to sound too eager to abandon the boy so I say, "Shouldn't we wait till the doctor comes, Cap'n?"

"Doctor! What doctor? We took the bullets out and put alcohol on it. What's a doctor going do beyond that?" He starting to scowl.

"I see one of your men has gone, Cap'n, and I is thinking, maybe he go for a doctor."

"No, he's just gone home to Fort Worth." He snorts a little.

I don't ask him how come the teacher has gone. I say, "I just thinking, seeing a doctor might cheer that boy up."

"Look, it'd take three days to get a doctor here, and in that time he'll either make it or he won't. What will cheer him up is some hot turkey, possum ... or trout." He coughs and snorts again and spits the mix onto the ground, puts a boot on it, and grinds it into the dirt like it were a cigar end and walks off. He say trout last, so he must think that it's second or third best.

I didn't want to bring Luke, I was still vexed at him. As I walk up to him he's watching this Ranger closely. "I bet he is of Dutch descent, with his lips the way they are." He sticks his lips out like a trout, and his eyes looks like they want to draw them lips.

"I don't think people like you talking about them things, Luke."

He turns to me, his lips still pouting. "Me talking about them is like you asking someone how they like their meat done--just a part of the job. You angry at me?"

I am, from the night before and from him telling me there is a doctor coming when there ain't. It makes me so angry I daren't even talk about it. I say, "No, I ain't angry. I'm going shooting game and picking herbs. Is you coming?" and I walk away. I found it hard giving him respect sometimes, even though I try give some to everyone, no matter. But then I turn and look at him, and I trusts him, I have to, because I'm worried about being on the end of a rope. I say, "Luke, let's get out of here."

He stares at me. I think I have made a foolish mistake till he looks over at the scout. "We wouldn't get far with him. Got to pick our time." Nearby, the scout washes his Confederate coat at the river. The part on the sleeve that looks like a twisted gold snake seems like the only part he cares on; the rest of it all raggedy with rattails on the hem. He starts to fix the three feathers on the back of his head, making them full, just like a bird do.

"Look at him there." I say, "He as vain as an old plantation miss," and we both bust up laughing at the notion of it. The scout shoots us a look, and when he do I just know it--I hadn't had before, but he's watching us. I mean it's his job, and don't ask me how I know it, but he expecting us to run.

We went hunting, and I shot two squirrels, which is plenty if you chop them up and put them in rice for flavor. As we walk back to camp I ask Luke, "What's the plan?"

"Already told you."

"Maybe my memory going from me, but no, you didn't," which is my way of calling someone a liar without saying so.

He isn't lying though, for he stops and says real slow, like I'm stupid. "Didn't I saaaay that weeeee had to pick our time?"

"That ain't a plan, Luke, that's deciding to go."

"Well, when I say 'r' you ready, you be decided, and we go."

"I is decided. What I wants to know is, when that will be?"

His forehead scrunches up and he looks at me, like I'm a skeeter in a room he's been trying to swat at for an hour, one that moves every time he gets close.

"Lord, give me the patience to put in your head what is in mine. I don't know, Abe, could be when an owl screeches and all the men go a-looking, because they think it's a white woman being attacked and she'll be all thankful when they rescue her. Then, while they're off chasing dreams of being heroes, we disappear into the night."

"It is not hardly likely, Luke, an owl doing that, nor a woman neither ... We could go now."

He laughs, creasing up his nose like you would at turned food. "You can cook food, Abe, but you only half-bake your escaping plans."

"Huh, what?" I say, and his eyes go all big like he pretending to be surprised.

"Well, where are the horses, or are you going to steal another?" He sweeps out his hand towards the trees, like he's throwing corn seed and not caring where it lands.

"Maybe ... I don't knows."

He snorts and says, "'Maybe ... I don't knows,' you say, and you were criticizing my plan. That's like the camel coming into a tent."

"What's a camel?"

"It's like a horse with a big long neck, big lips, bulging eyes, and long eyelashes for keeping out the desert dust."

"How is what I is saying like a camel?"

"Well, there is this camel you see, and one star-filled night he comes up to an Arab in his tent and sticks his lips in because it's cold. The Arab lets him, and then he sticks his head in, and again, the Arab lets him, and he keeps stretching his neck in and then his shoulders and again--"

"The Arab lets him?"

"That's right."

"So, do the camel end up in the tent, is that what you is telling me?"

His eyes get bigger, but they ain't mocking now.

"That's right, the Arab wakes up next to a camel. What I'm saying, if you had gotten the gist of it, was that we, or you, don't want to go stealing any more horses, or anything, anything at all, that will catch up on you. Do you understand what I'm telling you?"

"Yeah, Luke, it ain't hard getting your meaning."

"I do believe that I heard they are going near the Rio Grande on our next ride."

His odd eyes start to move about quickly, like maybe he thinks we're being watched.

I say, "How comes?"

"I don't know, but it's the best place to escape."

"Lord, I'm feared of the water, Luke."

"Don't be. A man destined to hang shouldn't fear drowning," he laughs, and I say nothing. "Sorry," he says. I guess my face is telling him I don't think he's funny. "Look, Abe, I don't know when it'll come, but we'll know the right moment to go, and if you see it and say it, I'm ready. I hope everything will yet turn out well, though I don't know exactly how that might come to pass. Don't unsaddle our horses when we get near the river."

Now I'm thinking, *That sounds like a plan after all.*

Next morning we go a hunting again. We saw turkey feathers but no turkey, and even though we got nothing at all it was good to be away because the Irish boy kept making lots of noise. When we come back, Billy walks towards me, Cactus Jack along with him. Billy hasn't shaved, and his eyes are sad and sunk and dark all round, but not from gunpowder. He's no shirt on, and I notice that though his shoulders are wide and his arms are strong, he has a skinny chest with a small potbelly. His color reminds me of a brown and white horse because even though his face and forearms is dark tanned his body milky white.

"You a cook, ain't you?" Billy asks. I say nothing. He twists his pumpkin head and puts a hand up to his ear like he's pretending to be deaf. "What?"

I look down at his suspenders that're blowing in the wind. "Yeah, I is."

"You cut things, don't you, like meat and such?"

"Yessir," and I'm thinking, *What's he getting at? Don't he know that I do.*

"Then I got a job for you."

Billy scratches his head and folds his long arms, as if the terrible thing he about to ask me is nothing more than boiling an egg.

# 7 DOCTORING

BILLY STARES at me. The big blonde brows over his dark deep-set eyes are like two fingers have been put there by God to keep out the sun. "Mare's leg is turning bad, what with the flies, and we're going amputate it off before it goes green. What I'm hoping is that you're the man for it." He put his hands on the sides of his belly, and when he takes them away to wipe his nose they leave streaks of Mare's blood.

"Oh, Master Billy, cutting a chicken's leg off, that ain't same as cutting a man's off, that ain't the same thing at all!"

"Don't call me master. I've never been one. You telling me you're shirking," he says, pointing to Mare, "after that boy lost a leg trying to get your gun back, just like thousands and thousands of souls died fighting over whether you darkies should be freed, or not?" He points at me. "Now you won't do one simple task that's to your suiting." He turns his head away, though his milky body keeps staring at me, his nipples like accusing eyes.

"I've no stomach for that, sir." I say. Cactus Jack looks at the ground, his lips pressed tight together, I'm thinking, *He don't have the stomach for cutting legs neither.*

The captain comes over. "What ails you, Bill?"

"This stupid nigger won't help."

The captain strokes his beard. "Bill, look now, if he's stupid, like you say, how can he be a field surgeon? That boy is a forlorn hope. If you take his leg off you'll only be hurrying his death along. He'll bleed a river; he already has." The captain looks sorry that I'm caught up in the Rangers' squabbling at all, but says no more and goes away. It's not that I afraid to cut the leg off, Morton. In a way Billy had sense asking me. It's just that if it went wrong I knew I wouldn't be thanked, and to be honest, I think the captain was right, least about Mare living anyhow.

I look at Billy. He looking sad, he sniffs the air, then he stares at Luke. "You there--ever done anything like this before?"

"Well, cut the leg off a cow one time," says Luke proudly.

"All right, you can do it. Only we don't have us a saw, just a knife, but it's a big ol' knife and sharp. His leg is broke where the bullet went in. Just cut through. We'll chip any sharp bits of bone back with the knife, sew her up ... shouldn't be hard." Billy grabs Luke by the sleeve and pulls him over to where Mare lay on the ground.

A little ways off, the captain and other Rangers are sitting on this old log that is resting atop another old log. I walk up to him. "Cap'n, we got no food in the woods. Maybe I oughta go looking again."

He doesn't look at me. "It's all right, Injun Dave got something. You can stay watch if you want to."

I don't want to. "Maybe I'll lay under a tree out of the sun, Cap'n. Lord, I think I must be part Mexican." I laugh, but it was hollow as the log they sitting on. I had heard him say before that Mexicans like sleeping in the daytime.

The captain's face doesn't move. He sits beside three other Rangers, their faces still as carved stone. After a while his lips move. "Don't blame you, son. It's not a picture you want to keep seeing in your head." I go sit under a tree. I don't see it happening, but I hear the whole thing. All because Billy Pender wouldn't let his friend die. The captain was right. That boy wouldn't survive having his leg off, and once the whole tribe learned the captain weren't for it, Billy wouldn't be getting much help.

So I'm laying under the tree and I hear them cutting Mare's pants off. Soon after the captain starts shouting at Luke from the log. "What you doing?" he says, and he asks Luke why he's wasting half a bottle of liquor on the boy's wound, when the leg ain't even off yet. I see Luke move the bottle a few steps away in case he'll grab it without thinking.

I am looking away mostly, but after a while I guess Luke is cutting because Mare is screaming. I hear what I guess is a punch and Luke calling Mare a little bastard. After a while Cactus says, "Chloroform don't work so good on Irish. Don't know why, maybe it's like alcohol and they need more than most folks."

"Tighten the belt, hold his arms," says Luke. A minute later he says, "That's it, I'm done." He holds up his hands and starts walking away.

Billy stops him. "What? You can't do that. If you're taking a horse over a jump you can't say half ways over the jump, I'm done jumping. You got to keep on jumping ... You said you did it to a cow one time."

Luke is staring sick-like at his own red hands and shirt. He looks up angrily into Billy's eyes. "That cow didn't punch me in the face, and I didn't reckon I'd have blood shooting in my eyes, did I? That cow didn't bleed."

"Lord Almighty, of course it didn't bleed. Dead things don't bleed. Mare is still very alive."

"Well, he's your friend, you go do it."

"I told you I can't, my hands shake ever since I got the malaria." Billy holds out his hands and shakes them like he's playing a piano on the back of a moving wagon.

With the captain a ways off, and not seeming to care now, Luke has his courage back. He turns away from Billy, walks off, and jumps in the river clothes and all. A while on Luke as he's coming back meets Cactus Jack, with both his eyes looking glassy now, on his way to wash after helping to finish up the sewing. For Luke had left a flap of loose skin to pull over the stump.

Luke walks over and he sits beside me. "Cactus broke ranks, I see."

I look over at the Rangers. "The logs resting on each other, looks like a cannon," I say, but either he can't hear me or he don't care because he just stares away.

A little later, the captain walks off into the trees to do his dirt, I reckon, because he has paper with him. We're both watching.

"Look at how the captain goes," Luke says. "He don't swagger or stroll. He's always marching, except when he's sneaking up on me."

"How would you know what he like when he's sneaking up on you, Luke? You got eyes on the back of your head? I been thinking, maybe he fight at Vicksburg."

"Why?"

I keep my face straight. "Because I hear that is where the gray-jackets starved inside the city walls and they left with nothing to eat but rats and donkeys, and the cap'n, he don't seem to abide any wasting."

Luke thinks a while. "Devil told you that. I don't know how you know, don't think I want to either."

"So, whenever I come upon something like that, you think it's the devil? No, Luke, maybe it God whispering in my ear why people are so." As I'm saying this, Luke is picking at his rice. I never told you about that, Morton. The day before the captain, he asked me to find chores for Luke. So I asks him to cook rice, but while I'm doing that the scout drops a dead raccoon at my feet. I'm ready to cut it right there but the scout shakes his head and roars a little like a bear and he starts to dance a little, too. I knew what he was trying to say, but I acted like I didn't. Then he got annoyed and said, "Bear." I nod, to show I get his meaning, and I go about half a mile away into woods before gutting it. When I come back with the skinned coon, the pot that's supposed to be only a third full of rice is flowing over, and Luke is laying under a shade tree nearby. You might think everyone in the world knows what happens rice when you cook it, but not Luke Sprague.

When Captain Wilson saw the rice, Luke was still sleeping. He kicked Luke's boots and shouted at him for being so careless. Luke started arguing with him and told him to wait a cotton-picking minute so he could explain how he'd only used a small bag. The captain acted like Luke was trying to provoke him--I guess white folks don't like cotton-picking, either in a turn of phrase or as a day's work. He couldn't abide the waste, and told Luke he had to fill up a bucket with rice and keep it with him, at all times, till it was gone.

It was enough rice for one man for two weeks, and Luke had to eat it all now in a few days before it turned.

"Luke, why not tell the captain the truth" I say, "and he'll take you back to Austin?"

"Well, then I might be freed and bushwhacked, or jailed, and I'd miss Washington. I've to be there in a few weeks." We're quiet for a time till he says, "My brother was at Vicksburg, during the siege."

"See, that is the sort of thing that will have you getting along with him. Ask him if he was there, too."

"How would I broach that subject? He does not like me, Abe. I can't just waltz into the woods right up behind him, where he's squatting and a-groaning, and say, 'Hey there, Captain, excuse me now, but I notice how your pieces of shit are lying upon each other there ... reminds me of a little cannon. Which reminds me of the war. Say, you weren't at Vicksburg, were you?' He'd take out that bayonet he's got stuck down his boot, stand up, and say, 'Gimpy, I shwear to God, are you trying to provoke me again?'"

"I hardly mean you to say it to him, if he's takin' a shit, Luke. I mean pick the right time."

Luke become serious and goes quiet for a time. "When he was eighteen my brother told me one of his jobs was slopping out latrines, carrying two buckets on his shoulders hanging from a stick, like it was milk, to throw over the walls around Vicksburg into the Mississippi. All the while bombs the size of barrels screamed over his head sounding like pigs getting their throats slit. One day he bumped into this low-ranking officer, said sorry and all. They were the worst, he told me--always trying to look important. Anyway the man went crazy because onto his boots went the soiling filth of a hundred men. Those boots were given to him by none other than General Pemberton because he'd swap his gray coat for a blue one come the night and go out and steal from Grant's men, or spoil, or burn their supplies. The officer beat my brother without mercy till he got restrained by two men."

"So, what of it?"

"Well, maybe nothing, but maybe it was Captain Wilson."

"Sheesh, Luke, come on now, he ain't the devil. It hardly likely he the cause of every bad thing we know of. The captain ain't the only Southern man with a temper now, is he?"

67

"Credit me with sense, there is more. The man was missing teeth because he'd gallop holding the reins in his mouth, so he could have a pistol in either hand, but if the horse stumbles, *Crunch*, your teeth are a memory."

I thought on it a moment. "Come on, Luke, the captain ain't the only Southern man with missing teeth." I grinned then Luke did, too. Whether or not he fight at Vicksburg, maybe it was wise for Luke to stay away from him.

Next morning, with my eyes still closed, I smell mist and hear crows cawing nearby, whispering secrets to one another. When I look, I see them strutting around our camp in among the sleeping bodies like thieves. Two of them are tugging at the blood-stained bandages on Mare's stump. Billy is lying face down on the ground next to him. I get up and shoo them away, and I walk up to Mare. Both his eyes are like glass, just staring up at the sky, with not a blink.

## 8  SOUTH

WE BURIED Mare later that morning. Billy was the most upset. I was sad, too, but mostly thankful I didn't have to be doctor anymore. Billy wanted to bury him in a Catholic cemetery, but the captain didn't want the hassle. Cactus Jack said, "Texas clay is good enough for any man." Everyone agreed.

Cactus left us and headed off on the wagon to Austin. Don't know why. Maybe so he could find out things for the captain. The rest of us quickly break up camp soon after the burial, fixing like there a pressing need to move on. I don't know where we is going, but it was south all along. It meant I was going to be late getting back to D.C. The journey home would take me three weeks at least, and I had to be there in two.

I knew every day I was overdue was a day my wife's momma Lizzie would spend complaining, like a drip in a roof, about where I was, what I was doing. It was because her husband had been a tomcat who sometimes took his supper with a different lady, and her suspicious eyes used look at me like I had a liking for milk and giblets, too.

Later on the same day, we made camp in a horseshoe-shaped clearing in a woods, and the captain sent us off to get game. I counted that a blessing, for Billy kept eyeing us like we was bad ones, but like he waiting on us to do something else wrong before he'd take action.

"That's how an angry Texan looks like--it don't mean he's going to do nothing," Luke says, though I wasn't sure.

When we return that evening, before supper, I hear an English voice coming from the camp saying, "Stop! Let me go."

Luke stands there, chewing on a piece of grass, looking like a village idiot.

"And what's he supposed to be?" says Billy.

"An Indian," says the captain, who is lighting a cigar.

"An Injun! What? He's like no redskin I've ever seen."

Of course, I knew who it was already because the captain is standing in front of his stagecoach with the picture of a big-eyed girl having knives thrown at her, and written on its side, in fancy cream-colored letters, is "The Great Punjabi." Yes, sir, the same one I'd met when I was escaping in the desert with my hands bound, and I started thinking, *He might say something terrible, because he knows my name.* The driver is wearing a sheepskin jacket now, and he keeps hollering and arguing. Billy throws him to the ground.

"Just shut up that guff you're spouting, you hear? I'm in no mood you want to go making worse. I buried my friend today, and you can keep him company in the next life if you keep hollering on like that." The man stops hollering.

The captain says, "Easy, Bill, easy." He looks up and smiles. "When is the full moon?" His eyes sparkle and his face and coat light up as the cigar tip glows like a tiny sun.

"Two or three days--haven't checked the almanac."

"We've two prisoners, two miscellaneous--we best head back to Austin. Tell the boys."

"Still by the southern way?" says the Dutch-looking Ranger, who is called Steve.

The captain coughs and looks like it's a question that don't need asking. "Naturally, and we're leaving at sunup. I still think they're going come after us."

"Who? The niggers?" says Billy.

He don't say who "they" is, but I'm thinking *It got to be the Buffalo Soldiers*, looking for revenge for what the Rangers done to their friends.

Who else could it be?

A mischievous look comes over the stagecoach driver, and his eyebrows pucker up. "Now, if it isn't my old friends Abraham Brown and Luke Sprague."

Luke is shocked the man knows his name.

The captain's nostrils get a little bigger, the start of a grin. He stares at Luke. "Thought you were Dick and Gary?"

"Thought our names didn't matter."

"They do now," the captain says smiling, like he hunting and just found fresh tracks. He walks off.

The driver gives Luke a hateful look making him uneasy, "what is your problem, friend?"

"You're no friend of mine." The driver sounds Irish now. He takes out a knife and a hunk of dried meat and starts cutting bits from it. Luke tells him it is not his fault that he's chained up. He says back, "I'm chained because you drew me like an ape. You're lucky I am. I might cut your heart out if I could reach it."

Gavin takes his hat off--it's like a red bandage wrapped around his head. He takes a piece of paper out of it, opens it out, and throws it at Luke. It flutters in the air and then settles near Luke, who picks it up. It's a wanted poster that says, "Gavin O'Neill ... The Thieving Irish Bastard." On it he's drawn with no neck, crazy eyes, a pug nose, and a big mouth with missing teeth, and he's holding up a bottle of rum like it's a club. It's an ape in a suit.

Luke smiles. "Well, they caught you. I can't have drawn you too badly."

"You drew yourself like Napoleon Bonaparte," Gavin says, talking about Luke's cameo on the poster. "And you drew me like something from Harper's Weekly." Gavin frowns and pushes his knuckles into the ground, like a legless cripple trying to get somewhere. Luke shrugs and tells him it is where he gets his ideas from. Gavin says, "You could have made me look better. It wouldn't have been hard. You didn't make yourself look like the Hunchback of Notre Dame, did you?"

"Who is that?" says Luke, happy letting the man show his learning.

"An ugly little man with a clubbed foot who rang bells in Paris, France beside all the gargoyles, his brothers in stone. He fell in love with this beautiful girl named Esmeralda."

"Well, there's hope for us all. I've a bad leg, maybe a beautiful girl will fall in love with me,"

Luke laughs, leaving Gavin to simmer in his anger.

I get ready for cooking, and Luke gets wood and makes a fire near to Gavin and the Indian prisoner who is close by. After a time the knots in Gavin's forehead start loosening. He says to Luke, "What happened your leg?" Luke don't answer, which is odd, for he such a prying man himself. "Why don't you like talking about it? Did you shoot yourself in the foot? And you call yourself the Fastest Draw."

Luke's jaws clench. "That's to do with sketching, not shooting."

"Are you mad? There are dudes out there who'd blast the life out of you, just to say they shot the Fastest Draw."

"Well, guess I didn't think about that," says Luke, a little annoyed.

"I don't think you did." Gavin smirks and starts putting bits of fresh meat I'd given him onto the end of a stick and holding it over the fire. As light and shadows from the crackling flames wrestle back and forth across his face, he gets comfortable. I ask him what sort of knife he has. He tells me it's from India, called it a Ghurkha knife, says he used to wear an army redcoat and shine its buttons every day. The heat there made him crazy--Doolally he called it, which is a place in India where the British soldiers wait around with nothing to do. He tell us he got sick of fighting Indians.

I didn't know why he'd come to Texas then so I start chuckling.

The native, sitting nearby, is just staring ahead like we ain't even there. I don't know can he even understand us. Gavin sees me laughing and asks me why. I shake my head and tell him it's nothing. When I gave him the meat before he'd told me to go and get a coat from his stagecoach because it was getting cool, and he noticed I didn't have one to go over the shirt he'd given to me. I got a patched up old coat of a bluish charcoal color then, and I didn't want him thinking I was mocking him now in case he'd mistake me for ungrateful.

Gavin stares into the embers for a while and smiles. "Would you like a ride on my elephant? Special good price for you, dee dee barp barp," he says, in the strange voice he used when I first met him, and he starts wiggling his head from side to side while he speaking with it. Then he laughs out loud, but to himself mostly.

I say, "What's that mean ... dee dee what?"

"Don't know, just something I heard a man in India say one time."

"If it means nothing, what you say it for?"

"Don't know ... don't know." His eyes start moving about quickly then he stops and looks at the native. "Who's the chief? Want something to eat, Mister Apache Man?" Gavin offers him the food on the end of his knife. The native looks confused. He jumps at Gavin till his chains hold him back and he can't go anymore. I'm guessing he's afraid. That or he don't understand Irish. "Gosh, even fiercer than an Apache. Must be Comanche," says Gavin, and he eats the food himself.

The Irishman talked on and on, telling stories. One, I recall, was about these four men in India. They were making cloth with their spinning wheels, and when they were done they'd put it away for safe keeping. But mice kept coming to nest in the cloth and chewing it till it was no use. So they got a cat to catch the mice, and each man was charged with the minding of a leg of same cat. Now this cat cut itself one day, on his front right paw, and the man who supposed to be minding it, he put a bandage and some oil, or alcohol, there to heal it. But the cat got near a fire a few days on and his paw, it comes near the flames, and it catches on fire. So what did the cat do? Only ran for the big pile of cloth and it all burns. So the other three men were angry with him, and one says to the man who bound up the cat, "Look what you did, it's all your fault."

"Naw, it ain't. What took him over to the cloth? Only the three legs you supposed to be minding."

I ask Gavin, "Who was right and who was wrong?"

"They're probably still arguing," he says, and he laughs out loud again, even more than before. Then he told me they went to a judge and he blamed the three men for what happened, not the one man.

That night was the strangest I ever had. As I lay down, the skeeters started having a drinking party and I was paying. So I opened up the purple bottle Mare had gave to me, and I splash what is lavender onto my neck and ankles and that keeps them away. It hasn't rained much in weeks, but it's raining hard that night. Maybe the Indian was a rainmaker, if you believes that, because it came out of nowhere and the clouds didn't have pregnant bellies earlier on that day, as I recall. Soon, even with the noise of rain tapping on leaves, inside my lavender cloud I feel peaceful as a baby in its momma's arms. I don't know if it really happened, or if it was only a dream, though it seemed real enough to me. After a time the rain stopped and the camp was silent. An owl screeches three times and the ground starts to shake and buckle. It's like something big is pushing up the earth. I look and see the head of a catfish come up out of the ground near to me. It's as big as a stagecoach, bigger even, and the mouth of the fish opens wide and out from it steps Sam. Sam wipes slime off himself and says, "Thank you, sir," to the catfish and stands there just like he's cock o' the walk.

His hat, with the crossed swords on it, is starting to rot. The scratches on one side of his face are gone, but the other side, where the cap is pulled down, is scary looking. His big pink tongue is the color of a boiled ham.

From inside the fish come screams, and the whore that died, she pokes out her head, and the man I bought the horse from, he's there, too, along with some of the other Negro soldiers that got killed. It seems full of dead folks. Even my father is there. Sam sees me and smiles. "Heyyyy, house-nigger, how you doing?" The misty night air is still around him and his chest that is like a big blue barrel ain't moving. He walks around the camp and starts shooting sleeping Rangers one after another, in the head, but his gun makes no noise. He just keeps saying, "Bang-bang" every time he fires. Sam stops and turns and looks at me, he walks towards me. His face a shade paler now, and the spit on his tongue makes it shine like a fish belly. He laughs and holds out the gun for me, which I think I already have, but when I look at the ground where I set it, it's not there. "Thank you for the gun, house-nigger. You was right. I was only minding it for you."

"What you doing, Sam?"

"Me, I'm thinking about killing me some Rangers."

"Where you come from, Sam. Is you in hell?"

"No, I ain't in hell. I come from the belly of the fish. It's a place between heaven and hell."

"What you doing there?"

"God was going to send me to hell, but I say sorry and I meant it, then the Lord starts thinking reasons why I shouldn't go there. All my whoring--was because there ain't but one woman for every ten men in these parts, and all my gambling and drinking--why that's just boredom because I can't read a good book to pass the evening time. He show me the door to heaven and told me I can walk on in, once I forgives the captain and once the Irish boy whose guts I shot out forgives me. Seems I is damned if I do and damned if I don't. But God tell me that Irish boy will forgive me if I forgive the captain. It's all like a spider's web and there is tangled lines and dead flies. Say, house-nigger, you're not sore at me for taking your gun, is you?"

"No, Sam, you didn't know what you was doing, I reckon."

"Ain't that the truth."

"How comes you don't just forgive the captain?"

"Hell no. He shot me in my prime of life. I don't even have a child left in this world, all over a stupid gun. You had it easy, house-nigger. I got sold down the river when I only a baby child, taken from my momma's arms, ended up breaking red Alabama clay, driving a beast, been driven like one, too. Then you get free and have a few years respeck for yourself, then bang, in a moment you're all dead and gone. That can't be right, house-nigger, can't be right at all."

"Guess it ain't, Sam, but you've got to have known it were wrong, what you did."

"Suppose I do, but getting all them bullets in my belly." He looks down. "That's a harsh thing to happen a man over a drunken foolishness."

"Guess it is, Sam."

"You right it is. Now you sure you got no bitterness in your heart? I'm in the belly of the fish till all my debts is paid."

"I don't think I do, Sam."

"If you do, I can give you one of my maggots to put on your heart. It'll eat up all the bitterness till it's all gone."

He holds out a maggot between two fingers that's wiggling like waterweed in a stream.

"No, thank you, Sam. I forgive you. Anyhow, I don't know if you is from hell or not, so I can't go taking gifts from you."

"But you already did." He grins, and I look down to where he's looking and see the gun inside my belt. He looks up, and below where his cap is pulled, maggots move under the skin. In parts it's eaten away to the bone, and where an eye ought to be is a hole.

Behind Sam is the catfish. Mare's head pops up in amongst slimy heads. He's crying, till something pulls him and he disappears into the deep where there is wailing. Maybe it's a Mexican child, or a dog, because I hear one barking.

A maggot falls to the ground.

I say, "Why don't you forgive, Sam? There's no joy in this world anyhow, just trouble."

Sam curls his upper lip and licks it with his pink-gray tongue.

"If you not happy here, house-nigger, I'll take you 'long with me. Don't sound like you is enjoying where you is at, don't sound like it at all. You coming?" Sam grabs my legs and starts pulling me along the ground.

"No," I say.

"You sure?" He keeps dragging me like he's hauling logs, till I come near the mouth of the catfish.

"No!" I say.

"Stop that talking," a voice says, "or I'll box your ears in." I'm awake again, Sam and the catfish are gone.

# 9 DEL FUGA

NOTHING MUCH else happened till a few days after we buried Mare, and during that time we was travelin' quickly south. We supposed to be going west to Austin, but it weren't my place to give directions to the captain. I Don't know why the captain didn't bring us in, or let us loose. Although he was spoiling for a fight with the Buffalo Soldiers, I don't think he wanted the death of so many, certainly not the woman or the two Rangers. But that's my own reckoning. I couldn't tell by his face if he cared at all. I think he needed to go to the desert to think for a while, or till things had blown over.

Luke and me were a small concern after all that happened, but the captain, for sure, knew that we were lying after Gavin said our real names.

I think maybe he was thinking Luke had led me astray, and he disliked his corrupting ways upon me. Though perhaps he just hated Luke because Luke was odd, or cocky, and he wanted to teach him manners, like an angel sent by God to show Luke the ways of good comportment.

I do think he liked having me around, not for the food I cooked, but because I acted how he thought a Negro should, always mannerly. The captain had a thing for manners, but it was a narrow road to tread upon, with little mercy for those who would stray from its path.

As we pass a sign for Los Ebanos, Luke gets happy about it, and he tells me the only time he hear tell of it is to do with rustling, which meant it's a good place to cross over to Mexico. Soon after, the captain sends one of his Rangers away on an errand. I figure he might be getting a new fugitive list in a town somewhere, but, even if he's not, seeing him go makes me want to run all the more.

That day we're going in a real strange way, weaving like a snake, southwest for a few miles, then southeast for the same distance back again. I don't know why and I don't ask, but whatever the reason, it was serpentine. After a time I hear a noise going rowp-rowp and it's getting louder. A small ball of dust comes out of the distant heat, flying low over the ground like a bird, and it's heading towards us. The captain smiles, but there's something sad about him, too. He dismounts and runs out to meet the ball of dust, which turns into a bloodhound, which he calls Buddy. He'd been missing for near on a month and looked it.

The hound puts his front paws on the captain's shoulders, and he steadies himself and starts dancing with that ugly dog, like they're a couple of old drunks. Buddy has bags under his eyes, hanging down like old pockets full of coins. The captain kisses him on the head and the dog licks his bristly chin. This goes on till the captain pushes him off and squats down, like a frog about to jump. He puts an arm around the hound, throws his head back, and starts howling. Buddy throws his head back and howls, too, with his matted tail slowly thrashing like a whip, then faster like a snake's rattle. "You hush now, Buddy. You hush, boy. Sit here, boy. Don't you move." The dog do that. "Anyone feed you?"

The captain walks to his horse and brings back a canteen, letting Buddy drink from it like a suckling baby. When he done, a few Rangers pick him up and say, "Three cheers for Buddy." They throw him up in the air, making his ears fly out. When he falls his lips go up to meet them. It like watching a bird fly low over still water, and the way its wings look like they're in a mirror below.

It occurs to me then maybe he dragged us all this way just to look for his ugly hound. But the captain had other rabbits to chase down at the border.

We move on.

In the plains as we approached the Rio Grande the sage got thicker. The sage bush was a glorious purple, like its flowers were getting ready to drink even though the sky clear blue. The captain knew rain was coming. He said so. He knew a lot of things like that and was real good at telling signs. Like later that day, he knew the storm was coming for he held out his hand and said, "Storm is coming." Don't know how he knew. I think he could feel the hairs tingling on his hand like when you hold your hand near velvet curtains sometimes.

Later, as shadows start getting longer, I smell river. We come to one and go along it till we get to a woods. There, we pass a shantytown of Negroes living in ramshackle huts made out of carpets, fruit boxes, sticks, and lumber. A mile or so after, Captain Wilson yells, "DIS-MOUNT," and he tells the Rangers to make camp in amongst a clearing of live oaks. The trees were more wide than tall, with branches so long they touching the ground, weaving in amongst each other like a giant wicker basket.

The captain comes up to us on his horse, I mean me, Gavin, Luke, and the native. He takes off his black hat, shakes his long curly hair, then looks up at the sky and across it like it's full of stars, even though it's still bright. "Storm is coming, later on." And without looking at us he says, "By the way, and so you know, we got extra powers when we're near the border. Any prisoners found trying to escape will be under *la ley del fuga*."

The captain looks down at us and we stand there looking at him, as he let his words that we don't understand sink in, and me and Luke start nodding like they're good and sunk. "What's that mean?" asks Gavin, who is honest about being ignorant.

"It means, if you run we can just shoot you, or if anyone tries rescuing you."

Gavin frowns. "You can shoot us?"

"That's right ... Just don't go roamin' off on me." He looks at me. "Abraham, go shoot game in the woods. But don't go too far, you hear, or you'll end up in the Rio Grande." Then he turns his head and slowly rides away.

It feels like he's daring me. Maybe he is and he wants us to run, because what happened at the Negro bar, and he wants to keep his story of it clear, with no muddying from Luke or me. Though the Captain, he still, seems kind of nice to me, and I can't figure his thinking out, can't figure it at all.

Luke stares at me a few seconds. "Let's go shoot game?"

Though I'd shot two squirrels with it, I say to him, "I ain't using this gun. It's got blood on it, makes me sick just to look upon it." Luke took it. A bow and some arrows are leaning out of the stagecoach window. I guess it was taken from the Indian and a Ranger has kept it for a keepsake, or it's for the courthouse. Luke walks over without asking anyone and pulls them out. He wasn't really one for that. Maybe it's because he an artist and used to doing things without needing leave from any soul because he had no boss or wife. He hands them to me. *Do I look like I can use these?* I'm thinking. But I don't say it ... At least he's trying.

We grab a lamp and go into the trees, find a trail, and walk along it till we come upon a stream. There's lots of ebony there and black walnut, too, which if you ever sees them, nothing grows in the ground near to them. They must have a poison in them or maybe they just want to be left alone like a bitter old man, because they have big old cracks in their bark like wrinkles. Luke says, "Let's go along the stream. You might get an animal going for a drink."

"Yeah, Luke, maybe even a bear, and with a bow an' arrow it'd need to be big as one if I'm going hit it, and it would have to be standing right in front of me, too. So close I can ask him what kind of day he's having and he might say, 'Not bad'. Then I'll say, 'Sorry, bear, I got to shoot you with this here bow an' arrow, but don't you worry none. Even where you is standing, I still might miss'." Luke offers to swap me the gun for the bow, so I stop fooling around and tell him, "It's all right."

We walk through woods along a crooked trail that hugs a winding stream. The side of the stream is brownish gray, from the rainwater running over the floor of the woods, but the middle of the water is clear. There we see a young colored woman, no more than eighteen, with big eyes, like a deer. Her head is covered with a tied red kerchief and she's wearing this sun-faded blue-print dress. She is standing in midstream filling a brown jug.

81

She turns and sees us. The bottom of her dress, which she'd been holding against her calves, falls to the water and she puts a hand to her chest. She is a bit shy, even a little scared. I take off my hat, so she sees my eyes. She smiles. "You scared me near to death."

"Sorry," I say.

"It's all right." Her voice is sweet. It feels like my bones being warmed.

"Scuse me, girl," I say. "Do you know a good place to shoot food around here?"

She laughs at me. "We don't shoot food. You mean animals for food, like raccoons and possums?"

"Yeah, of course that's what I mean, girl."

"Further up river." Her face gets scared looking again. "Just don't stay out after dark so close to the whole moon. You might run into the devil. He can drink a whole bottle of whisky in one mouth an' breathe fire like a dragon."

I laugh. "Fire like a dragon? That's crazy, girl." A wind starts blowing that's cool against my shirt, and it sticks to me like molasses on a stick. It feels kind of nice and not so at the same time.

"I'm just saying don't stay out after dark, that's all." She lifts the jug onto a shoulder, tilts her head forward till a bone looking like a knuckle appears at the back of her neck through the skin, and she walks off along the side of the stream and then she's gone, into the trees. She don't interest Luke. He's looking up at the trees like there is ghosts in them, and the Spanish moss is their beards, and it's not the wind that's making them sway, it's ghosts' hands, the ghosts of banditos and smugglers, and they're stroking their beards, wondering out what they're going to do with us all.

Luke smiles in his odd way. "She may be crazy, she may be not, but she sure sounds earnest." I'm thinking, *How comes he thinks saying she sounds like some man he know one time is a useful thing for me to hear right now?* So I don't ask him. But I did find out what earnest means years later from a colored schoolmistress, who laughed at me for near on ten minutes when I told her, I thought it's just someone's name. Though who knows when or how you learn the meaning of a word.

Still, as I see Luke staring up at the trees, I'm thinking *He's often a strange sort,* so I dare not pry when he in that part of his head. Like on one of them phrenology skulls, I wonder is there a part of the brain that says, *Strange things that ain't got nothing to do with what's going on,* because if so I reckon that part of his brain must be bigger than the rest of it. Anyhow, I'm just willing myself not to get spooked, probably because it's the sort of thing a young woman might do. And maybe if Earnest sounds like a young woman he spooks easily, too, and I laughs at the notion of it.

It's still bright, though the last rays of sun coming through the trees will soon be gone.

We keep walking on, watching, listening, hoping for something to shoot.

We see two strange white-headed ducks floating on the water that's swirling downriver towards us. Luke takes out the gun, but as he do, his foot snap a twig and they fly away.

We walk on a bit and hear a few whistles and see a green light shooting above a muddy foaming stream that's flowing into the clear one. It's a kingfisher and it slows and sets down in an old graveyard, where the gravestones are made out of stone, not wood.

There's been heavy rain that day and the ground must be too hard to swallow it up, for the gravestones are under a foot of water. It dating back to before the wars with Santa Anna, because the names I see not covered in moss are Mexican. Trees growing between the plots are twisting the ground with their roots, tipping gravestones forwards and backwards. The bird starts banging the little fish's head against a gravestone. It hears us, turns to look, bobs its head up and down a few times, and flies away. I go up near where the bird was. The fish is still there, alive and gasping for water. His eyes are like circles of oil on polished silver plates covered with jelly. One of the eyes is bust in with blood flowing through the jelly, and under his opening and closing gills it looks red as liver. I leave it be and look along the gravestone. On top it's covered with old fish scales. I guess the bird had been there before.

I like most graveyards, but not the forgotten ones. This one was peculiar, though, and I was glad when we moved on by it. The woods are beautiful at night, and it bring me back to happy days as a child.

Strong moonlight makes the Spanish moss glow, and lightning bugs are keeping us company. Frogs are croaking, owls are hooting, and cicadas are going sceeeee, sceeeee, like they're all in a band that's been playing together a long, long time. I feel a part of that, too, even though I'm trying to make no noise.

We walk on. Trees and dark night get thick and close around us like water over a sinking turtle's shell. Above us the full moon shines through a hole in the trees, with branches around it looking like the veins of an eyeball. Our lamp is lit now and we come to a big pool. Luke is carrying his bucket of rice, and I have the burning lamp in one hand and the bow an' arrows in the other. I put them on the ground and say, "If you shine it on the water, we might get us a catfish napping." I roll up my sleeves and wade in. Luke ties an end of the bow onto the lamp's handle and holds it out over the water.

The sounds of the slow, easy, bubbling river and bugs being breathed out by the woods gets louder as I wade further in. Then I try to be still and breathe slow as I can, while I watch the water for dark things a-moving below my hands, which are ready as snakes' heads.

I see a large fish swimming to where the light is shining on the water. I'm thinking about nothing else. I see a leech on my hand, but it's small so I just keep thinking about the fish. Even though I hear the fear in me say, *Oh, it's small now, Abe, but you don't think 'bout him now and he'll have all your blood, till he's like a newly twisted blood sausage. With not a hog in sight, just a paler looking Abraham Brown, like he's just been bled by a quack to kill de fever.*

Whoosh, I grab the fish and it must be fifteen pounds if it's one. It's a catfish that looks like it has a big moustache. It starts acting like a gentleman who's been arrested for the wrong reason, like he's saying, *Take your hands off me at once, sir. Don't you know I is a gentleman?* It keeps flapping his head from side to side while Luke is standing there idle, watching me struggle.

The fish slips out of my hands and splashes back into the water.

I slaps my thighs. "How comes you ain't helping me?"

"Well, because I'm on lamp and rice detail here. Why aren't you using the bow 'n' arrows I got you?"

But as I'm getting my words, I'm thinking *the ghosts be calling to us*, letting us know they've made up their minds, as a banshee scream goes through the woods, raising roosting birds out of their sleep and they don't like that, and start squawking to say so. I jump out of my skin, but only for a second before I back in it again. There bound to be a reason for the hollering.

We walk towards where the sound is coming from and duck behind a bush. In a clearing are two men that have what looks like flour sacks pulled over their heads and tied around their necks, with holes cut in the front to see with. I don't know is they Kluxers, but they might as well be. The screaming is from a Negro who is on his knees beside them. I hold the lamp low to the ground--I can see them clear enough by moonlight. One of the nightriders holds up a full bottle of whisky and takes a gulp from it, then he blows it out onto a flaming torch, making him look like a demon breathing fire. "I need to quench my thirst before I take your soul to hell," he says in an old raspy voice.

"God help me, pleassse," says the Negro.

Ol' raspy voice upends the whisky and drinks near the whole bottle in one time. It don't seem natural that he can do that, it don't seem natural at all.

Then the other one says, "An' I'm the ghost of the war come back to tell y'all, you're not free no more, yeah. I didn't take enough niggers souls with me. I need to be taking some more, yeeeeee-haaaww," and he stops talking and starts laughing and drinking. They are stirring up ghosts that should be left sleeping, like voodoo priests, letting in the spirits that haunt the woods to take over their souls.

Soon I overcome my fear, but it turns to hate. I whisper to Luke, "Let's shoot 'em."

"They're just fooling around."

"You crazy? They're scaring that man from his wits. I got to stop it."

"I am no John Wilkes Booth. If you want to play the hero go right on ahead."

It hard knowing what to do and it so muggy, too. Sweat is running down my brows, stinging my eyes with salty drops. Nearby these bullfrogs are shouting at each other. It's like one is saying, *I'm bigger than you is, and the other is saying back to him, No, you ain't,* and they keep doing that back and forth, over and over.

Hundreds of cicadas are shaking their bellies all around me, busying my mind with the sound of an army of baby rattlesnakes.

I go to take my gun from Luke, and he stops me. "If you fire it others might come. Let's shoot a flaming arrow and scare them away." It seems like an idea to try--I've none better. I take out a kerchief from my pocket and tie it to an arrow tip. My lamp is turned down so low it looks like a bottle a child has put a few lightning bugs into for fun. I tip oil onto the kerchief. We're close to them, maybe thirty feet, no more. I put the arrow in, set fire to it, pull the string back, and aim for a tree between the Kluxers. My shaking hand has a skeeter on it. Its fat belly is filling up fast with blood.

The sound of cicadas is coming in waves. As they start to die down again Luke whispers, "Aim close to the crackers." He puts a hand on my shoulder and starts to guide me, like he thinks he's Geronimo or someone like that. "Not there, you'll hit 'em. Back a bit. Now fire."

He claps me on the shoulder as I fires the arrow.

At the same time, Raspy is drinking back, till the bottom of the bottle is up in the air and the moon is dancing inside the glass.

I don't know does he see something shooting through the trees looking like a giant lightning bug. I don't know do he even feel it, because it hits his chest and he keeps on drinking. Maybe it is a demon after all. Flames slowly start to flicker like they are just thinking about what to do. I guess his clothes are soaked in whisky or some other spirit for up they go, conflagrating on him. The flames are like bats out of a cave on an evening, just a few at first then they're everywhere.

He starts screaming, and the Negro starts screaming, and Raspy is burning, and he starts flapping around like a chicken that's just got its head lopped off with an ax. The other one throws his torch away and hides behind a tree. Raspy stumbles in the dark and falls. A second ball of flame comes up from his chest and he gets up again and he's dancing from side to side, hopping from one foot to the other, screaming. "Oh Lord, oh Lordy, damn you to hellll ... Aaaahhhaa ..." He gets on the ground and rolls over the flames, then he's just gone, like he's fallen into the pit from where he'd come from. But he's not gone. For I can still see something glowing. And his friend jumps into what is a hollow and starts to hit him with his jacket.

It's like the woods stops to listen, because all I hear is, "Aaahhhaaaa" and the sound of the jacket beating against him, sounding like bellows on a fire. A few seconds go by and we hear, "Aaaahhhaaaaa" again, and the sound comes back from the deep of the woods, like it's an owl or a night bird from far, far away.

I feel sorry for him then, even if he is like a demon from the deep. The glowing stops, the second nightrider helps him up, and they get on their horses and ride off. The Negro is still hollering, and me and Luke run over. I squat down beside him. My nostrils soon fill with the smell of burning hair and what smells like bacon cooking. I put my hand on the Negro's shoulder to ease his fearing. "It's all right, they gone," I say.

He shakes my hand away. He's about forty, bits of moss and twigs is stuck in his curly hair. He's shaking, with his eyes wide with fear. His brow is wrinkled, like bark, and shines brown, white, and orange in the light of my lamp. And he's got a gray leather pouch tied around his neck. He sees my face and Luke's and calms down, wiping sweat the size of lemon pips off his brow. His eyes get smaller. "The devil one, he on fire."

"That no devil," laughs Luke. "Them nightriders use false bellies of leather. Then pour a whole bottle of whisky in them and you darkies believe it, because it don't seem right. Everybody knows that."

"How comes you don't tell me this before, Luke?"

His face is glowing orange and his nose shiny white and yellow. "Well, Abe, I credited you with enough sense not to think it was the devil himself. I mean, he was crying on the Lord, which is quite a clue. Anyway, why would he stop all his war and mayhem to appear to us?"

"I knows it were men, Luke, and the devil, he can be everywhere. He got a third of the angels doing his bidding."

He's mocking me, but that's white folks for you. They're not so clever about things of the spirit. That's because the slaves brought the beliefs from Africa. I don't think them all good, mind you. I don't go for magic or voodoo, but I do know there's bad spirits, that everything ain't superstition. Just like any people, they can be bad, pretending they is good. Though I laugh at it now because, for a moment, I did think it were a demon from the deep belly of the earth.

But that don't mean the devil weren't there whispering in those men's ears.

The Negro says, "How can I thank you?"

I ask him his name. It's Richard. But before I can refuse his offer, Luke says, "You got any food there, Richard?"

"Yeah." He fetches this bag a little ways off and gives it to Luke, who smiles because it's moving and clucking. Luke thanks him, then Richard, he just walks off and he's gone.

"Luke, we're taking all he has. And how we going say we got chickens?"

"Just pluck 'em and call them small wild turkeys, babies even." He sneers. "And I'm not taking, he was offering. It's right that he do, considering what we just did for him. Let's go and get the Rangers to track down the nightriders."

I can see then how everything will work for the good. The chickens will keep them happy, and while the Rangers are off looking for nightriders, we can escape. Nothing said on the matter, but I knew then we were going to be free of the Rangers that very night.

We go back to camp along a trail, easy enough, for a full moon shines through holes in the sheet of leaves pulled over the woods, like gas lamps on a dark street. From the edge of the woods we're guided back by the campfire. But as we walking to it we see it flickering. Rangers are running back and forth. The fire gets put out. Something is wrong. Luke stops a panicky-eyed Ranger named Joe, who is running by us, and asks him what the matter is. Joe's lips are quiverin'. "Captain Wilson fell in a fire."

Then Joe done run off. Did we ask the Rangers to track down the nightriders? No sir, they wouldn't have had far to go. Hee-hee, know what I'm saying. I mean, I almost started giggling, it so plain he reaping what he sowed. But when I come up to him and I see the captain, by the light of the moon, Goddamn! He's like someone with the rabies. It reminds me of a dog I see one time that had been run over by a stagecoach wheel--and same thing, he asked for it. But still, I felt sorry for an animal with its back broke.

Beside the captain is a burst water skin with a broken arrow sticking in it. He brought fire on himself or God did. My bottom lip falls, for now I'm thinking, *Maybe it ain't God at all*, and all this clamor is going come back to get me.

Billy grabs my arm. The wet on his eyeballs is shining in the moonlight. "Help him, give him some tea, do something."

"Give him as much whisky as he can hold, sir. What's tea going to do?" He knows I'm right, too, but he ain't happy hearing it. He rubs an eye and his nose like he's near to crying, like the captain his father, or a very close friend.

Seconds later Billy is gone. I'm alone with Luke, as the Rangers are busy, running to the river, filling their hats with water to cool the captain. Then a fear hits me. What if he wakes up from the raving and his mind is clear? "Gimme my gun back." I take the gun from Luke and push the bow an' arrows on him. I'd been careless, too, because when I was standing next to the Rangers with the bow before, looking at the arrow in the water skin, I'm lucky none of them say, *Hey, looky what he's got in his hands right there.* The Rangers should have just lifted him and carried him close to the river instead of running round for water. But I didn't say that to them. Maybe they were acting stupid now that their head was gone.

Luke says, "Now is our chance to skedaddle. We're close to the Rio."

"We can't run," I say. "I'll get blamed for this, too." Trying to kill a Ranger on top of stealing a horse--two horses. It's like the camel in a tent again. It's like I got a camel's head way into my tent, maybe even as far as his shoulders. But fear is making it worse because, truth be told, maybe it's only like the camel's neck is in my tent. I turn to Luke. "Hey, how big is a camel's neck?"

He glares at me. "What! Pardon my rudeness, Abe, but I don't believe I care. What's it got to do with our lot anyway?"

"You talked about it first."

"No, I did not."

"Yeah, you did, the camel in the tent, you was talking about it before."

He blows out a heavy breath like I'm exhausting him. "That was a thousand years ago."

"Come on now, you just being silly."

"It don't make sense you talking about it now."

"So when you think it right to start talking anew about something, huh?"

"When it makes sense, how about that."

"I see. Hmmm ... anyhow, Luke, I'm staying here. I don't wants to run no more."

"No more! You haven't even started."

"I've been running my whole life, Luke." I look at him with pride, though I'm nearly about to cry.

He frowns in a mocking way, then he get serious. "Captain Wilson is not going to want to explain to a judge why he had a bed sheet over his head when he could have two dead corpses."

It's a real good point he's making that I can't argue with. Though I do still think it were a flour sack, not a bed sheet. I just didn't mention that at the time though because it weren't necessary. I calms myself down and say, "All right, how we going to cross the river then?"

"Let the horses do the crossing."

"I don't know, Luke, leaping into the dark like that, it's sue-side."

"No, it's a cinch. They call them wet stock. Smugglers bring horses over the border all the time--riding the Rio, they call it."

Then the tables get turned because he says, "Maybe we shouldn't go." Then I start trying to convince him we ought to.

"No, we is going."

I hear metal clinging and clanging. "Don't forget I helped you." Gavin is beside us holding out his chained wrists, like a begga' with a bowl.

Luke frowns at him. "When d'you ever help me?"

But before Gavin answers, the Indian prisoner starts going, "Oo-weep, oo-weep," real loud four times.

Gavin's brows come together in the middle, and the hairs in them spike up. He don't look easy--none of us is. "Something is wrong. They say other Injuns just handed him up."

"Who do?" I say, and I squat down low, ready to run.

"The Rangers," says Gavin.

Luke looks at Gavin with doubting eyes. "How could they know about that?"

"Soldiers taught them it by giving them poxed blankets."

"Be wary of enemies bearing gifts," says Luke.

The native keeps going, "Oo-weep, oo-weep," making lots of noise. I don't know what is making him cry out. Maybe some sound that we don't hear.

Buddy starts to howl like he knows something is sneaking about in the trees. He's right about that. There is.

Gavin says, "Lads, are we for running, or what?"

Luke takes off his hat and slaps his thigh with it. "Yes, we are. What about the coonhound?"

Gavin's eyebrows bunch up like caterpillars do before they about to step forwards. He scratches a big sideburn like he's thinking. "We'll have to kill it, of course."

I hear a twig snap and I know then our plans are undone. From behind a tree, covered in night, someone says, "*La ley del fuga.*" I hear a gun cocking and see Billy and another Ranger, walking out sideways like mud crabs from behind the tree. Billy's eyes are rolling round their sockets, back and forth at us all, his gun trying its best to keep time with them.

"We heard you boys, every last word. While that hero lies dying up there, you think you're going to just up and a ... secesh from our little group here. No sirs, you will not be doing that. You was even going to kill Buddy."

Billy's legs are standing real wide, like he has the ghost of his horse between them, and his eyes are hurt and betrayed looking. Like it's us that's injured the captain, which it was, though I don't think he knows that. He looks even sadder than when I didn't make the captain a cup of tea. I'm thinking *I'm dead again*, though I ain't as scared as times before.

Gavin and Luke start to talk at the same time. "See-cesh?" Luke says. "What you talkin' about? We're only talking, we're not going anywhere."

"What in the blue blazes," Gavin says, "does *la ley del fuga* mean anyway? Tell me now. I've a right to know."

"First, you're damn right you're not going nowhere," says Billy. "Second, it means the law of flight."

"It's from the Mexican wars," says this short Ranger standing beside Billy named Llewelyn Sexton. Llewelyn has straight hair down past his jaws, a tiny upturned nose, and a big mouth that is smiling like he is proud of himself. "Now, which one of you boys wants to--" And those are the very last words he ever did say. Because just then his eyes roll up, he chokes, and he falls to his knees, grabbing at his throat. Then over onto the ground he goes, stone-dead. It's not really in the spirit of *la ley del fuga*, not that I know much about that law.

He really should of just shot us down if we're escaping, but we're not running. Maybe we have to be running and that's it. And how comes they is the last words he ever did say? In case you is wondering, it's because an arrow has just gone through his neck like a skewer through a pork belly. It's an Indian raid, which is the reason the Rangers didn't question me when they'd seen me with the bow. Maybe they knew trouble might come for us when they took the Indian prisoner.

There is lots of noise, and Rangers start shooting. I'm no general and no expert in the military things, but I do know that Indians are about the best horsemen in the world. They able to run and jump on a horse while it's moving. But these ones, they just seem to be, I don't know, in the woods whooping and running. I mean they're whooping over here and whooping over there. They couldn't have surprised no one with all that clamor.

Bow strings start snapping, arrows fly through the air, going like a whip do before it cracks. I see one stick into a Ranger's leg.

There is a hollow in the ground, like a shallow grave, next to me that I jump into. Morton, I would have pulled the earth round me, like a blanket, till all was quiet, if only I could've. An Indian, his face painted blue by the light of the moon, grabs Luke by the hair and flashes a knife at his throat. Gavin throws his knife at him and it goes right into his belly. Then Gavin jumps up and pushes it home, using both hands, right up into his lungs. I can still hear Gavin's chains and the air escaping out of the Indian, and he whooped no more.

Much as I would like to crawl into the earth, I'm part of it all, yes sir, because I have to fire at a charging native who has thoughts of putting an ax into my skull. He falls like a scarecrow that's just had the back stick pulled out of it.

I say, "Lord, take his soul." One minute I'm thinking *I'm going to die*, but a minute later, I'm thinking *This is going to make me free*. I get out of my shallow grave and shake off my fears. I think Luke can feel it, too, for he throws his bucket of rice down, and I shoot Gavin's chains. The noise is getting louder. Maybe you hear more when you're excited. The Indians are whistling at each other, whistling like eagles, howling like dogs. I guess it means something to them. I hear horses screaming, too, because arrows hit a few.

The Indian prisoner holds out his hands for me to shoot his chains, but I don't. Even though I'm trying to get away from the Rangers, they're the devil I know. And who can know what these Indians might do and the stories people tell about them. If his tribe wins they can break his chains, so good luck to you, sir.

Then again I was never a slave. If I'd been one, I might have helped him.

I know Seminoles in Florida looked after runaway slaves. But when Custer's army got killed, an injured Negro had his pecker cut off and put in a kettle by an angry squaw. That's nasty, even if she was upset. Anyhow, no favors were given from the black to the red that night, for an Apache war party is a scary thing, even though there was no more than a handful, maybe eight, nine, or ten of them. Might not sound like much, but if you were there, in it, Lord, it was like a part of Gettysburg and no less danger. It only takes one bullet to kill you because you're not watching the whole thing, just your own patch.

The man I shot didn't say nothing, he just die. I don't know which is better and I don't know if I'd be silent or screaming. Thankfully I am ignorant as to how Abraham Brown would fall should he be hit by an arrow or bullet. Something did hit me above my shin without me knowing and left a scar, though maybe something I run into just cut me there.

Dog barks, bow strings snap, and horses scream. Gavin, me, and Luke run to the horses. We had grabbed our bedrolls but left our canvass tarps behind at the bivouac, all presents from the Rangers, and we mounts up and ride on, with moonlight guiding us, towards the river. I hear someone near me cry out, but I don't look around.

The ground starts to fall, and soon after we're at the riverbank.

I take out the gun that saved my life. I never asked for it, and I don't want it. I think it almost knows what I'm going to do, as it shines in the moonlight, like it's wishing me to change my mind. But that is made.

I throw the gun into what I think is the deepest part of the water.

"What's that noise?" Luke asks.

Gavin don't answer.

"I think something jumped," I say. Which ain't a lie because it had regular jumped out of my hand into the water.

The Rio Grande is not wide, but it's strong, Morty, like looking at a sheet of black velvet being quietly pulled beneath you.

We're on a sheer bank looking in at it. You could be fooled to thinking it's slow. Then a branch would come along, moving like it has a pressing errand downriver. I'm afraid to go forward for there is still gunfire echoing from the camp, with the odd flash of gunpowder, like lightning from a distant storm. Soon it'll be blowing our way, so we have to be on ours. I hear Buddy through it all, howling with his head held high. Then the moon say goodbye for a time and a bit.

Luke says, "You ready?"

"No," I say.

"Have no fear, it's nature and nature, a river and a horse, dos amigos. Just enjoy it and let it happen. Yah!" I hear him whipping his horse either side with his reins and plunging in, then we all do.

As we go over the edge, the horses' bellies hitting the water sounds like claps of thunder. My face hits the back of my horse's neck. It feels like getting a punch in the nose, and there's the taste of blood in my throat soon after.

It's not so bad near the bank, but in the midstream the river wraps its hands around the horses' legs and starts pulling us along, like driftwood. My horse rears a bit and neighs like he's going to throw me. I expect the worst for a moment, because I can't swim. So I do nothing. Then the horse, it just goes calm, and we go along with the water's power. I bump into Luke. He's trying to come towards me and he's beside himself, or hoping to be. "Darn it, my horse is steering like a greasy pig. Abe, swap horses with me." I don't answer. He's no jockey, and if the horse and river are amigos on a ride, it don't mean they've asked him to come along. "It's my gimpy leg. I can't control him. I'm going to drown." His horse keeps jostling, and I move up beside him. He jumps onto the back of mine. After a while he asks me when I'm going to move across to the other one, whose straps I'm now holding.

"I'm not moving across," I say. "Why you think I'd go and do that for?" We keep arguing till the moon comes out again and the bank of the Mexican side tells us we're safe and to argue no more.

*****

Abe strikes a match and lights a pipe he has neatly stuffed with dark tobacco. He waves the match back and forth till it goes out. Wafting smoke soon embraces his face and creeps over his hat.

"I expect the captain came after you."

Abe inhales, making the end of his pipe glow the manifold colors of a sunset. "How comes you think so, Morton?"

"He seemed to think he owned Texas--why not Mexico?"

Abe laughs. "But Rangers, they ain't supposed to set foot down in Mexico."

## 10  BEASTS and BONES

THAT NIGHT in Mexico, Luke and me slept near the river for fear of riding through a nighttime land of snakes. We had the horses stood nearby in case we had to flee. Though if the Rangers had followed us then I think I'd have just given up. The ends of our bedrolls were as soggy as jelly roll dipped in tea but we slept on them anyhow as the center's was dry. Gavin wasn't with us, and I figured him dead. Not that it would have been rude for him to run off without saying nothing. It's just I'm sure one of the voices in his head would have made him say goodbye, in some highfaluting way, rather than just up and go, without so much as a wave. Though maybe if the river had taken him it would have been a mercy, considering what did happen to him.

We wake early next morning to the sound of chachalacas. It was Luke that seen him first. Although my eyes are still shut, even with the noise of the birds, when I hear Luke's yelps, I jump up and the blood stops cold in me, Morton. Because what I'm seeing would raise up the spines on a dead porcupine. The first thing I say is, "Oh Lord, no," and I covers over my eyes.

For there a little ways off from us is Gavin, standing with his back to us, with the feathers of an arrow sticking out of the back of his head. He must hear us yelling, because he turns around and it gets worse. Worst thing I've ever seen. An arrow has gone all the way through his head and an eyeball has been plucked right from its hole and is stuck on the end of the arrow, half a foot from his face, hanging there by a fleshy thread ... no lie.

Gavin stands there swaying gently back and forth. And then he speaks. "What's happening?"

Luke is looking at him, squinting his eyes, like he would to see where the sun sitting in the sky. "Nothing, Gavin, we figured you dead ... Good to see you're not."

"I can't see too good, and I've a splitting headache. I don't even remember drinking. Can't walk right either." He takes a few steps, but they was shaky looking. But Gavin ain't a slow one for figuring. He can tell we're troubled. "Is it bad?" he says.

I can't talk. He's lost an eye and me a tongue. I'm standing there with my mouth wide open, just watching him sway, like high corn in the wind, but there's no wind now, not even a child's breath of it.

"Tell me, boys, is it bad? I've a right to know."

"Well, Gavin," Luke says, "an eye patch ain't going to cut it."

"In the land of the blind, boys, the one-eyed man is king-- wahoo." Gavin laughs for a moment then he walks, and it's quickly now. He gets up on a pile of smooth rocks stacked by the river and holds his hands up high, like someone noble, and he stands there for a time. But the rocks cannot abide him being king. They slip from beneath his feet, and he falls onto his backside.

I remember outside Ford's theatre once these actors were playing to get the crowds to come. A man told me it was about the ghost of Hamlet's father, visiting him from the dead. I say that, Morty, as it reminds me of what happened next. I'm right in thinking Gavin wouldn't say goodbye in a common way because he says, "Luke, Luuuukkke," like he's the ghost, and he crawls over to Luke, with his head bent low, then he raises it up high, he's still kneeling. "Luke, I'm dying. Promise me you'll never draw an Irishman like an ape ever again."

"I promise you, Gavin. Come on now, you're going to pull through here."

Then Gavin keels over stone-dead. Or so we think. "That was disgusting!" Luke says. "My God, how did he ever survive the night?" But he has a chance to ask him himself, for Gavin gets back up and asks can he have a drink. Luke shakes his head. Either he don't believe what he's seeing or he don't got one to hand.

Gavin says, "Dee dee barp barp," then he keels over dead again.

Luke picks up a stick and pokes him in the ribs, like a Roman would. I suppose he's guessing he finally is dead, for his voice sounds like he's talking about someone no longer living. "That eye spooked me."

"You couldn't ... look him in the eye," I say. And I laugh, but it's not from the belly. "Let's bury him, Luke."

"Good idea. You do that."

"I meant both of us. I'm tired."

He scrunches up his eyebrows and stares hard at me, making me feel guilty. "Not too tired to be making jokes about a dying man."

We try to scrape back a hollow in the earth, but the ground gets hard as rock after a foot. We pull him in and make a cross out of driftwood and part of his shirt, and we cover him over with many stones. The last place to put a stone was over his face, which was not pretty given all the stones pushing against it.

"Let's say a few words before we close the casket," says Luke. "Gavin, you were not a handsome man in life. Death has been no kinder. Rest in peace, *hermano*."

Luke looks at me. I lowers my head.

"Lord, forgive Gavin his sins, don't forget the water and clothes he give to me, and save him from the fires of hell and the worms and demons that be there."

Luke put a big stone over his face, he had to work around the eye, which was there poking up like a prairie dog keeping watch.

We mounted up and continued to ride along a trail beside the river.

After a while the ground gets swampy, with the trail disappearing altogether. We don't really know where to go. The nearest thing to a signpost, by the Rio, is a palm tree with palms pointing to all places and none at all.

We decided not to hug the river in case we were smelt or seen, and to keep it simple we agree to head south for a little while, into the sun, then west towards the coast, and when we get there we'll go back north again to America, then quick as we can up to D.C. Both us hoping Luke's prize money is still there, and me that my wife and her mother don't kill me.

Luke reckoned the desert the best place to be to keep away from the hound, which he kept calling a coonhound, as if it'll only come after me. Maybe it made him less afraid to do that. Though I think one man's ass is the same as another's, at least to a dog. We weren't going fast, but we still hoofing away miles like horses shivering away flies, traveling on as though the warm air blowing from the north were a dog's breath we had to keep moving to avoid. Soon we're riding on a shiny, rocky desert trail. "*El sendero desierto*," Luke called it, though I'm thinking then that he don't know much Spanish at all and is only bragging.

Even after drowning it in the river, the captain's gun was still giving me trouble, for Luke says, "When are you going to shoot something?"

"Ain't got no gun, and I ain't your cook no more."

"Where is it?"

"In the river. It had blood on it."

"All guns have blood on them, or could have." Now Luke's face looks like a punished child's. Neither us ate the evening before, what with all the Apache clamor, nor that same morning. In fact, Luke hadn't eaten much in three days, ever since he'd been forbidden all other foods except rice, and he'd only been picking at that. I say, "Where's your rice at?"

"I threw it away, as you know."

"I would've eaten it. Better than being this hungry."

"Throwing that gun away is crazy. A few children with wooden guns could hold us up now."

"You're not telling me you afraid of chillen, is you? If those Indians captured you and made you one of their own, they'd have called you 'hare foot' because you run like a hare from everything like you scared of it, even a child."

"I got held up by children once down here. If you care to listen, I could tell you about it. I reckon they're the meanest thing in creation, meaner than adults by far."

I don't care to hear about it, and we keep quiet for a time. Under the Mexican sun, all the bad stuff, like pity for yourself, and whatever else there be in the soul, kept rising to the top, like drowned dead men in a river, asking to be spat out in words.

After a while I know I'm not being friendly. I say, "Sorry, Luke. Chillen ain't meaner than a bucket of rice, is they?"

"Don't mention rice to me again. If I survive Mexico, I'll never eat another grain of it."

"Not even with beef or chicken? No, sir, I'm making no promises about rice. We're still guuood friends."

We're both quiet till I start to sing:

"Miss Caroline Girl, yes ma'am.

Do you see them buzzards, yes ma'am. Do y--"

"I'm starting to like it." Luke says.

"Oh, yeah."

Luke smiles. "Yeah, and I think I got a plan owing to it."

Soon, as part of that plan, I'm lying out in the sun with my hat over my face, waiting many minutes. Till I hear a swishing sound nearby.

I see shadows from the sides of my eyes and hear petty squawking and bickering. I stay still as a corpse as they move closer--buzzards, that is. I wait till one comes right up on me. It flaps near to me and smells musty and nasty. It pecks at my ear and I try to grab it, but it fly away. Lord, the pain of it. I still have the scar on my right ear. Luke is nearby in the shade, "Grab it before it pecks you."

"I'm waiting for it to get closer. If you want to try, go ahead."

"I already explained, I'm a hombre blanco, you're a *hambre Negro*--I mean a hombre Negro. I'd fry in that sun." He's looking at me and he's between sun-dizzy and fearing. "Your eyes are all loco. I bet you could turn cannibal."

"If I did, I sure wouldn't eat you." And to myself I say, *You speak so much manure I bet you taste like it.* He's talking crazy, and it's clear the sun has warmed up his brains.

I got so hungry, lying there waiting, Morton. That when a silly-eyed runner bird walks up near to me with a green lizard wiggling in its mouth. I thought, He's just trying to make me jealous. When it sees my hungry eyes it runs away till he turns into a dust cloud.

Finally I did catch a buzzard and we cooked it inside a cave shaped like an overturned bowl. As the grass and twigs on the fire crackle and echo, Luke, staring at me, says, "Sorry about your ear."

"I bet you ain't."

"It's true." But I can't tell by his eyes if he's being truthful or not.

We put off eating long as we could. When we take the pieces from the fire, they nearly burnt black. I say, "You go."

"Well, normally I'd want the biggest piece, but maybe I'd do better with the smaller." We pick up our pieces of meat, both waiting for the other to start. But seems as I cooked it, it only right I bite into it first, like a captain staying last on a sinking ship. Even if it is a demon bird, maybe it won't taste like one. I chew on it. The taste don't come to me at first. Luke bites into his, but it looks like it's bit him back because his eyes close tight as babies' fists. "This bird tastes foul." He says.

"It don't taste like fowl to me."

"I mean bad foul, not bird fowl."

"Yeah, it sure do. Still, it's nice to get one over on them buzzards," I say, feeling my ear.

But Luke ain't listening or caring. He's staring into the fire, with proud eyes, thinking of former glories. "Ate a tasty Mexican cow once during the war."

"You come down here during the war?"

He looks at me and frowns. "I did not! I was Texas Home Guard, the West Pointers."

"That a fancy college, ain't it? D'you go there?"

"No, we were on a bluff overlooking the Rio Grande, and our group were on the west bit of it."

"How comes you was there?"

"Keeping an eye on the backdoor, for blues."

"See much fighting?"

"Not really, but we shot a cow one time."

"Was it a union cow?" I smile.

His eyes narrow.

"Well, no, it was just a stray longhorn crossing the river. I doubt it had taken sides, Abe. She was hit six times. It was me that hit 'er in the head.

"Fleming Condell was fifteen. He wanted all the glory to hisself, ran forward and claimed the mortal blow. How I wish his father had given him his wish."

"Glory hallelujah, I shot me a cow." My words bring him back to the fact he in a cave in Mexico eating buzzard.

"As a theater of war it was no Shiloh, true, but we did serve with honor."

"What was his wish?"

"That he be sent to war."

"Luke, is that the famous cow?"

"What do you mean?"

"The one you gained all your doctor's learning from, for amputating?" I say, joking to myself, but keeping my face straight.

"Yes, Abe, it was. My servant wanted to cut it for me, but I wouldn't let him."

"You'd a servant! Lord, them Yankee boys was lucky if they'd proper boots."

"It was our fathers who called us West Pointers." He pouts his lips. "I called us the SYROC regiment."

"How comes?"

"SYROC--it means we were too stupid, young, rich, or crippled for the regulars."

I laugh. "Excuse me. So you a crippled one, right?"

"Not necessarily."

"Which one was you then?" I say, and respectfully, so.

"Don't matter," he says, looking away, as though he'd had enough of my questions.

That's the first I heard about what Luke did during the war. I didn't ask him about it before, as I reckon he'd feel sorry for himself, with his limp. I figured that's where he'd got it from anyhow. The bird tastes like gall to me and we out of water to wash it down with, which is probably why I'm being catty, that and the heat and all. I throw the meat onto the fire and wait for Luke to finish his. When he do, his face looks like he's eating an unripe lemon and his throat looks like a bird's that is swallowing an eel. "Abe."

"Yeah."

"I'm thinking you were lucky the first buzzard bit your ear. "

"How so?"

"Normally they go for the eyes first. If that second buzzard hadn't seen blood there it would have went straight for your eyes."

"Thank you, Luke, that's good to know," I say, even though his plan near blinded me.

After eating we travel on through waterless country, mainly just sand and pebbles, with brown ground naked as breasts. Except for prickly pears and rain-carved canals that's telling you it's rained and dust that's telling you it's gone. It got so thirsty, Morton, I felt like dying. Luke says, "The land offers no sadder sight than a dried riverbed." I tell you it's weary work keeping another man happy when you've got a job doing it for yourself.

A hot east wind blows up soon after and the dust gets bad. When it clears I see a light, like a mirror in the sand. My horse moves faster. Getting closer we see it's a small pool with sweet water.

I nearly fall off my horse because he's so thirsty. He run up and puts his head in through the watery mirror up past his eyeballs. We drank our bellies full, filled our bottles, and moved on. Nothing much happened till a few hours later. We hadn't seen many people, except in the distance, and the dust was hurting my eyes, so I didn't really care what there was to see. I did see a few donkeys, tied to a boulder, a little way off. I saw nobody nearby, but still I'm thinking, *Something ain't right.*

We soon come upon two big rocks that are either side of the trail, and behind them stood a big cactus flowering with pink blooms. When it gets hot sometimes things move, but you don't expect to see two rocks standing up, for that's what happens. They stand up, turn around, and one of the rocks fires a shot over my head. The rocks are wearing gray ponchos with brown stripes, and they're pointing rifles at us, and laughing deeply through their dark open mouths.

A third comes from behind the cactus. He's tall and eagle nosed, wearing a big straw hat, and he has a rope tied round his middle. I guess he don't like his poncho flapping in the wind. He has two guns up in the air, and his big yellow and brown teeth are laughing and shining in the sun--one of them is gold. They come over shouting at us to give them money and order us down off of our horses.

We get down. I have a wallet and other money, stuffed down in my boots, but I don't go for them. Maybe they don't think I have much--and I don't act like I do.

One of the rocks comes over and empties Luke's pockets. All he has is an empty wallet, the wanted poster of Gavin, and a piece of charcoal. A rock starts shouting at him in Spanish. Luke says, "*Tranquilo, amigo.*"

The bandito asks Luke, "Why you got a Ranger's badge? You a Ranger?"

"No, I'm not a Ranger. I just rode with them a while."

The bandito doing the talking is the leader. He's small, with long-healed scars on his face, probably from fighting as a boy because he's still young, maybe about twenty-two. "*Maldito,* Ranger." His frown suddenly goes. "I know you've money. You can trust me. You give me money and you go." He starts nodding and smiling, and he don't look real bad, only like he's doing a job and is just mean enough to get it done.

The other rock is sulky looking, with eyes that have different plans about where to look. Luke tells them that he's got no money. The leader wants to know why Luke has the wanted poster. He tells them he's an artist, but they don't understand. So Luke goes behind me, asks me to lean over, and starts drawing on the back of Gavin's poster. Lord Jesus, what is he going to draw?

When he's done, a minute later, Luke gives the leader the drawing. The cactus looks at it, too, then at Luke, and then at me. I don't know how he's going to act. He wants to know which one he is. Luke points at the drawing. The cactus starts laughing. The leader do, too, even though he's made them all look ugly.

"Where Pablito?" asks the cactus. His dark sunken eyes are laughing and his rubber lips are stretching wide as they can across his face with his smile as he points to the sulky rock. Luke points out Pablito on the drawing, but Pablito don't laugh like the other two. He calls Luke a gringo pig and points a rifle at his teeth. Pablito is half cross-eyed, for one of his eyes keeps looking straight on while his left eye keeps looking right, and Luke has drawn all this, you see. Then a strange thing happens--a wind whips the poster out of the leader's hand and up into the air. It twirls a few times then swoops down and sticks to the needles on the true cactus tree, piercing the poster where Pablito's face is.

Pablito walks up slowly to the poster and he's still as a rock again. But not for long, because his sulky face shows fear. He blesses himself then he runs, runs like it means something to him. The other rock and the cactus walk backwards, towards the sun, still pointing their guns at us. They get on their donkeys and go after him. We watch till they're gone and travel on.

It really hot that day, and as we traveling along I see the bones of a longhorn, bleached white as cotton. Its ribs like a giant mother-of-pearl comb, combing the sands and shimmering like snakes. Now if you had bet me after I saw the longhorn's bones moving I'd soon see another dead beast's belly move, and I'd be the one making it move, I'd have lost my money. For sure enough, that's where we is later on that same day. We're inside a whitewashed, mud brick house, in a hollowed-out cow, and we're jumping up and down quick time.

It was an old-style winepress. And if you've ever wondered do a Mexican farmer figure two men taking some of his grapes is stealing? The answer is: Yes, he do--at least this one did anyhow. Light coming through a window shines on the barrel of the farmer's gun, and I guess you know who he's pointing it at. His dark eyes are bugged out and angry, with hardly no trust in them. His hair is black and straight, like it's been clipped beneath a bowl. His moustache is big and bushy, and he's wearing a white shirt and a brown leather jacket with short sleeves.

"His clothes are too small," I say. "Remind me of a frog shedding its skin. How comes he's making us do this?"

Luke grins. "Probably reckons slave labor better than wasting his own flesh."

"It wouldn't harm him none," I say, for he's fat, too, a fat Mexican frog. Soon I'm feeling about wine the way Luke do about rice. "This how wine gets made? Look where it's coming out."

We stop to look at juice trickling out of the cow's asshole, like blood from a gunshot wound, into a foaming barrel. The farmer don't like us slacking and tells us, "Vamos," to hurry us on. The room becomes bright. A young boy and girl walk in through an opening door. They laugh at us and start calling us gringos. Luke don't like that--you can tell by his eyes--but they're just sweet and innocent. The farmer acts cross and runs them off, but he's smiling as he closes the door after them.

It's hard work stomping grapes. We have to put our hands on each other's shoulders to get the balance, because every time we take our feet out the grapes don't want to let them go, and they make a weird sucking noise to say so, like our feet are in the mouth of a giant leech. After about an hour Luke reckons we're nearly done.

The room gets bright again as the door opens and two Mexican ladies, one old and one young, walk in with two straw baskets full of red grapes the size of plums. The ladies tip their baskets and walk out again, doing it like there is more to come. As she going by, the young woman smiles at Luke. Her teeth shiny and white, and none of them missing, except one of her eyeteeth. She has pretty hair, long and black, almost blue as the barrel of her daddy's gun, like the way you see on a crow when all its feathers are clean and the sun hits them. She has big brown eyes and a pink flower in her ear. She's like a lovely flower herself.

A big yawning dog, with gray eyes and a long wet tongue, is walking alongside her, following her in, and following her out.

Her mother's teeth like an old forgotten graveyard, where tree roots has moved headstones from where they ought to be. The sun has baked her skin, and it looks like someone took a sponge, dipped it in grape juice, and touched both her cheeks with it. Her eyes are dark in color but bright. Like when she looks at us it's like she's not angry with us about the grapes we took.

The cow winepress is sitting on logs, crossed like an X on both ends, like a sawyer's sawhorse. Under the barrel are mud bricks to build it up. The cow's legs are sticking in the air, and it's tilting towards the back end where Luke is at. When we done the farmer stands, kicks out his stubby legs to get the blood flowing, and gets us to step out. His eyes and gun still on us. I get out slowly, onto the bricks, but Luke he put a hand on one of the crossed logs and jumps out the back. As he do he clips the edge of the barrel, with a heel, and starts falling backwards. He grabs the rim of the barrel, that's full now, and the juice starts sloshing.

Luke falls to the floor, but like a cat do, he's all right. But the barrel spits out a gallon of juice, and it sways and sloshes. One of the mud bricks below the barrel explodes to dust. The farmer drops his gun and leaps for the barrel, but he trips on a loose flagstone.

I close my eyes, thinking, *The floor is going to go red in a wave of juice.* The farmer is flailing and bawling on the floor, his white shirt stained red, like the winepress has just given birth to him. Luke stands up and holds the barrel. Me and the farmer run up, the farmer kicks a mud brick under the barrel, and we all stand back with our hands held out. The barrel stays still. The farmer looks at us. His suspicious eyes close, but when they open again they have trust in them.

That evening we all sit down to a fine meal to celebrate the end of the harvest. The family is Catholic, for there is a smiling statue of the Virgin Mary, with the nose broken off, standing on a brick jutting out from the wall. As they pray before eating they cross themselves. Luke, who about as Catholic as Martin Luther, do so, too, trying for the girl's attention. The mother had a round earth oven that looks like a giant, curled up armadillo. She serves up beans, pollos, tortillas, and it's all good. But while we're eating chickens start squawking outside.

"*Los lobos,*" says the farmer.

His wife shakes her head. "*Leon.*" I think he was mixing up coyotes with wolves. Anyhow, the farmer gives her a look as if he's more interested in proving which animals are outside than saving chickens' lives.

He picks up his shotgun, and he and the wife go outside, leaving Luke, me, the pretty teenage daughter, and the two children. Luke don't waste any time. He looks at the girl, points to his chest, and says, "Lucas."

"Aracela." She smiles back.

"Aracela, what a beautiful name. Aracela *hermosa.*" The girl starts to play with a lock of her shiny black hair.

Luke's top lip is wine purple after drinking a few cups of it. The blacks of his eyes are the size of pennies now. Candles on the table glow in both of them and on his teeth, too, for his mouth open wide. She is looking back, with her face tilting to the side, as though she is brushing her hair. On the table many flies and moths lay dead, or twitching their wings, burnt by the candles they kept flying into. Luke frowns at them. "Daaaamn, it's like the Wilderness of Spotsylvania down there." He looks up and smiles at the girl again. "She is ripe as a peach."

I say, "What you doing, Luke?"

107

"I wonder has a handsome stranger ever told her she's *hermosa* before. Ever heard of bull-wire?" I shake my head. "My brother Bob has Texas rights on it. It's like barbwire. Now he's got a pretty young wife and my father's pride. It's hard getting a good woman when you're white. You can't just jump over a broom. She has to be from the right family and have good character. I tell you, Abe, wouldn't mind just moving down here where there's no rules, where you can do as you please."

"Luke, I got married in a church. If there a broom there it only for sweeping up with."

The little boy has eyes like an owl. He walks off and comes back with a small wooden box. "What you got there, hombrocito," says Luke. The boy lifts the lid and takes out a cockroach the size of a small bird, no lie. My mouth drops open. I never seen one that big before, and I've seen big ones working late in kitchens. Anyhow he wants Luke to look at his "cucaracha hermosa," he calls it, and he starts to pet it. His big sister, she hates it.

When the farmer and his wife come back Aracela screams to get the roach off the table.

The momma says nothing, just picks up the roach, brings it to the round oven, and throws it in. Then she bends down, looking inside the opening, her face a-glowing. The cucaracha makes a run for it and gets out the opening. She hammers down but misses. It tries to sidestep her, but she slaps it. White goo comes out of its tail, and she throws it back into the fire.

The woman washes her hands in a bowl, then takes a damp cloth to the table. She wipes away all the bodies and there is no flies now, except those stuck in the little lakes of wax on top of the candles. It's like looking at ants stuck in sticky tree sap, with their surprised eyes, and pincers, open and frozen.

The little boy starts bawling. Between snot and tears he do a lot of pointing, telling his daddy that Lucas has been calling his big sister hermosa. His little sister nods, her face all serious, like her brother's words is true.

The farmer's dark bugging eyes ain't happy when he hears it's not only his chickens being eyed. Luke laughs it off, so do Aracela, but like I say, the farmer, he don't like it. Then the little boy went and stuck his face into a straw mattress that smothered the noise of his bawling.

I stretch and yawn, as it's time to be away from the family. So the farmer brings us outside to a whitewashed shed with a downstairs and a loft. That's where we slept. The farmer gave me a hog-fat candle and a pistol for the "*los lobos,*" he said, or the "*leon,*" which is a mountain lion, I guess. Back then, Morton, people loved givin' me guns. It had a curly, Mexican type, design on the brass of its handle, and though it looked good, it so old I thought it might explode. That's if I ever got to use it, and I was hoping I wouldn't have to, not after all the trouble with the last gun I had.

I'm a light sleeper by nature, and I didn't get much sleep that night. I blew out the candle and turned in, but the farmer had a donkey and it kept making a noise like bad plumbing. It sounding like someone is grabbing it by the tail and pumping water up from the earth.

As I try to settle down to sleep I start thinking about a story Gavin told me back at the campfire.

I might mention at the time Gavin was drinking a green drink from a bottle he wouldn't share. He start to tell us about a king in Ireland, once upon a time, called Larry Lynch. Now this king wore a hat instead of a crown because he had donkeys' ears and wouldn't let anyone know about it. Every year he'd have to get someone to cut his hair, and afterwards he'd get the man killed by having someone chop off his head. So they start having a lottery in Ireland to see who'd have the unhappy job of cutting the king's hair. One time it fell to this young man, who was the only son of a widow. So the boy goes to cut the king's hair and sees his big ugly donkey ears and he knows right then he going to die. He begs King Larry, "Don't kill me. I won't tell nobody. I'm my mother's only son." So the king lets him live so long as he don't tell no one about the donkey ears. Now the young man has this story in his belly that won't leave him. It's like a curse, but he'd made his promise. So he goes to a priest and tells him his problem. The priest tells him, "Go to the forest and tell your secret to the trees." He goes to the forest, sees a willow tree, and he tells it, "Larry Lynch has donkeys' ears," and the curse gets lifted. Soon after, the king was going to be having a feast. The harper, who was to play at it, had a broken harp, so he goes into the forest and sees a willow tree, cuts it down, and makes a new harp.

Later, when they were having the feast, instead of music the harp says, "Larry lynch has donkeys' ears," over and over. For it was the same willow tree the boy told his problems to. How about that. So the king's big ugly secret was out. He took off his hat and everyone saw the truth and the people laughed. The king laughed, too, and no more barbers got their heads chopped off.

When the farmer's donkey stops, and I try to sleep again, the dog comes in and starts sniffing at my pants. I had dropped a portion of chicken on them, and I have to shoo him away for near on ten minutes, till he stops bothering me down there. I had tried to close the shed door before, but it was stuck, so Lord knows what can come and go as they please, pestering me. Anyhow an owl outside starts making noises soon after and I think I can hear Buddy, howling in the distance, though I guess that's only in my mind. Then I hear what, at first, I think is a screaming child, but really it's a cat and it starts to fight with I don't know what.

When I'm nearly sleeping again I hear a wolf, and that chills me because I'm on the ground floor, for Luke had claimed the loft to himself, or so I thought. I guess I got to sleep, but I can't recall how or even when, for I'm woken later by something moving outside. It's like someone is blowing out candles because beams of moonlight start disappearing from the wall, one at a time, till a dozen are gone. Then I see how big it is, whatever it is. But it don't make much noise, which means it's sneaky. I pick up the gun, pull back the hammer, and hold it out arm's length away from my face. It so old looking Chris Columbus must have brought it over with him, and I'm worried if I pull the trigger it might explode and it'd be the end of the gun and my face. It gets heavy after a while, but my fear won't let me put it down. I can't hear whatever it is now for my heart is so loud, and that and the wind are all I hear, coming through the door. But now this thing, it's so big, it's blocking out the wind. It moves closer.

I see two green eyes shining low, like candles in a faraway window, lit by moonlight coming through loose lumber in the wall. I wait till it gets right up near to me for it's not a Colt revolver I'm holding and I only have one shot. I'm scared it'll spring before I shoot, and by the time Luke or the farmer get to doing anything, if they'd a mind to, there won't be nothing left to save.

While I'm thinking this, I still don't know what the dickens it is. Maybe it's a mountain lion after all. It comes closer--I think, because I can't see its feet. I'm wondering are its eyes like lights at night. Like if you stare at them hard and long they seem to move closer to you and away again.

Then it pushes forward towards me. I fire at its eyes, BANG! The eyes disappear into the night.

The only thing I hear is my ears buzzing and Luke shouting, "What the hell you doing down there?"

"I shot me a wolf."

I'm about to ask him the same thing because I hear Aracela upstairs. A door slams at the farmhouse, steps walk towards us, and I see a light getting brighter. The farmer, holding a lamp, pokes his head round the shed door. Aracela ducks her head, and he don't see her. Luke tells him there is "*lobos*."

The farmer nods. He lifts the shed door up, closes it--as easy as a book--and he goes off back to bed. The rest of the night I slept peaceful even though my ears were buzzing. I had come against a wolf and lived. I felt like a hero, and I'm glad I did, Morton, for that feeling ... it didn't last long.

# 11  HUND BEGRABEN

A BE STOPS talking for a while. I say nothing till a peach tree orchard running by the train's window prompts me. "You say Luke thought the girl was ripe as a peach, but to me she sounded unripe, and if she'd been plucked early. It would've caused no small resentment on behalf of the peach tree."

"What do you mean, Morty?" Abe says, shaking his head. "I don't get you at all."

"The farmer, I don't think he would have cared for Luke's shenanigans with his daughter, he being a peach tree of sorts." I laugh awkwardly. Abe winces, then smiles before continuing.

\*\*\*\*\*

I'm getting to that, Morton, and yeah, Luke didn't have much luck, least when it come to peach trees anyhow. Next morning, I get up and walk outside, into the yard, to see the Mexican sun. It's like the landscape is the same, but you know you're in a different country, for it feels so. Like there's a different angel watching over the land, watching over you.

Angel or maybe demon, for we'd yet to learn what else Mexico had in store for us.

Distant blue-brown mountains are starting to go red as a shy girl's cheeks. The early sun has made the clouds into fields of pink cotton. Pretty, but it's also shepherd's warning at that time of day. But I ain't no shepherd, so what's that to me?

The donkey is lifting its tail, swishing flies away, for they're out already. I see under its tail these big white ticks are sucking on its asshole. It's a home for them, I guess, but a real ugly thing to see right before breakfast. But I wouldn't be getting any of that.

For that day, Morton. I was lucky to escape with my very own life.

I walk through the yard.

Flies are flying around the farmer's dog, too. But he ain't paying them much heed, nor me either. *He must be sore at me for shooing him away so much the night before*, I'm thinking. So I go over to make friends again. I say, "Hey there, good dog, time to rise and shine." But we sure ain't friends no more because the dog don't move. So I pet him and he's cold.

I turn him over and he's stiff, too, and right between his eyes is a bullet hole and his face is blacker than a skillet, his mouth is open, and his tongue is hanging out. I look around me, and no one is watching. I'm thinking, *What am I gonna to do?* So I drag the dog behind a building and I run into the shed and climb the ladder to get Luke.

Aracela still has her clothes on, Luke is in long johns. I shake Luke's leg. "Luke, we best go."

"Whyyyy?" he says, waking.

"Look see. We just best."

"What about my fiancé?" I don't know if he's joking or still drunk.

Outside the farmer is calling for Aracela and also calling *perrito* for his dog.

Luke, when he hears the farmer, recalls where he's at, and comes full awake. He shakes Aracela. She hears her father calling and blushes, for she sees me looking at her.

She starts to smooth back her hair. It's loose and raggedy, with bits of hay in it. She looking like a princess at supper the evening before, but now she's wearing the night she had in her hair, and her father the sort of man who'd hold a gun on you for picking grapes. But this farmer, we're in his country, in his farm, and in God knows what else. And that's just one *in* too many for him to put up with I reckon. We best leave and quick.

The farmer still calling for his daughter, and his dog. And I don't know which is worse.

Aracela goes to a window, at the back of the loft, climbs out, and drops to the ground outside.

The barn door gets kicked, then it starts to shake, sunlight bursts through as it slowly opens, and there stands the farmer with his shotgun. "*Donde estás Aracela?*" Even though I'm still upstairs I can see his lips moving under his bushy moustache.

Luke grabs his clothes and we both get down the ladder. "Sorry, señor, don't know." Luke says. "I don't speak *espanol muy bueno.*" He was speaking it fine the night before.

The farmer looks at the ground, where dark drops of blood are calling to him. He follows them till he sees where the blood stops and something has been dragged, and he follows the draggedy trail.

My stomach is feeling like a piece of dripping cloth being twisted by a fat Negro woman washing clothes, by a river, would. A woman who is sparing the sun all his work and laughing as she does. The farmer sees his dog. He pulls it back to where I found it. I'm standing at the shed door now. I whisper to Luke, "That no wolf I shot last night, it were the dog."

"You shot their dog! Why?" Luke's lower lip drops.

The farmer kicks the dog. It moves like something that's dead. That is, not much at all.

Then the farmer sees his daughter running. Their eyes meet. She stops between him and where Luke and me is. Luke is trying to pull on pants over his long johns, and we're moving quickly towards our horses, but not like we've done anything wrong. The farmer lifts up his shotgun and aims, but he don't shoot, because of his daughter.

The two of us run now, behind a shed, and jump on our horses.

Luke drops his clothes, but holds onto his boots by the skin of his teeth. The farmer comes around the shed and, as we're riding away, fires, sending Luke's horse into a gallop, and mine, too, owing to Luke and his horse catching buckshot in the ass. When he fires again we're far enough away to avoid being hurt.

The farmer, comes after us.

I turn and see him following on his donkey. He looks like a mad frog in his tight jacket. He's slow but real dogged--the farmer, that is. The donkey just looks lazy, like he wants to be in his barn, chewing on hay.

As the day warms up, the farmer starts gaining on us. When I think on it, it was Luke's fault really. He said we should go up where there were many pines and the trail led to this narrow gap between two rocky cliffs, but it made it all the worse because now we're riding over rocky donkey-loving land. We came out the other side onto this dry, sandy prairie and the ground started to fall.

Above us the sky was blue as a hyacinth except for circling black specks and the odd wisp of a cotton-colored cloud. Far ahead, where yellow ground met with blue, was a dark circle like a dot. It grew like the center of an eyeball and began to look like a stone head. I couldn't believe my eyes, but sure enough that's what it was.

It was ten, eleven, maybe even twelve feet tall. Its lips were pouty, and its nostrils were flaring like it upset or mocking somebody. Maybe it didn't like the sand that was blowing up into its mouth and nose, or maybe someone had touched his daughter. We said no words and let it pass us by like it were a dream that would go from our minds. Where the stone head came from or how anyone got it to that place is something I do not know. The land begins to drop even more into a valley, and before us the ground seems shiny and white. It was salt. We pass a stone church with a cracked bell and a few houses made of mud bricks. Then I see a little Mexican boy with his hands and face covered in blood.

*****

The Georgia landscape floats by our window. Pine trees have long black shadows saying it is nine o'clock, though it is hours before that. Ahead of us looms a sharp turn, and beyond that a steel bridge traverses a river. A gleaming trestle encages a dipping sun. Beyond that a cave entrance, lurking in a hillside, hungrily awaits the train. I interrupt Abe. "What of Luke's untended-to backside, during your escape? Surely it was troubling him greatly."

Abe swats his hand and shakes his head.

"It was fine, Morton. If anything it caused me more trouble than him." My expression told him that I didn't rightly follow. "I'll get to that," Abe tells me as the train goes dark and the rattling gets louder and echoes. He stops. Apparently it'll need to be sunlight before he'll recommence.

*****

The boy, like I said, had blood on him. Beyond him were folks with big straw hats, and by a river there were sheep in a pen made of sticks and boughs. There was more buildings and it looked like a village square. I could see carcasses and joints laid out on hides. It looks like the people setting up market. The people looking at us, but with no concern, nor for the farmer, just being busy with what they was doing. A little white dog with a black spot on its head was following the farmer. I don't know where it came from, but maybe it related to the one I shot.

We passed beyond where people lived and finally, I don't know what happens, but I guess the donkey got thinking *it's a waste of time*, as I hear shouting. I turn to see the farmer get down off the donkey. He starts pulling at it and yelling and waving his fist at us. The donkey keeps complaining, and starts sounding like bad plumbing again. We're both stopped and looking back now. The farmer points his gun at us and fires. Luke slumps down on his horse like he's hit. Then he laughs and sits back up again. We move on, and from a distance the donkey sounds just like a train braking from far, far away. That train don't start again for we go over a rise, and we see and hear the donkey no more. But the poor little dog it keeps following us.

A few hours after we free of the farmer, we come upon a pool, with bubbles rising up in it like a boiling stew. In spite of coaxing, the horses won't drink from it. A lizard lay beside the pool with his feet in the air, like the last thing he do before dying is try to tickle the sky. It all under the shade of a cottonwood tree, growing there by itself, and beneath the shade of its clattering leaves sits a skeleton, dressed in men's clothes. Soon we're under the tree. Luke asked me to take out the pellets from his ass, a job he could not do himself. I sharpened two matches with Gavin's Gurkha knife, taken from a snuffbox I had down in my boot, and go to work.

Luke was laying belly down with his bare buttocks showing. After hardly any time he says, "Can't you hurry? It stings like hell."

"I ain't no Chinaman, Luke. The pellets keep on slipping." I was not used to using little chopsticks.

He stay quiet then, just lying there staring at the skeleton. "I'd love to draw him. I wonder what race he is."

"You should draw him. He be the first man you ever did that don't complain about it."

"What you reckon he die of?"

I'm just about to take out a pellet and it slips off my sticks. "He gave up hope. Said to himself, What am I doing out here?"

Luke laughs, even though I'm not trying to be funny.

Then the dog comes over and begins to lick Luke's bloody backside. "What the hell is that?"

"Little dog."

Luke put a hand back, he grabs the dog by the head, then throws it aside. He tells me soon after the skeleton has a satchel under its legs and asks me to go get it for him. I do that, and I go on looking for pellets. He asks me for a match a minute later. He has a cigar in his hand now. I light it for him.

"That skeleton stinks, but the cigar is good."

"Didn't notice it stinking."

"Why do you figure that happened back there?"

"With the farmer? He didn't like you fornicating with his daughter."

"Well, you shooting his dog didn't help. An' I didn't fornicate with her. I tried to reach for her nether regions, but she said she didn't want to get embarrassed. Wouldn't let me do anything except kiss her. Catholics for you."

"Didn't know she could speak English."

"She couldn't, she just said, 'No *embarazada*,' but the meaning was she didn't want the seed of Sprague in her belly ... That vaquero was a mean cuss."

"What's a vaquero?"

"It's a Mexican cowboy. *Vaca* means cow."

"He didn't have cows, Luke, just that dead one."

After a while I hear flies a-buzzing nearby, which they weren't before. Though maybe I'm only hearing them now as we ain't jabbering on no more. I think little of it. I start singing, "Shoo Fly, Don't Bother Me," but the flies pay me no heed and get louder and louder. I look around to see what's drawing them in.

A few dead bats are on the ground, not far from us. Behind them is a large hole in a hillside of rock. Squeaking is coming from there, and every now and again when the wind turns it smells like when you're walking by a slaughterhouse, and the cottonwood leaves above start clattering. The little dog goes over and shakes a dead bat at the mouth of the cave, then drops it hoping it will move.

"There is bats in that cave," I say.

"*Da liegt der hund begraben.*"

"What do that mean?"

"It's German. It means that is where the dog lies, already told you."

"Maybe you did. But it don't make sense, not even in English."

118

"It means that is what is causing the smell. It's the root of the problem. When people bury a dog they often don't do a good job of it, then after a while it starts stinking. Means you're right is all, about the bats."

"I think I'm done."

I wash my hands in the pool and sit back. I start to relax because our thinking is we're safe, Morton, from the sun, the farmer, Rangers, everything. Till after a couple of minutes I hear a noise like stones falling, and I look to where it's coming from. A man's head comes over a hill a hundred yards in front of us, like a wary wild turkey. Feathers are sticking up out of his head. I think it might be Dave, the Ranger's scout.

Then I hear barking and I see Buddy moving fast, though his legs seem like they're moving slow, flailing in big loops like scythes. His head is bobbing up and down and his ears are flapping like wings. He's barking, but the wind is blowing at his face, and the sound only carries now and then. I don't know has Dave seen us. Luke gets up. I hear a hiss and see the cigar floating in the pool. I don't run for the horses, for the scout would have put an arrow or two in my back before I even fell from the horse, and while I lay on the ground thinking about that pain Buddy would rip open my throat like the crust on a blueberry pie.

The barking is getting louder. We put the cottonwood tree between us and the scout, and go into the cave's mouth. We climb up a little and see something like giant teeth coming from the roof, like white spears, or like you see under a stone bridge, but a thousand times bigger. They gently glowing too, like fungus do at night in the woods sometimes.

Soon the cave gets dark as a shithouse on a moonless night, though it smelling far worse. Luke is out in front and I'm close behind behaving like a blind man that's lost his stick, just feeling about in the dark. Till I touch Luke's clothes and clammy wet walls. Then the air turns to poison, burning the inside of my nose, and stinging my eyes like I've lime dust in them. It smells like ammonia on a hospital floor. Suddenly, our boots start to sink. We're standing in bat shit. From up above we hear whistles and screams. I hear something moving near to me, but I keep stomping onwards. The noise must have been Luke falling, and he held out his hand to steady himself.

For soon after, by a line of light coming through the wall, I see beetles there walking up and down his hand like people on a busy street.

"Don't put your hand in it," he says.

"It's bat shit--I'm not gonna."

"They're just words coming out my mouth."

"What's it smell like?"

"I guess bad. Not going holding it up to my nose now, am I." They was stupid things we was saying. Of course, a place like that ain't no good for thinking.

There's gnats there, too, as many as in the woods. And they so small I've a few down in my throat before I even know they're there, and I swallows them. I keep coughing, not because the flies or smell, it because the air so bad. It dustier than when you're banging an old rug out the back of your shack with a stick. What's coming out of my nose must have been a foot long, no lie.

I have no idea how long I can stand it, Morton. Not knowing how to find the open air and, not only that, heat coming from the bats is making us sweat, too. The only joy is when bats flapped near to me, fanning my face, and none of them crashed into me.

We hear Buddy inside the caves and his barking, rowp-rowp, echoing out like fingers searching everywhere for us. I can't see, but soon after I know something is moving, near to me. I'm wondering, am I going to get bit or shot? Then a terrible thing happens, because I can't see, I light the hog-fat candle from the night before that I had stuffed down in my boot. Maybe Buddy will see me now, or Dave with his arrows. But I have to see, too. But Buddy ain't near me, Luke is--and Buddy, that ain't the terrible thing that happens. See this. My candle touches off the wall and a light dances out and sticks to it. A flame like ants on fire starts crawling up the walls, like an army carrying blue torches.

The roof starts burning like lightning flashes rolling across the sky. I can see firelight through pink bats' wings, like they're flying lampshades. It's gas, and bats up above us start screaming and falling from the roof like burning rocks.

We duck low and I don't get burned, though all the air gets sucked out of the cave and our lungs, like a squeezed bellows, till the candle starts to flicker.

We run towards an opening near to us and get in, like we'd smoked ourselves out of our own holes. We keep moving through a chamber--the bat colony don't live there. Just as my lungs about to burst we feel cold fresh air being sucked toward us, and we hear trickling water. We find a running stream and follow that till it falls into a hole about the width of a big man's belly before pouring into a pool in a chamber below. I hold the candle into the hole. It's like looking into a sick child's throat. When I put the candle behind my back, I see a light, like sunrise, coming from the lower pool. We're thinking, *It must open out onto something.* But there is no way of knowing if we go in that hole, drop down maybe four feet before hitting water, how deep it will be. And if it ain't deep would there be a way out, or is there only cracks letting light in? I think on it and say, "We got to go on."

Luke's face is white, orange, and scared looking. He looks into the hole then into the dark behind me. "Give me the candle, I'll pass it to you." I guess that means I go first. I shy about going till we hear howls echoing again and no bats. Luke pushes by me, sliding down till his head and arms are all that's above the hole. He stops moving. The howling is getting louder. I don't know what's wrong with Luke. Maybe he's caught on something as his feet are down the hole like a breech baby.

As the stream slaps against his dimpled chin, like it's a ship's prow, he tells me his backside is stuck. Maybe it hurt from the shot, or maybe it's swollen. But it sounds like he be complaining is all. His elbows are pressing down and his fingers are spread out like a piano player's, digging into the rock under the flowing water. I reckon if I push he'll fit right enough. The noise of howling is nearly surrounding us now, like it's coming from the walls. I stand on his shoulders and he pushes through, yelling and swearing at me, like a baby who'd rather not be born. I hear a big splash, an echo, a little splash ... silence.

I look into the hole. It's twisting a little at the bottom, and it'll take some turning to get through. As I'm doing that, I hear something behind me. I look through my legs, because I'm kneeling, and see the small dog running towards me all filthy and wagging his tail. I breathe easy again, hearing nothing except gurgling water. I turn and sit up. A huge shadow stands behind the little dog.

I stays calm as it's just the little dog, the candle, and maybe even my mind playing tricks. I grin at my own foolishness and start to put my feet in the hole. The shadow starts creeping towards me. But the little dog ain't moving and the shadow's tail ain't wagging neither. *That's peculiar.* My heart and lungs stop, then I knows it. They start again. I hear a hellish rowp come rolling down the tunnel. Behind the little dog comes the running shadow. It's Buddy looking like he's been chewing on soap with lines of spit suds swinging from his teeth like ropes. He starts going rowp-rowp. Echoes make it sound like a whole pack of dogs. The spit lines from his rubbery, pink and black gums start shining--he's that near my candle. The little dog starts barking at Buddy, whose angry eyes are red and hurting from his time with the bats. Bags under his eyes are falling down, showing pink flesh. I never this close to him before to see the bits taken out at the end of his ears by rabbits, fleas, other dogs ... who knows. I keep moving down, holding the candle out in front of me. I got another hand at the top of the hole, and it looks white and blue the water so cold. Buddy scrapes the stone on the mouth of the hole with a paw. It's like frost is falling on me. I shake the candle at him and whip out running wax, hitting his nose. He yelps, snarling as he backs away. Then he comes back snapping at me, crazy-eyed now, like he's rabies. He's not a young dog, maybe six or seven, and his teeth are worn down with red tips, though they'd still take off an ear or worse.

The little dog starts growling and Buddy pounces on it like it's dinner, or maybe he thought it the cause of his burning pain. Buddy grabs its throat and shakes it. He drops the little dog and it looks dead as a dead bat, then Buddy comes back for me. He goes to bite my face but ends up snapping air and water. He snaps again and grabs a hold of my chin, piercing it.

I pull my head to the side and get free, and he snaps onto my collar and starts pulling it towards him like it's the leg of a rabbit that's down a hole. His muzzle scrunching up like an angry furrowed field. I feel his nostrils blowing air on me. My collar rips off and comes free in his mouth and he falls back. He drops it and leaps for me, but instead of biting me I see his balls flying over the hole because Luke has just pulled my legs and I'm falling down onto him.

I don't go under the water and my candle don't go out. For all his barking, the hound scared to follow. He looks down the hole then starts howling, like all of a sudden he knows he's lost. I'd fallen into a chamber that's cool, peaceful, and bubbling like a baby. We move on into a tunnel where the water is flowing slowly. We follow it along, hoping to see light, drinking as we go, because the water so pure. Our feet touching bottom mostly. I swim a little, too. Though back then I wasn't really able to because I was never taught. I'm only using one hand, as I've the candle in the other. After a few minutes we start to see daylight then blue sky. The water falls into a box canyon that's about as long as three boxcars, as wide as one, and as tall as two houses to the top, and it opens onto a rock table. In front of us is a drop, about twice my height, into a deep pool. With nothing to do, but go forward, we jump in and go under.

When we come up, and get out, Luke's hand is clean of bat shit and beetles. He smiles at it, holding it up to the sun like it's a precious glass he's just polished. We sit at the bank for a while, resting like lazy turtles on river logs, knowing we're safe from anything coming from behind and in no hurry to start a hard climb still wet from the pool.

As I sit there looking at the water's flowing and foaming, watching the sun play on the froth as it swirls, I see something shining, like the water is smiling with teeth bright as diamonds. I don't think on it, but a minute later I grab my boot. For I know that shining thing that's been sucked down a hole at the far end of the canyon by now is a silver snuffbox that I'd been leggin'. It's worth money in its own right, plus it's carrying most of my money and my matches, too. I say nothing to Luke in case he'll mock me. I take my boots off and empty out the dirt. I wasn't thankful for that bat shit at the time, but that hound wouldn't have liked walking on it. I'm certain he didn't appreciate smelling it. It slowed him down, and without it I'd have been hurt bad for sure. Praise the Lord he didn't hurt my chin so bad. I've done worse myself shaving. We couldn't hear much coming from above us, just wind whistling and whipping the rock table, and an eagle in the distance sounding like it's crying. We didn't know how far we'd traveled from where we'd first gone in. And if we climb up how far we would be from the Rangers.

But after a short while we see a way up that looks easy enough. The stone smooth as polished wood and don't have much plants growing out of it for grabbing, or deep cracks for putting feet and hands into. But they were there if you looked.

It was slow going. The rock was plastered white in one spot because it under a hawk's nest. We try to go around it and stop halfway up. Above me, it's like there's black fog coming out of the rock. Or maybe it's morning mist being burned up by the sun, though the hour for that has passed. My ears start to buzz again. I think they're just remembering the shot in the barn. But as we climb a little more, the buzzing gets louder. The mist becomes bees, and hanging under a rock we see combs of honey. Luke's eyes are falling out of his head. The bees are ignoring us, mostly just floating by, like we not even there. They sure look delicious, them combs, but after the buzzards I have no mind in me to go grabbing for them. Luke reaches out a hand but stops. He pulls out Gavin's Ghurkha knife instead and pokes it in a comb that looks full and frosty. Honey dark and orange starts oozing out. A few bees go down to the honey, but they look calm enough.

Luke laughs, pointing at a comb. "That one on the end has no bees. Would you like to try?"

"No, Luke, I wouldn't. An' if we is taking turns doing things it's yours because I laid out for them birds."

"But Negroes are so quick."

"I ain't going round calling myself 'Fastest Draw', is I? You is. Sounds like you is the fastest. I ain't fast at nothing, unless it's peeling potatoes."

"I cut that man's leg off for you."

"I never asks you to now, did I? An' that still don't make it my turn, because them birds after that."

His eyes wrinkle. "You *maldito* house-nigger, I have to go do everything myself now, don't I?" He holds a hand up like a snake, snaps it in, and pulls out a comb with no bees on it. I want to punch him, and at the same time I'm wondering am I going to get any of it. It's looking like he's earned his wages for his courage, and maybe I don't figure into it in his mind. As I look at him eating I'm angry at myself for not been braver. But then a bee lands on him, lands right on his forehead. It walks around there for a bit, like a dog might do before taking a shit in the garden.

Luke's eyes turn up till I see the little red veins on the bottoms of his eyeballs, and his nose crinkles up like creased paper. We climb down onto the shelf where the old hawks' nest is so we can stand. Luke swats off the bee. He picks out the sting like it's a piece of lint from his coat and flicks it to the wind, laughing as he starts chewing comb like a goat.

"You just standing on hawk-shit there, Luke."

"No, there's rocks under it."

"You sure?"

He presses a foot down and looks at me like he is, and why am I wasting his time. As he chews on he sees something. He leans over, picks it up, and puts it to the back of his head. It's a hawk feather, and he sticks out his chest proudly, like an Indian brave.

"How do I look?" he says.

Like a turkey plucked of all of its feathers bar one. But before I can say something another bee lands on his head and stings him. He starts getting panicky now. He swats it away, then chews on like nothing has happened. Next thing, seven or so bees try to attack him, like flies to a dead badger's eye. He throws the honey to me, it sticks to my shirt like a lump of glue, and he starts haymaking his arms like a kingfisher do to stay still over the water. His eyes start popping like his skull is laying goose eggs, as more bees try landing on him. The shelf starts to break because where he's standing it's no more than chalky old hawk-shit that crumbles like old cheese. He kind of falls, and throws himself off the rock at the same time.

As he's falling down the height of a house, it's like he's grabbing at a rope that ain't there. He crashes into the water. The feather twirls in the air like a dust devil before gently floating down like a buttonwood seed. The noise of splashing bounces back off the canyon, and I just knows it then that we're caught. I eat some comb, wipe my mouth, and throw the rest away. I don't move. The bees leave me alone, which was the hand of God to me, and I waits and I listens, till I hears them ... what is footsteps coming from above.

# 12  HARD KNOX

A SHADOW appears at the top of the canyon. Small stones fall from where stands a Ranger called Knox, who I never spoke more than a few words to--he just another one of the tribe to me. He has square-like brown eyes and graying, bluish hair, even though he still young looking. And though he white, he's dark as a squaw. He sees us and tells us to stay still, that he'll shoot otherwise, but we ain't going nowhere.

A Ranger throws a rope down with a noose on it. Luke, from the bottom of the ravine, put his foot into it and they hoists him up. Then the rope gets thrown down for me, and I do the same.

When we get to the top, we're left sitting on the edge. We're just looking out at the rock table and into the swirling canyon below, waiting. Luke's face has swollen, but only a bit. I'm guessing he's taken out the stings before the poison had the time to do its work in him.

After enough time passes for us to get our fears up, a voice from the past calls out, "*Hola, amigos.*" We turn our heads and a shadow walks out from between blinding beams of sun.

It's the captain, and he comes into view when his body shields our eyes from the light. How he looks like in the day is now closer to how he looks like at night, for his head is covered again. But this time it's not a flour sack. It's with a bandage that go around his head over his nose, and another bandage is wrapped tight around his skull at the forehead. Beside him is Billy, who walks forward, grabs our collars--or what's left of mine--and lifts us up. He marches us back to the pool, where our horses are at. The Mexican farmer is there sitting on top of a fine horse, probably belonging to the Ranger who died in the raid.

The farmer edges up alongside the captain, and looks happy now he's gotten his revenge. He turns to leave, but the horse ain't used to him, and sticks its feet to the ground. I guess he don't have much luck bending donkeys, horses, or girls to his will. He go round the pool a few times till finally he gets the horse to go back to where he'd come from.

The captain a changed man with his locks burnt like corn stubble. Like a day or two after a hurricane when the wind is still blowing, though you know it's spent and ain't going to rise up again. I also notice, besides the Ranger I saw killed in the Indian raid, two others are missing and they don't have the native prisoner now. They make us sit down under the cottonwood tree. The captain looks at the skeleton lying there. "Howdy. What did you die of, mister?" he says, but in a serious way.

A few Rangers get pots and pans from a pack mule. We're going to have lunch there, for there's not much shelter elsewhere nearby. As they're banging pots and pans Buddy comes out from the cave and shakes off its dirt like a man shaking off his fears. He starts barking at us. The scout comes over and leashes Buddy, then he strokes his feathers at the back of his neck till they come together pointy as a knife. A knife he'd like to cut us with, for escaping him, because he's looking at us with defying eyes.

The captain yells, "Settle down, Buddy," and the dog stays quiet after that. The captain turns to us. "You surprised how I look?"

"Yes sir, and troubled for you, Cap'n. Praise the Lord you still alive and all. We was thinking it best to run from the natives." I'm wondering, *Do he think we cause his burns?* Though his face is mostly covered, I can see his eyes staring at me.

The top buttons of the captain's jacket are undone, and bandages are wound round his chest, too. "Thank you for your concern. Sorry about your friend."

"You dug him back up?" asks Luke.

"Yes, had to see which of you it was."

Luke's eyes get bigger. "Was he still dead?" Some Rangers start laughing.

The captain's eyes get smaller. "Gimpy, that's the strangest thing I ever heard. You buried him, you ought to know. Now, I think we'll eat." He turns to Luke, grins, and says, "You never did finish your rice, did you? But don't you worry."

His words take the air out of Luke's lungs like a fork stuck into a cooking pie. The captain nods at a Ranger called Joe. He's a small man, country type, with a weak chin and straw-like hair, not from the color though--from the not combing. He has pale-green bugging eyes that are red around the eyelids, and his eyelashes are a peculiar looking red with blonde tips. Joe's upper lip stuck out straight, like a duck's bill. Don't know why it did because his teeth weren't bucked so there no need for that really.

Anyhow, Joe fetches a bucket from a mule. He looks at the captain then holds it out to Luke, who is starting to breathe in and out like he's snorting, till the fear in his eyes turns to rage. "Aaahhhaaa." Luke hurls the bucket into the pool. As the bucket sinks clumps of rice float up and push the cigar, which is in the middle, to the edge. His face is all red. "Damn you if you think I'm eating another bite of that foul shit." All a sudden Luke's face goes white and he looks sad now and cries out, "You white trash bastard, you're not supposed to be down here. It's Mexico."

The captain don't blink. "Hard telling what is Mexico ... sometimes."

"No, it's not. There's a big river in the way. It's called Rio Grande." Luke's eyes start getting damp.

"We cross lot of rivers, boys. Mostly they look the same ... watery." The captain walks up to Luke and stares at him. Luke falls to his knees and looks out at the desert. He don't look scared or sad now, only like he accepting what he thinks will be his death. The captain looks out, too, but sees nothing interesting.

"White trash? No. I'm not white trash. My father was a skilled man, a wheelwright. He worked for hisself ...

"My momma, her people had land till they all died, all except her. She had to marry my father when she was not much more than a girl--can't be easy marrying a forty-year-old man when you're only fifteen." The captain squats down, getting close to Luke's face. "YOU seem to think I've treated you wrong." He touches his chest. "ME, I never treat anyone wrong. Unless they've got bad manners. Now, you lied to me and I let that go by, then you ran off. Now I try to be fair, I do, but I shwear, when someone lies to me then runs off after they've been warned, how can they expect to be treated like they was a good old boy? You answer me that now." The captain so near to him, Luke could've smelt moonshine from his breath.

The captain stands up and gets Luke to stand, too.

Luke starts to cry. Maybe he'd seen a few public hangings and heard sermons about good manners before ropes got tight. He starts blubbing and his legs start bending like saplings in a high wind. "You're going to kill me?"

"Nope, not for calling me white trash."

"You're going to hurt me, though."

The captain looks angry. He raises a hand as if to hit Luke, but puts it down fast with hurting eyes and sticks his tongue out between his missing teeth and hisses from the pain of it. "No, I'm not." The captain looks at Billy, who swaggers over. "Billy is." Billy presses his lips tight and punches Luke. He falls straight over, like a chair would, and his face hits the ground. A line of bloody spit goes from where a tooth lay, on the dirt, back to Luke's mouth. We all look at it for a second till the spit line sags and breaks. Billy grabs Luke's collar, he pulls him up to stand him, and slams a fist into his belly.

Billy looks around for orders from the captain, who is holding his chin with one hand, lost in thinking. "Oh," he says, coming to, "you want me to say something? Just go on, you got permission." The captain scrapes a boot on the ground, like he's ridding it of a stone stuck to the sole. Billy holds Luke's right shoulder and boxes his left ear, then his hand dives, like a swallow, and fly up into Luke's ribs. Luke keeps on whimpering. Billy looks again at the captain, who says without looking, "Another one in the ribs, Bill," and Billy, he do that. He about to hit Luke again in the face, pulling his arm back for it.

But the captain shakes his head and Billy lowers his hand. "That's for implying my parents were white trash," the captain says. "They don't deserve that. You boys don't know the power we have with *la ley del fuga*. It's the power to kill you if I so please. Now, can you get on your horse?" Luke nods, holding his belly. "You shure?" says the Captain lisping.

Luke looks up, his mouth all bloody. "Course I'm sore."

The captain clenches his jaws. "Are you S-U-R-E, not are you S-O-R-E."

"I am B-O-T-H."

"Mount up. I'm bringing you boys back to Austin." The captain turns to the Rangers. "Let's get out of here, boys, this place stinks."

Morton, that's what we do. We mount up and head north. I don't know if it's the same way we'd come. With the sun glaring off sand and rocks you're mostly looking at your horse's ears and someone's bouncing back, and even that ain't easy because they were good riders. It hard keeping pace with them, and it dusty with so many as they go before us, like a cloud, with the captain at the front. We did pass the Mexican farmer's house. His pretty daughter had a bruised eye, which is probably the only thing her and Luke Sprague had in common, that and one missing tooth.

The captain saluted the farmer, who waved back at him, and he waved at the little boy and girl, who smiled back. The little boy had a Ranger's badge in his hand and looked happy now.

The girl's mother looked teary eyed and the little girl looked scared--when she saw Luke's face, that is. He was ahead of me. Anyhow, we didn't stop till we came to the Rio Grande.

We rode along it till we come to the place where we buried the Irishman. They hadn't done mighty work of burying him again, for a buzzard is chewing on the stumps of bloody fingers sticking out between rocks. The captain told one of the Rangers to put more rocks on it and he wanted to know why it wasn't done right before, but the man said he'd done a good job, that the birds must've moved a rock or two.

We went to a place where the Rio is narrow. The captain called a halt, though he didn't raise his hand over his head, as before. Under the shadow of a tree a gray-haired Ranger named John changed the captain's bandages.

The bandages stained yellow, like old newspapers, in places for his chest badly burned. John says to the captain, "Maybe we should leave you in San Antone."

"Say that again, John, and I'll blow your head off. We're four days from Austin. I'll see a doctor then." The captain is sipping from a bottle and looks dead drunk. But if he thinks that we the ones that did it to him he hasn't said. Maybe he thinks he deserved what happened, and yes, he did, though it's still hard to look at. I sit down with Luke to a breakfast of the tastiest beans, tortillas, and donkey meat I've ever had. The farmer must have given them all to the Rangers in the swap for the horse he got and the help he gave. Luke's face is swelling fast. Both his eyes are closed, down to slits, mostly from the bees, that is, not Billy. His forehead has a big white bump in the middle, and the rest of it is red.

I still got anger in me towards the captain, Morton, hatred even. Though seeing the ghost of Sam shook my bones and I didn't want to die with so much hate in me, for I might have been dying again soon enough. That's till what happens next changed how I felt towards the captain, changed it for good. It make me go from hating him to caring for his very soul. I say to Luke, "I need to see the cap'n, I just got a sign from the Lord."

"What you talking about?"

I pick up a tortilla I'd been about to eat and I look closely at the brown burnings on it. All excited I hold it up. "Can you see it, Luke? It's all here--a beard, two eyes, hair down past the jaw ... no mouth, but it's nearly all there."

"Well, what is it?"

"It's the face of Jesus, on the tortilla."

"I can't see it."

"Not everyone could."

"I can't see anything."

"It's a sign, for sure, he about ready."

"Who is ready for what now?" Luke asks, barely listening as he eats his beans with his fingers because he weren't doing so well with the spoon.

"Him, the cap'n, he about ready to take Jesus into his heart. All that burnt flesh is like a hard field that's just been plowed, ready for seed."

Luke keeps chewing. "Jesus in a tortilla or not, unless you're talking about baptizing him in the Rio for twenty minutes, you'd best leave him be."

"Can't you see the hand of God in all this, Luke? Anyhow, I feel I need his forgiveness."

"Forgiveness!" He shakes his head. "The hand of God guided an arrow into his chest. He's a violent drunk of a man--the jury is not still out thinking on that one. How could you pity him, Abe? After what he's done to me. If his brains were on fire in hell, I wouldn't piss in his earhole."

"That's just the Lord bringing him down before bringing him up again."

We did nothing for a while, unless you call eating and not talking something, till finally.

"Abe, if you want to preach to him you are going to make orphans of your children, if you've got any, and orphans of mine before they're even born. That's if you start talking about our walk in the woods and stray arrows, or maybe you want a rope round your neck so bad. You're too impatient to get to Austin before that happens. I know people, Abe. I can get free and you, too--if you're innocent--but not if you're a corpse ... Then it's too late."

"I knows all that, Luke. It not just about the tortilla. Only wish it was. It's just the other night, well ... the ghost of Sam done visit me, too, like Hamlet's father do to him. And if the cap'n don't repent of his sins, he's going to see hellfire for sure."

"Ghosts, tortillas, Jesus--are you crazy?"

"So you think that man who wrote Hamlet is crazy?"

"No, I don't, but he was one of the most famous men who ever lived."

"What if he think of it before he 'come famous? Is he crazy then?"

"I don't know, Abe. Look, you'd a dream, or nightmare, just forget it."

"I knows that's maybe what it is, but it's on my heart to speak to him anyhow."

"Abe, I just heard him tell that man over there he'd kill him and that's someone he probably likes--and he's pickled. He isn't near us is--?"

"Nope."

"All right, now are you going to waltz up there and say 'sorry for all your pain, Cap'n, but it were me and gimpy that burned you up, and don't you know Jesus loves you? Oh, and I'd a dream the other night. Lawds, don't you know, but it were nigger Sam from beyond the grave. And unless you give up your sins he'll take you down to the devil.' Whatever you tell him, Abe, do not talk about me. I'm hurting in every part of my body. I don't need any more pain. I'll just die if I get any."

Luke empties his bowl into his mouth, puts his hat on his face, and falls back onto the ground. But something inside of me is at me to speak.

So I get up and I walks towards the captain. When I'm about ten feet away from him, Billy holds up my way. "Get back to where you was," he says. But the captain waves me on, and I get to talk with him alone as he sits under the shade of a cedar elm tree, fanning his face with his hat. He still had the bandage around his forehead, but he hadn't put the bandage back on his face, though it's not so badly burnt there. His eyes look sad, the lids smeared with fresh gunpowder.

"What is it, Abraham?"

"Cap'n ..." I sit on the ground with my legs crossed. "I'm sorry for your pain, truly I is. Don't know the right way to tell you this. But sometimes things happen and there's reasons for it. Don't mean that they should have or that it a good thing, just that they do, if you understands me."

"I'm listening." His mind clear as moonshine now even though he seemed drunk earlier.

"Like I say, I'm sorry for what happen to you. I'd never do nothing to harm nobody. Don't think the Lord would want me to."

He looks up at the sky. "That a fact, Abraham? If that's so, why in the hell," he looks at me, "did you shoot a fiery arrow at me?"

I freeze, but like I said he looks calm. "So you know it was me?"

"Yes, I know it was you, or the other one." He waves his hand towards where Luke is lying like he's swatting away a bug.

I shrug my shoulders and hold out my hands. "Because I thought it a demon, then just a bad man, and I didn't even aims to hit you. It's just that--"

"Abraham, I don't know why you did it, and I am in agony as we speak, but I'm not angry at you."

My hands are still out like I'm trying to catch raindrops, even though it's sunny and big blue skied. I put them down. "You not angry?"

He shakes his head gently. "No, not anymore."

"How comes, Cap'n?"

"I wanted to shoot you, and I'm in my rights to. But I got thinking, over the last day or so, if you hadn't of done this, we wouldn't have had watchmen with guns drawn and ready expecting a raid. I'd have lost a lot more than one man. Maybe I would've lost my own life. Fact is, I probably would've. I suppose you think I was wrong giving that darkie a skeer, but I thought it was right. They need it, them niggers, or else they'll 'come like the ones in the bar, all swaggering and swelled up, acting like they're beyond our law. But there sure was a blaze from that nigger moonshine. Guess they had the last word."

He grins a little, as if someone has gotten the better of him.

"Them soldiers is dead, Cap'n. You got the last word. If you lives by the--"

"Hold on," he says, his face scowling a little. "I sent Mare in to get that gun, and they struck him on the face and pushed him out onto the street. They the ones that's living by the sword, not me." He points to his chest then pounds the ground with a fist till dust comes up.

When the dust blows away I say "Cap'n, if you say you sent in Mare and give them fair warnings, I believes you, I do. But sending Luke and me to that town and acting surprised about what happens, why that's like throwing a stick of dynamite in a river and wondering where all them dead fish come from." I wait, and after a time his eyes move from being still. I know he's thinking on my words or putting them by for later. I go on, "Cap'n, what you did in the woods to those shanty Negroes, that ain't right."

He looks at me with nothing showing on his face. "I've no quarrel with those shanty folks--good luck to them--but niggers running around in the dark with chickens I will not tolerate." The captain gulps back a big swig of moonshine. "I will say two things to you."

He looks in my eyes. "First ... don't tell any of my men that you're the one who shot that arrow at me. That's for your own skin, not mine. Or that you saw me skeering that darkie in the woods to anyone, you hear?"

"I hears you, Cap'n."

He put his hat on and moves it about till it sits right.

"Second, when we get to Austin, I'm going to see you get justice." He seemed to know I'd been accused of horse stealing and murder, but he didn't say that, or even how he knew.

"Hanging?"

"If hanging is what you need."

Now it was my turn to cry, the captain had that way about him. "O Lord, but I didn't kill no one or steal no horse." I rub my sleeve over my eyes.

The captain stared at me without blinking. That was another thing about him--he never blinked. "Son," he says, "you were acting guilty from the moment we met. You lied, and then you ran." He looks to me like he's taken a jump and there ain't nothing he can do but land. "You don't sound like the sort of man who would kill, but there is evidence against you, and you two and the native, I consider, will be the last men I bring to justice."

That was the first I'd heard of the Indian who I thought must have been killed dead in the raid, but he wasn't, as I soon found out. I could tell the captain wasn't angry with me, and I could see how the men gave him such loyalty, for he put their safety before his own pain. I didn't talk to him about God, as I don't think he'd have thought it anything other than me trying to save my own hide. My talk with him was over, and I went and sat down beside Luke again.

We crossed the Rio Grande easily ... there was a ferry.

At the other side were two Rangers with rifles, they had the Indian prisoner trussed in chains.

With the two Rangers was the Ranger the captain had sent off before at the camp. He had a new fugitive list and wanted posters of Luke and me. Luke's poster had a reward of five hundred dollars and said: "Wanted Dead or Alive for Murder." The poster looked fine, except the reward was too high. But I was on the fugitive list and Luke wasn't, so something was wrong with Luke's poster.

We said we were innocent and not much fuss got made as they had pegged us as guilty anyhow. The fact that we--or Luke--didn't give our true names when we run into them made that seem even more likely.

Luke was wondering why and how a poster got made of him. What we think happened is, after they lost me, the Cruikshanks came into town. They got new guns and then they see the Johnson brothers' brother. It were pure luck, good or bad, depending on who you is. And they shot him. Mother Johnson hears the noise. Maybe she's in town getting supplies and her son is waiting for her, before bringing her home. So she sees him dead, and she finds out from the Cruikshanks, why they killed him? They would have told her that they are just doing their job, and showed her a poster of her son. It's him all right, but with a small picture of Luke drawn on it, too, bragging about how he "The Fastest Draw, Austin Texas." Because Mother Johnson called to Luke's office with a locket holding a photo of her dead son. She looks calm enough, but for her staring eyes, gray as limestone, and wayward tresses slithering out from under her blue bonnet. She asks Luke can he do a portrait of him, letting on she's a sweet old thing. Luke don't know who her son is, because he is busy training a new telegram operator, the fishy looking man I spoke with, because he was going traveling.

When she sees the rogues on the wall, she asks, "Do you have any self-portraits?" Reckoning he'd be kinder to himself, for she didn't want her son drawn, like the wanted men, looking so ugly and bad. Luke shows her a picture, but she tells him "it ain't flattering enough" and asks to see if he's "got any more handsome drawings" of his face. He searches for a few more portraits at the back of his office, taking his time because of the interest she's showing. He finds some and gives them to her to look at, and continues talking to the man he was training. She lost interest and quickly left.

Luke reckoned she stole a portrait of him while he was talking because crime ran in their family. They all had similar-shaped skulls, he told me when we saw them all later in the courthouse. He told me he hadn't seen it in her, but told me the new operator told him after she'd gone, "That lady, either she don't like us or she's plain mean."

I think when she saw Luke and reckoned, "Fastest Draw" to do with making pictures, not shooting bullets, she got her sons to come after him. When Luke and me escaped she had them get a wanted poster done up, so someone else would shoot him. Which is the picture the captain now had. I am pretty sure that is what happened, Morton. Luke told me it was certainly drawn by the fat Negro preacher from Nineveh, this small settlement about ten miles from Austin.

*****

As Abe told me this I had a picture in my mind of two men riding into a one horse town. They are both bearded, stocky, and questionably hygienic. They pull up outside a church, dismount, and stare into it from the door. Inside, a fat, sweating Negro is giving the sermon about the grizzly bear and the unbeliever to three children, unaware of the men.

"One day a man was walking in the woods listening to all the beautiful sounds and smelling the flowers. Now this man, he didn't believe in the Lord. But one day a mean old grizzly bear come up on him and he says, 'Lord, save me.' God said to him, 'But son, you always saying you don't believe in me. 'That's true, Lord, but can you make this grizzly here a Christian?' So the bear puts his paws together, and what do he say? He says, 'Thank you, Lord, for this food I is about to receive'."

The children are still laughing as the men walk into the church. It's the Johnson brothers. The preacher ushers the children away, and they walk out past the brothers. Marvin tells the preacher they're Rangers and asks can he redo a picture they got. The preacher tells them his price and that it will take a few hours. They tell him they're pressed for time. He tells them, "If that's so, go to the man in Austin who draws real fast."

When they show the preacher the picture they want redrawn he realizes Luke Sprague would never want this business, for it is him. So he reluctantly draws up a wanted poster, and they pay him and leave. Maybe that's what happened, but I don't know, I wasn't there at the time. Abe begins to talk again, ending my daydream.

# 13 PURPLE

WE RIDE for four days, and Luke's face go back to the way it was before Billy and the bees. Then me, Luke, and the Indian spent a night in Austin's jailhouse. That evening, out through bars, I watched the red ball of sun get swallowed by a grape-colored sky and darkness fell. Then came stars and the sickle-shaped new moon, looking like a giant toenail cutting stuck there in the sky.

On the street out of the indigo-blue night came lights swarming towards the jail. It wasn't lightning bugs it was a lynch mob. But even so I wasn't scared, Morton. A few jailers loaded lots of guns and weren't letting anyone in. This one jailer, the part between his lip and nose twice as long as normal, which Luke pointed out to me in the middle of it all. The jailer wore spurs inside the jail, which makes no sense, like the way he talked. You may've noticed how Texans can talk either real fast or real slow. He out-and-out brave about doing his job. He talked down a lot of men who came to the door and got angry with men in suits who reckoned they important. He point a shotgun at them and then ever so quickly says, "Lessyouajudgeoralawyermoveonnowori'llscatteryou."

Because I had been accused of killing a tax collector, there no lynch mob for me. That mob was there for the Indian.

When we get to the courthouse next day it's not a trial, it's a talk about seeing would they have one, going on what they had against us.

It got so hot from bodies and sun coming through windows that I pulled my chair back to where a woman sat cooling herself with a turkey tail feather fan. But she stingier than bats in the cave, for she leaned back and wouldn't share her air with me. We're made to stand. A man walks out called Judge McAdoo. He a man about sixty, with smart, gentle brown eyes and ropes of weaved black and gray hair combed over his head. He has a red face, but his nose ain't bumpy in spite of this, so I don't peg him for a whisky drinker. If he's anything against Negroes it don't show. I'm sitting next to Luke on one side of the court. The captain on the other side, sitting next to a lawyer who if he said anything I don't remember it. The judge says, "This is a wanted poster for Luke Sprague, but he's not on the fugitive list. Why is that?"

The captain slowly stands. "Don't know as yet, Judge. Thought you'd let us lock him up till we found out. It's by order of the Governor, and I'll be hearing from him soon, so I'll rectify anything not in order. You worry none about that."

"I seldom worry about anything, Captain Wilson," says the judge, smiling firmly.

"Glad we have that in common, Your Honor."

There politics mixed up with it, too, for that native had killed these white folks and their children. The story was in all the Texas papers, even national ones, causing an uproar. I don't know why they thought he did it. Maybe some native from another tribe told the authorities. Or an arrow with his mark on it got pulled out of a body. Or maybe he stupid and had a blonde girl's scalp hanging over his wigwam door.

Getting the Indian was a special job given to the captain by the Governor, as I guess his way of doing things was known. Once he'd caught the Indian, he was able to settle some old score with those Negroes in the bar. For he knew he'd have lots of sway if things went bad. With Luke and me after happening along, he knew they might pick on us.

139

I guess the captain thought we were a godsend, though what happened at the Negro bar was never talked about by the judge. Luke, who told me we didn't need a lawyer, jumps up. "Your Honor, you've seen me working in this court. That poster is fake, made by lawless men trying to stop me helping the sheriff." There was a short fat sheriff in the courtroom, but he didn't seem thankful for anything Luke ever did. In fact, he even looked a little pleased at Luke's trouble.

"Abraham Brown, what do you say to these charges?"

"Judge, I killed no man and stole no horse. I'm a cook. I even cooked for them Rangers. I'm in Texas searching for my kin. I got a note here saying I owns that horse."

The judge asks to see it. I take it out and give it to a man who brings it to him. As he doing that the captain says, "I heard tell of people getting someone to sign over a horse under duress then shooting them."

I swore I'd say nothing about the shanty Negroes, but I got to thinking how I feeling put upon before, and how I ain't no more. I knew he'd think I was betraying him, but I had to. "Judge," I say, "when the captain finds us, we is in Mexico."

The captain jumps up, with paining eyes. "That is a lie. A band of Rangers would know more about Texan geography than a Northern Negro."

People in the court are making noise, as though they of the same mind. And two men in particular who sitting there with their old momma, her in her blue dress and bonnet.

The judge bangs his hammer. "I've no proof of where you were captured." Luke jumps up telling him he has proof. "Address me as 'Your Honor'." Luke starts taking off his boots. The judge says, "Sprague, you need to be putting clothes on, not taking them off. Sit down." Luke is still in long johns and tugging at a boot, and he's hopping now. "Sit down, Sprague. Many times you've sat here sketching without theatrics, why not today?" Luke can't get his boot off, then I understand what he's doing. I start helping him. The judge's face gets redder. "You'll both be removed and tried in absence," and he keeps banging his hammer, "if you do not sit down."

Luke's boot comes off with a weird sucking noise. "Exhibit A, Your Honor."

"What are you seeking to prove with your crippled extremity?"
I take off my boots, too.

"No, this is my good leg. We were on a farm down in Mexico crushing grapes in a winepress. That's why my feet are stained red--or purple in the case of my mulatto friend here."

"What of it?" says the judge.

"There's no grapes grown 'round these parts, so how did we get grape juice on our feet, Your Honor?" The judge gets quiet when he realizes the truth of Luke's words.

"A Mexican farmer can vouch for this?"

"I would sooner not ask him. We shot his dog--by accident, of course. I was engaged to his daughter as well, but the marriage didn't happen. He didn't approve. We'd to run out of there. He blasted me with shot, too, right here." Luke points to his backside, and the judge bangs his hammer, for almost the whole court is laughing. Because Luke is talking to them all like he's on a stage.

When it quiets down, the judge waves for Luke to sit. "This courtroom does not need to see your Exhibit B." He makes one more bang of his hammer. "We're in recess for ten minutes." It turns out the judge wise as Solomon, even if for the wrong reason. He picks up my note and walks out of the courtroom. When he comes back we're told to rise again. "Be seated. I checked the jail book. It seems that Luke Sprague was indeed put in jail along with Mr. X, beside which the jailer has written, 'Abraham Brown'. In my hand here I hold my own tax papers, signed by Mister Symmes. The writing on these papers matches that of Prisoner Brown's bill-of-sale. What I fail to see is how Prisoner Brown could force someone to sign his name, if he's illiterate. That means not able to read and write, son." He looks at me. I stare back, saying nothing. "As for the case against Luke Sprague, his defense is so bizarre, I believe there is a spirit of truth to it. I hereby find no case against these two men. They are free to go. Captain Wilson, I cannot prove you went out of your range, but I suggest you stay in it. I don't know what happens in Corpus Christi, but I must remind you this is the state of Texas. It is sovereign, and the rule of law operates here most of the time."

The judge bangs his hammer down, but that don't mean we start rejoicing just yet. Because Billy is looking at us in an unkindly way.

141

And inside the courtroom are the Johnson brothers and their momma. She'd been there knitting through the whole thing, and while she doing that, her sons was putting nooses around our necks with their eyes, thinking evildoers' thoughts about us in their skulls. They not happy looking at the outcome of our freedom, no sir. Luke walks over to Judge McAdoo and tells him we're wanted in Washington and that we've been delayed by the Rangers.

So the judge orders the captain to get one of his men to guide us to Galveston, in case anyone acquainted with an old wanted poster of us might shoot us on sight. When the judge left, Billy told us he didn't want to see either of our odious necks in Texas again.

Then the most surprising thing that ever happened to me did. The captain says, "Shut up, Bill." Billy gave us a look and left, then the captain he says to us, "If you two fools had just been honest from the start." He opens a clenched fist and holds out five dollar coins to Luke.

Then the stupidest thing I ever heard happened next. Luke says, "No thanks, we're provided for. Buy ointment for your forehead with it," in a tone both pitying and mocking.

The captain still had a bandage over his forehead, and it was stained red in a circle in the middle like there was a wounded eye below.

"It's just something for on your way, but as you like." The captain said as he put the money back in his pocket. "Cactus Jack will ride with you to Galveston. After that you're on your own." He clapped us on the shoulders and walked away.

Luke called to him, "By the way, sorry about giving you my wrong name. My real name is Luke Sprague, the Fastest Draw."

The captain turned. He looked up at this circle window with four panes in it. The light was shining right through it down onto his face. "I know your name," he says.

"Well, don't you forget it."

The captain don't blink at the sun. He turns to look at Luke and says calmly, "I won't." Then he turns and walks away, and that's the last we ever saw of Captain Levi Wilson. He was nothing to look at now. Although his face was nearly healed, his hair, like our fear of him, was mostly burnt away.

142

We went outside with Cactus, who was probably the nicest out of all the Rangers. He even gave Luke old clothes to wear. For when we went to Luke's office before we left, it had been tossed about. The door was wide open and most everything inside was gone, even in the back room where Luke had slept. There was just a phrenology skull on the floor lying on its side, made by a man named Fowler in London England. It had his address there and all, written on the side, though what it was I don't recall. I guess it ain't important.

Luke put the skull standing, right side up. He left it there and we go. We were like two birds who'd escaped from a net with no broken wings, and only a few ruffled feathers for our trouble. I'd like to say we had learned our lesson and become wiser men, but the trouble with nets is, if you're a bird, they hard to see.

On our way to the coast a hurricane hit Texas, and we lost a day's riding waiting in a barn. Cactus Jack said little on the journey, and a few days on, in Galveston, we said our goodbyes. The hurricane weren't as bad as the one that killed all those people in 1900, but it still bad. Lots of the houses there looked like they were no better than piles of matchwood.

I remembers how the sunlight sparkled off the waters, like a thousand winking eyes, as we stood on the shoreline watching waves slosh and foam onto the sandy beach. Gray-white clouds charged past the sun, like galloping buffaloes, making the water light up like lightning flashing under the sea. Beneath milky foam danced beautiful colors, of emeralds, indigos, and sky blues, pretty as a peacock's plumes catching the sun. And soothing sea breezes kept kindly fanning us like a momma would a newborn.

No boats were sailing for a few days, for the sea still angry after the storm. But we booked a ride on a boat called the Nacon, and were able to sleep onboard while it waiting at the wharf. As we going for a walk before it set sail, I told Luke about my money situation and the great lack of it.

"Why didn't you say this when the captain offered me money?"

"Because I scared to say anything, Luke. I just happy not being dead."

"Doesn't matter. We didn't need anything from him anyway. We can trust in providence."

We walk on.

Seconds later, Luke stops as he sees what he thinks is providence in the shape of a man and a boy walking towards us.

"The Wandering Jew," Luke says. Ben Herzog was his name, wanted for the crime of charging high interest in four states. He dressed normal for a Jew, with a black hat, coat, beard, and so on. Luke stuck on his Ranger's badge and we walk up to him--I walked and Luke swaggered, to be truthful. The boy with Ben was about eleven years old. "I know who you are, mister," Luke says. "I'll do you a favor and not turn you in, if you give us traveling money."

The Jew stares at Luke, the long curls either side of his face are swaying in the salty air like palms. He lifts up his hands like they're a book he's reading from, shrugs his shoulders, and says, "Sorry, I haven't got any money."

He starts walking away, but Luke puts a finger on his chest and stops him. "Yes, you do, and you broke the law."

The sun is shining on Ben's spectacles. He takes them off, puts them in his jacket, and smiles. "Not really, I didn't." His face goes grim and he starts to tell us how he come to be a wanted man. "This rancher kept asking me to lend him money," he says, gently bowing back and forth as he talks, "so he could buy cows. I tell him I'm a tailor, not a banker, but he keeps asking me. So I lend him money and he doesn't pay me back. So I follow him, from Texas to Wyoming, on a cattle drive and he doesn't pay me anything, but he gets the law against me, saying I'm charging him high interest when I only said that so he would forget this crazy plan. He wasn't going to pay me anything anyway, so what difference did the interest rate make?" He shrugs his shoulders and smiles, as do his son.

Luke looks confused, like he don't know what the man is talking about at all. He says, "Mister, I'm being kind to you by not bringing you to a lawman. I'm in dire need of money so you give me some now and you can go wander off again."

Ben laughs. "I'd give you the coat on my back, but I already told you, I've no money."

Luke beckons to him. "All right, the coat, hand it over."

"I wasn't being serious," Ben says, but he sees that Luke is. "All right, all right."

Ben takes off the coat, takes the spectacles out of the pocket, and gives it to Luke. As he walking away I feel bad. "Let's give it back, Luke. It's the only one he's got."

"He's a tailor; he can make up a new one."

Which is true enough, I guess.

I say, "Maybe there's money in the coat's lining." I mean, he was a Jew. So we lay the Jew's coat on the ground and divide it between us, each taking a half. I start feeling about for money in the silky lining. But Luke rips at it, and he sees no money, and then I start to rip at it, and I sees no money. In the end, the lining, it was a big old mess and no money was found. Of course, Luke blamed me for that, too, even though I was only trying to help.

We set sail soon after. On the journey it started calm enough, till a white bird with the longest wings, you ever did see, flew screaming alongside us like it was running from something. The tips of its wings cutting the water like a knife. Then the sea got stormy and rough, like a peacock had closed its wings and shook them rid of wetness. I remember a squally breeze slammed into us, like a fist into a belly, almost turning the boat over. Stampeding foamy waves kept throwing buckets of salty suds up onto the deck.

The boat tossed about, with wind and water pulling us every which way. Up and down we going.

I tell you, I puked everything in me then I puked some more, and it were apple green and black, just staring up at me from deck planks, moving, back and forth, with the uppity downy sea. I'd a headache the whole time and my mouth dry as afternoon cotton. When the billowy waters settled for a while my pants got stiff and starchy as shirt collars from the salt and the baking sun, and up above the gulls were screaming and laughing at me.

"It's bad luck what we did to the coat," I said.

Luke was standing with his back to the ropes of a sail that he'd been holding. He looked at me as I retched up more bile, he opened up that coat like black sails, and the wind filled them up like lungs. "No, this is just blowing us all the more quickly to New Orleans." Then a gusty breeze blew him over and he banged his head on the deck and slid down towards me till his feet hit the gunwale. Luke sat up then and laughed mockingly at the angered water.

His hair was blown stiff and spiky, starched by the sea, for he had tucked his hat tight under his belt, what with the wind and its stealing mind. After a while his lips made a trembling O and his eyes opened wide in defiance of the spray that so briny it could cure your eyes good as pig feet. "Santa Maria," he says as a big wave, maybe twenty, twenty-two feet high, came rolling towards us ... It swamped over us like we were rocks. I didn't know was the boat going to sink. It didn't, but when the wave passed and the water sluiced away I saw the body of Luke Sprague a lying there on the deck, dead looking as a jellyfish on a dry beach. I don't know had he hit his head, but I reckoned it wasn't a bang that killed him--he went out with the splash.

I saw a rope and I thought it best to tie Luke's body to the mast and myself, too. So I put a rope around him and hauled him up to the mast. I put him sitting up, though he kept falling forward till I had him tied. He had not been a helpful man in life, death had not changed this. I guess I should have felt sad, about everything, but I didn't know what to feel. Although I'd lost my reward I could still sell his horse, which was in the ship's belly below, provided it hadn't drowned.

I don't know if you have ever been toe fishing. It is when you tie a line to your toe and you put your arms back behind your head and go to sleep under a shade tree, and if a fish comes along and takes your bait it wakes you. Back before the war I'd a lot of free time once my chores was done. This led to long, lazy days laying about toe fishing, listening to the field niggers singing as they picking cotton, the odd sound of the crack of a whip making me thankful I weren't one of them, smelling the grass and the pine and listening to the birds singing. Then you catch a fish and lay it on the bank and watch as it slowly dies. But every now and then even if the fish hadn't budged in a while and you thinking *It surely dead* it might start to gasp or wiggle again. I'm reminded of that because bubbles start to come from Luke's lips like it do on a crab sometimes. Of course, he weren't dead, Morton. How else could he have designed the coin? Anyhow, a short time later he moved his feet a little and then he woke up.

"Well, what ... where am I?"

"I thought you was dead, Luke."

"Well I ain't. Why am I tied up?"

146

"Thought it safest."

Luke pulls off the rope. "Darn it, you got tar all over my coat. What you gonna do next--roll me in a chicken coop?" The mast was black and sticky, you see. He said nothing more for quite some time, humbled by the wave, just let the life come back into him. The captain started to trim the sails after that, and it was slow sailing for the two of us I tell you. The only comfort I had was thinking *It would be safer by sea than overland*, if we wanted to dodge the men who'd come after us, as they might not know we free or even care. But some things are not for avoiding, and we did met our foes again in New Orleans.

*****

Abe told me that in New Orleans the trains weren't running all the way to Jackson, on account of train robbing, and the workers wouldn't work again until it was safe to do so. He asked an old fellow could they go by road, and was told that a levee had broken, flooding the river road to Baton Rouge, last he'd heard, but that a boat would take them. So they decided to go by river as far as Vicksburg and cross land to Jackson, Mississippi. There they could catch trains heading for Washington D.C., where they were both long overdue.

Luke's brother, who was at the siege of Vicksburg, said it was nice there, even though losing Vicksburg on July 4, 1863, is what cost the Confederacy the Mississippi and the war. For that river is like the handle of a valise, and once the Union grabbed hold of it they had the whole country, albeit after two more years of heavy lifting.

I say to Abe, "After the siege Lincoln paroled the confederate soldiers, and that when he was told this was folly, that they could fight again, even after the army of secessionists had been half-starved. He said something to the effect it was like someone blowing up a dog with a stick of dynamite, that, sure, the pieces might fit back together again, but the dog would never be the same." Abe smiled at that, as he'd heard Lincoln had been a good man for his words. However, Abe Brown and Luke Sprague never got to see the city of Vicksburg, as nature abhors straight lines not only in its rivers, but also in the lives of her people.

# 14 NEW ORLEANS

L UKE AND me are standing on a dock beneath a sky full of little clouds shining like mackerel scales watching the mighty river. The sound of waves hitting the dock's wooden posts sounds like a gang of cats licking milk.

A white steamboat in the distance has a trail of black and yellow smoke billowing out of what looks like two giant cigars with pointy black crowns. Its giant wheel is slowly chopping out a foamy trail that's following the smoky one up above as it twists drunkenly out over muddy flows of the Mississippi River. As the riverboat nears us it slows down. Its steam whistle blows, announcing to everybody *here she comes*. I love that city, Morton. I worked on a riverboat as a cook one time, but the joy of memories was soon gone. And as beautiful as New Orleans is, she not so pretty each time I put my hands in my pockets to feel what weren't hardly there. I remember the boat passing by us with crashing noises as its paddle wheel slapped muddy water, sounding like it saying *PO PO PO* over and over. And rolling waves shaking the timbers of the dock we was standing on like it were a raft on the sea.

Luke stares at the river with his mouth open, trying to take in the size. He turns to me. "I trust you can arrange a boat." I let him know again that I didn't have much money left, but he reminded me that getting him to Washington was my concern. We agreed to meet back at the dock later and he walked away.

I sorted out a deal quick enough, for a boat, and I walked to New Orleans past the big white church and on into the French Quarter. I took my fill of sights and nothing much besides. I have to tell my stomach not to listen to street vendors selling melon slices, my nose to ignore the smell of fresh bread and meat cooking, and my ears not to listen to silver scraping plates in restaurants. I got woke from dreams of eating by a scratching at the back of my head. It was a ladies' parasol, and the lady, who's dressed in a silk indigo hoop dress, says sorry and swishes away.

I walk on and see a black boy dancing with his cap on the ground to an old, white-haired Negro playing bones like spoons. War soldiers with missing legs and years are beggin' on street corners, hunched over like herons in a swamp with the brightness gone out of their eyes. People are laughing gaily up on the balconies. I see mulatto girls there. That's where they used to send pretty light-skinned slave girls--New Orleans--and it weren't for picking cotton.

The first thing I had to do is let Bolinda know I'd be home soon. Part of me was wanting to tell her about nightriders, giant catfish, getting accused of murder, even ghosts. But there is things not for telling, unless you've got eyeballs in front of you. And if those eyeballs start getting big, you can slow your words. I find a telegraph office, I go in, and the first thing I see on the wall is a picture of Luke, the one that the preacher did. As I look at it this short, smiling white boy, wearing a visor, round wire glasses, and hair parted in the middle, says, "Aren't you curious? That was put up today. You seen him?"

"Can't say so, sir. He looks regular enough." I send a telegram, and after that the man wishes me good day. He picks up an almanac and folds back a page. It was week thirty-seven, though I forget the date, and what else it said I don't recall. I ask, "How can someone get one of them pictures?" Of Luke, that is.

"We got copies, five cents each."

"For just a copy!"

"Yep, one of them I have is ripped, though. I'll give it to you for two cents."

"That's still plenty."

"Go on. I'll give it to you for sending the telegram."

"Why, thank you, sir."

I turn back to the wall and see another poster. This time, it's of me! "Wanted dead or alive for horse stealing," it says. A 100-dollar reward being offered by a Mister Theophilus Dupree--the man who owned the clothes store back in Austin--even though he got his horse back and I got mine. Those charges was dropped because it under duress. Anyway, this says, "Angry mulatto, dangerous to approach," so if you a bounty hunter you'd be thinking, *Shoot him, right? He dangerous. Why risk trying to catch him?* It reminds me of how that saying goes, "You might as well be hung for a sheep as for a lamb." That's what my father told to me when he going to be shipped off to Van Diemen's land for stealing a hare in Ireland, so he ran away to America instead. It means if every crime has the same punishment it don't matter what you do, Morton. You're dead anyways.

The telegram near cleaned me out of money and pride. So I squint my eyes and drag my foot and I go a-beggin' but I have no luck. On one side of this street a Negro tramp is collapsed on the ground with crutches beside him. A cap is lying where a leg ought to be. His face is badly scarred and he has powerful arms. A wealthy white man walks by him. "Secesh nigger here, boss. Pleeeease put some money in my cap." The passerby drops a coin near the cap. The begga' smiles as he picks up the coin, but something is bothering him. He looks up. His smile goes as he gets up and hobbles over to me. "No, no, move on now, you hear? This here's my stomping place." So I move on.

Over my head is a twisted iron balcony, where these white men in top hats are sitting, singing a spiritual about the Underground Railroad. "Swing low sweet char-i-ot coming for to carry me home ..."

I'm thinking *This has to be fate.*

"Excuse me, sirs," I shout up. "Can you help a veteran of the Civil War? Help me out, gentlemen. I'm so hungry I could eat my own hands. Have you ever in your life been so hungry you could eat your very own self?"

I laugh, and this man with an English voice says, "Which side did you fight on?"

I don't know what to say, so I smile and say, "The blue side."

He turns his back on me for a bit, shakes a champagne bottle, then turns and sprays it over me. They all start laughing, banging their table with knives, forks, or whatever. "Get lost, you bloody scrounger," the man says, and they laugh even harder. I don't want to judge them, but it's most terribly ignorant what they done.

I pull my hands tight over my hair, shake off the drips, and walk away, pulling at my shirt like a piston, drying it off.

Floating along towards me is a white woman in a bonnet and billowing black dress looking like a dark raincloud. She stops to step over a puddle, lifts up her dress, showing black lace-up boots as she do. They the kinda boots that'd tread out the desire to drink from your very soul.

"Excuse me, ma'am, I is hungry."

"For what, more liquor? Because that's what you sure smell like to me." She stops talking and looks me in the eye.

"No, not liquor. I'm looking for a help up."

"You are up, young man. If I give you something you surely will be down, in the gutter." She starts to float away.

"Please, ma'am ..." She keeps walking. "You stingy bitch," I say. It just fell off my lips. She stops a second but she don't look around and keeps going.

A little further on I sit on a porch of a boarding house called The Sunset, with an old faded picture of the sun on it. A Negro is stooping down next to me whitewashing the hotel's lower boards. His hair has a skunk line of whitewash on it, and it's splashed onto his blue jeans and bare feet, too. But he pays me no mind and just keeps on working.

I'm so hungry I'm thinking, *I must have worms* and if I do I need Jerusalem oak tea to kill them. And just as I'm thinking I'm done with folks, that Negro begga' comes up to me again. I'd seen scars like he had on his face before--on a tramp who got his face chewed on by rats. I'm thinking *He's just going to kick me while I'm down.*

"You hungry?" he says.

"Yeah, I is."

He throws his head to the side for me to follow and he hops over to an outdoor cafe. A white waiter is setting tables there with a bigotty look about him, which go when the tramp puts coins in my hand. I say to the tramp, "What d'you want?"

"Nuttin." He says.

I'm thinking, *Good, at least I got plenty of that.*

The tramp turns and hops away. I sit down and lay out my money on the table. "I want some shrimp, gumbo, chicken with spices, and cornbread. Thank you, sir. Is this enough?"

The waiter grins. "Nope, it's not. I can give you chitterlings and okra." I accept. Soon the food comes and it good. But just as I'm starting to eat, I see the purple veins in the red nose of Daryl Johnson, who has just walked out of a saloon across the street from me. Daryl puts his hands under his fat balloon belly, fumbles about, and starts pissing from the porch onto the street. Seconds later, two men dressed in black and white ride by. It all so strange now, for Daryl gives them a crooked smile. It's the Cruikshanks, who tip their Quaker-like hats back to him. Simon's jaws are closed tight and his prairie dog eyes looking about. Peter's mouth is still hanging open and his eyes still blinking as he smiles. Daryl fumbles his pecker back into his pants, nods to them, and walks back into the saloon.

I run off down Chartres Street with the waiter shouting after me, thinking I'd forgot to pay, even though I'd left money on the table. The Cruikshanks hear shouting, and they look about and see me. They try to follow but can't go fast because of the people in the way. I jump on the back of a stagecoach with no trunks. I hope it goes left. It does. And we travel away from the church and the statue of Andrew Jackson, up on his horse, and towards the river. I turn a corner and see they're still following, but quicker now. The street starts going to the right and I jump off and hurry under a bridge. A minute later I hear hooves pounding over my head. I thought I'd jumped into a fresh stream, but I was so scared I forgot to use my nose.

I think the only thing bringing the Johnsons and Cruikshanks together again, Morton, is maybe the Cruikshanks owed them for killing their brother. I figured the Cruikshanks only after Luke now, and I'm just a way of getting to him. Unless they'd seen a new poster for me, but that I didn't know.

Now, whilst my hands is covered in foulest filth, Luke's were holding a cup of coffee in a cafe. He told me he saw this pretty lady in a black dress there, wearing a fancy hat with a purple flower in it. She was sitting across from a young girl.

The lady takes off her hat and, while no one is looking, she starts to put bread rolls into it. She stops when the cafe door opens. A man walks in with white and red diamond-shaped patches on his suit of blue and orange. He's wearing white paint on his face and a red hat with three bells on the end of three prongs.

The man starts to juggle, but the diners ignoring him mostly. Luke just waves him on. So the man goes to the lady's table. Luke says she acts like she's interested, but when the man ain't looking she looks bored and pitying. She offers him a bread roll. He reaches for it but drops his juggling balls. She smiles a little, but then he swoops up his balls and starts juggling again. Her eyes roll, but it ain't from watching the balls.

Luke draws a picture of the lady on the back of a menu and walks over to her.

"Sorry, ma'am, didn't mean to interrupt." He hands her the drawing. It makes the lady look pretty, but bored. The juggling man walks off, maybe in a huff, and the lady laughs and puts a hand in her purse. "No, thank you, ma'am. It's all right." Says Luke who turns to go, but she takes her hand out of her purse and holds it out and says her name is Marie DuPont, a widow. She is French, and she is looking at him kindly.

But Luke realizes, what with his coat that looks like what Joseph's ten older brothers did to his before he was sold into Egypt and him wearing it over Cactus Jack's cast-offs, that he don't look like a dude, dandy, or anything good. He'd got it into his head that he wouldn't find love till he's wearing fine clothes, that cupid would hold his arrow till he's looking good. Even though this lady seems nice, he reckons any kindness shown while he's wearing the clothes he's in would only be one of love's false cousins, politeness or pity. And any talk of prizes in D.C. to stir up her interest would seem at best a wild boast and surely just a lie.

He don't shake her hand, he bids her good day and turns to go.

"It would be a shame for a man of your talents to not be paid." She says. Luke tips his hat to her and leaves the cafe. A while later he thinks, *Maybe it ain't fine clothes that makes a man good looking to a woman, but kindness,* so he goes back to the cafe, but she's gone. Then he sees the lady, with the girl, walking down a road going towards the bridge I'm hiding under.

The girl stops on the bridge. "Mom-ma, I saw something."

"Come away, Andrea. It stinks."

Luke comes up behind them. "Hello again. You waiting on someone?"

"My daughter thinks she saw something."

"What did you see, little lady?"

"A man, under the *pont*," says the girl, pointing at the bridge, I guess. I see Luke's reflection swaying in the inky, shitty water as he leans over.

"I don't see anyone down there. Maybe it's a troll."

"What's a troll?" asks the girl.

"He's an ugly, smelly creature who comes out at night looking for little girls who don't go to bed when they're told. They live under bridges. Don't your momma read to you?"

The girl laughs and screams a little, too.

Marie is maybe thinking, *He's only come back to talk to her about the dirty business of money again.* "Are you sure I can't give you money for your drawing?"

"Please, ma'am, I'm provided for. But you could give me one of them bread rolls you took?"

I can tell he's grinning.

"They are free, you know." She sounds annoyed.

"Of course, they're free, ma'am. But I only had money for a coffee. They didn't bring me any bread." I know his eyes would be getting big and innocent looking.

"I'm a little ashamed you saw me do that," she says. "If you sit down quickly after someone has left their bread and start eating, they will leave it and then you order a coffee."

"Well, ma'am, I'd rather go hungry for a week than see you ashamed. I've money coming to me and I can buy you all the bread you need."

"Ah! So you are testing me, to see am I kind, no?"

"Testing you! No, ma'am. I reckon you're of good character."

"Ah, that is a shame. I am of good character, but I could never respect a man who does not test people. For all you know I could be a bank robber."

"Well, if you were a bank robber you wouldn't be stealing bread now, would you?" He laughs.

"Pah! I wasn't stealing bread," she says, but now she's laughing, too. "Here, I will pay you for your drawing."

"I don't want your money, ma'am," says Luke as I'm climbing up from the sewer.

She doffs her hat quickly. Inside it rests half a dozen bread rolls looking like eggs in a nest.

She looks at me, wondering what I am doing standing there dripping wet looking angry at Luke. "Here, take bread, take two. Now, monsieur, please, the smell here is horrible. I must go. Goodbye."

"What's your name again? Marie what?" says Luke.

"You are standing on one," she says.

The woman smiles and walks away with the girl.

Luke said she was really beautiful, but to me, I thought either her eyes too big or her head too small and her chin just too pointy, though her smile was charming.

I remember her little girl had curly hair, wore a magnolia-colored dress, and had a baby parasol in her hand. I also remember I was angry. "Luke, you ask me to spend my last cent and here you is turning money down."

"Why were you under a bridge? That's a sewer down there, don't you know that?"

"Luke, them bounty hunters here. They still chasing us."

"Well, good luck, Abe." He holds out his hand, but pulls it back again when he gets a whiff of me.

"Good luck. So that's it?"

"If it was the boys after me you wouldn't be here talking, amigo. You'd have run away."

"Is that so?"

"I believe it is."

I take out the wanted poster of Luke. "Do you know him? If it's only the boys after me then who bring that here?"

Luke frowns, but he don't look too worried. "We should've got a piece of paper from the judge saying we're free."

"Sheesh," I say, as the foulest smelling water drips off my hands onto the dust, "paper don't mean nothing no more. They'd reckon you is lying, haul your bones off anyway. Then have you locked up, and be in no hurry about finding out if you telling the truth--that's if you is lucky!"

"I cannot be delayed any longer. We need to skedaddle."

"So now it's we again?"

"I believe so. Do you realize you just helped chase off the classiest lady I ever met?" He looks to where she'd gone.

"Classy! You were calling her a thief. It's not the kind of thing a woman wants to hear, Luke."

"Well," he says, his eyes big and mocking at first, then serious, "not taken by itself, no. But in the body of a conversation it wouldn't have been unpleasant, for I was fixin' on being charming until you crawled out from Louisiana's bowels attached with that awful stank." He looks at me like a lazy man would at a hard chore then he looks away and starts chewing.

I say, "You eating bread?"

"I am."

"Give me some."

"You're in no condition to get any."

"Then put some in your pocket till I is." He puts a roll away and I stick out my chest a little. "Luke, I got us a boat."

He smiles, and crow's feet step onto the skin beside his odd, dark eyes. "Good, Abe, well done. We're blowing smoke at last. With a poker game I might even win us a little money."

My bottom lip drops because he has it all wrong. "Ain't that kind of boat, Luke," I say. But Luke, he ain't listening.

# 15 HOGWASH

M E AND Luke stand on a small dock of the Mississippi for local boats carrying cotton and lumber up and down the river. Behind us is a brick warehouse with an indigo dye merchant's signage. In front of us is a leaky, low-in-the-water steamboat about thirty feet long. A battered looking Cajun, Monsieur Martin, is captaining it. He about sixty, with a white beard and white hair that he keeps combing over his pink scalp with a tobacco-stained hand. The whites of his watery eyes are a little sickly looking, rat tooth yellow, and shot through with red veins. He heavy looking, too, though mostly it's because he has on lots of waistcoats and jackets, even though it ain't cold.

Luke is staring at the boat. He don't look happy.

I say, "It's the best I could get. Sold the horses to the man's brother. He'll take us sixty miles upriver. Then we get another boat to Vicksburg. He owe me money, but--"

"Abe, when I said boat, I meant gambling, liquor, loose women, not Noah's ark with a malodorous Cajun who owes us money. It stinks, what's in them bags?" Old gunny sacks tied up on the boat's deck are rustling about like giant grunting maggots.

"They're—"

"Hogs. I can smell 'em. Can that man even speak English?"

"He sure can--I can't speak Cajun! And I don't want to be riding with hogs neither, but we got to get."

"What about food?"

"It's all taken care of." We walk a narrow board and jump into the boat. The Cajun pulls up the board and undoes the ropes, and soon we're moving. The Cajun starts shoveling coal into a stove. And after that he begin scooping water up from the deck with a bucket to throw over the side. I guess the boat's bottom has holes or loose boards and they are below water now. When he done bailing water he lights up a cigar. Two of his fingers are as orange as beaver's teeth. Luke leans over the side to fill his water bottle, then he holds the bottle to his lips.

"Easy, if you know what's good for your belly," I say.

He holds his hand up to keep me quiet and drinks nearly a half-gallon. Then, between breaths, he says, "All right, now what did you have to say, that's so important, it couldn't wait?" I say nothing. A minute later he pukes it all up onto the deck and stands looking at it sloshing in with shitty deck water and grease from the engine. "That water is bad."

I laugh. "No, it ain't. You supposed to sip it gently, like whisky. That's how comes she's a lady called Miss-issippi. Way you drinking it you'd end up with a sandbar in your belly."

A little later, Luke picks up this banjo and he holds it up to the Cajun, like asking can he play it, and the man nods. Luke picks at it and it annoys me so I walk to the other end of the boat. In amongst a pile of coal is a big old lump of lead--a bombshell, for weighing down the boat. There was another one at the front of the boat, too. Anyway I wipes over it with my hand and sit there. I get a surprise because Luke follows me and blocks me in. I can't go nowhere. I mean I got coal on my left and behind me, too, and on my other side is a mile-wide river. He laughs, and starts playing and sings:

"I just found my mother.

I'm looking for my brother.

No other man's brother will do.

"I got to find my brother, to please my mother.

Even if I search my whole life throuuugh, yee hawww."

He stops. "What do you think?" I say nothing. "It's said, if a really good player plays a fiddle, the sound changes for the better. Like you'll be after spending time with me, Abe." I turn my head away from him but he keeps talking. "I don't know if the same thing happens with a banjo. It's about you. You might find your brother on a farm. Then I could use *udder*, because rhyming *brother* and *mother* could tire out quickly, don't you think?"

"Uh-huh, I guess." I say and I feel something, and I look up and see Luke's head moving slowly towards me, with his mouth hanging open and his eyes big as saucers.

"Your eyes are green," he says, breathing onto me, "but brown around the center. It's like there's gold dust in them."

I pull my head back far as I can till it's pushing into the coal, cricking my neck. His eyes show hurt when he sees I don't want him so close to me, and he sniffs the air. "You do need a bath, Abe Brown. You smell worse than the hogs."

He skulks back to the other end of the boat, sits on a half-barrel, and starts picking strings slowly. As I listen to the sad boings and bings, Morton, I'm thinking I wanted to run away, but then he'd say that's just what I am--a runaway who can't stick to a spit and a handshake. I look out at the mighty river. Laughing Negro women are drying clothes along a levee, but like Luke and his banjo playing they soon pass along. Beyond them from the backwaters a fresh river flows into the muddy one. A little on is a big chestnut tree at the edge of the bank, where the river has washed away mud around its roots--they look so big, too, like they must go to the other side of the world to prop it up. With the waves of another big flood would it still be standing? I close my eyes, lay back on the coal, and feel the boat gently rattling into my bones.

I guess I slept for I woken by this loud steam whistle.

I looked and saw this giant boat going by and the whistle blower looking down at us like he all important, just because he wearing a river hat. There a woman next to him who blows us a kiss, but I don't catch it. She laughs and then they gone. We ain't in his way at all so there no reason for him to be making all that clamor.

His boat sent waves everywhere and rocked us for a bit so we had to slow down. As the ringing went from my ears I began to hear a low squealing. I look and see Luke is acting mischievous. A little pig is scratching open a bag with its hoof and snout, its nostrils opening and closing like winking eyes. Luke, without the Cajun knowing, rips at the bag till the pig pokes its whole head out. "Don't be doing that," I say.

"Hey, piggy ... If he wiggles free you grab him, Abe."

"You'd like that, while you stand there idle."

"That is unkind. I'd catch him, but ... Don't like saying it now, but it's my leg." He stares at me, trying to make me feel guilty, till I drop my eyes.

I hear a splash beside me. It's the Cajun throwing slop into a trough. He smiles generously. "Mangez. Hogs next."

It's not all slop. I mean there is apples and pieces of bread, too, but still it don't look good. Something dark moves under the trough. All I see is a pink foot; the rest is lost in blackness. It don't move anymore, just biding its time waiting still.

"Food all taken care of?" Luke says. I stay quiet. It discomfiting to me, because I got sold on the promise of food back at the dock. "Got to tell you, Abe, I never felt so impecunious in my life, looking in a hog trough and someone looking on like it's my suppertime." The Cajun is still smiling.

"What do impecunious mean?"

Luke turns to me. "You know what a picayune is?"

"Yeah, it's a coin."

"Well, means you've got none of them."

The little pig runs up and starts to chew the slop, like it's swine gumbo. The Cajun laughs. Then BANG! With no warning a shot fires out. Wood splints spit out onto the deck like a horse has stove in the rear of the boat. Squeals come from a pig-bag. Following behind us are two men wearing black Quaker hats in a small boat. It's Simon and Peter Cruikshank.

Simon's eyes look dogged and black and poisonous as pokeweed berries. Peter's mouth is wide open, like he's drinking in the whole river to pull us back to him. His blinking eyes aren't friendly no more--they stare coldly on at us like they is harboring a grudge. Beside him his skinny-as-a-skeleton brother holds a shotgun.

Peter gives up drinking the river and shouts at us to turn towards the bank. Water starts squirting into our boat. I feel sorry for the Cajun, but as Luke and me start fretting, he don't.

Luke shouts back, "Boys, we've been set free." But our engine is noisy and the words ain't as loud going back as they is coming over. Simon keeps pointing for us to turn to the bank.

I'd forgot about the Cajun for a while, but he wasn't going to let river dandies start taking potshots at his boat. He looks kind of calm and wild at the same time. That don't make sense, I know, but it's how he is.

The Cajun pulls a shotgun out of these leather covers, with an end shaped like a bugle. He aims and fires, buckling their boiler and making it spit steam like an angry devil. Its rattling sounds different now, like it's fighting for its life.

Simon must have been scalded, because he grabs a rope and jumps in the river. The Cajun starts reloading till a blast comes from where Peter is. The Cajun's eyes get surprised and dead looking, his mouth opens, and he falls over like a chopped down tree.

Our boat is sinking.

Ahead of us standing on the water is a pink and red bird, a scarlet ibis. It's standing on a sandbar we can't see. I grab the boat wheel and steer toward the ibis, hoping to ground the boat. We hit the bar, but it made the boat go high on one side and it starts sinking all the faster now. Brown water rushes in the back of the boat like rats from a burning building, flowing down the deck over my feet around the Cajun.

The Cruikshanks' engine chokes and dies. Luke grabs a pistol from the Cajun's waist and fires at them. The water in the boat starts crawling up my legs. I tell Luke, "I can't hardly swim."

He laughs. "This is the best way to learn. Me and my brother got thrown in a lake when we were boys. That'll learn you." He starts breathing in and out quick-time.

"Can't you help me, Luke?"

He stops breathing. "Abe, that gun won't fire till you shoot it."

Threads of the Cajun's hair start floating.

There's all these panicky noises and grunts; in particular is the sound of high squealing. The little pig is standing on its back legs splashing about.

Luke picks up the pig, blows all the air out of his lungs, then breathes in till his cheeks and chest are like bladders. He jumps into the brown water and drifts away, bobbing up and down like a cork. The back of the boat starts dropping fast with the lead weight. Bags with screaming pigs start sliding towards me. I see Luke's Chinaman bottle. I try to grab it, but the river takes it away. Then the other bombshell slides down from the front of the boat and it all about to sink. With nothing to help me I jump in and go under. When I come up I start choking, flailing about like a scared horse. I go under water again, for a second, and I think I'm dead, but the current keeps me floating. It keeps me alive. When I get to shore I climb these slabs of mud, like slices of bread carved by the river, where the bank has caved in. Luke walks up to me and stands under a big magnolia tree. I double over coughing. "Did you hear them pigs screaming?" I say.

"They were just cheering us on."

"Didn't sound like it."

"Guess not."

Peter and Simon's boat keeps floating on downriver, with Pete steering it towards the bank we're standing on. Me and Luke, him with a piggy in one arm and a gun in the other, put our backs to the river and go on. Soon we at a bayou covered with duckweed. Bits of old cypresses are pointing up, through the green, all bony black and shaped like stakes. We wade through her sleepy, swampy water, between stumps and cypress trees tall as ten houses, rising our knees up like we in a marching band.

Luke is sloshing three, five, now seven steps ahead of me. Roots of cypress trees are coming outta the water like black snakes wanting to crawl outta the swamp. Ahead of us billowy fog floats up from the bayou, brooding there like a woman with unanswered questions. Will we feel her venom? Uppity egrets looking down from trees begin screaming and squawking that shady folks is lurking 'bout, in their yard. They stop complaining and fly away. Luke stops and turns. "Hold him a second?"

He gives me the pig, which is struggling. I take it without thinking, before he wades on ahead. "Where're you going?" I say.

"You carry him, I'm crippled. We may need him."

The trees get smaller.

I see a black shimmering thing swimming towards us.

163

A *snake*, I think, till it dives and through duckweed up pokes a gator's tail. But soon we on dry land. We follow a scrubby trail along a ridge, atop a swale, and come unto swamp again.

I don't know can gators smell blood, because if they can, they would've smelt me. I feel a pain on my foot. I sit on a stump and pull off my boot with my left hand. It makes a strange gurgling sound. I pull down my filthy gray homespun sock that so full of holes it's past darning and see a line of leeches on my ankle like a litter of suckling pigs, right in the place where skeeters bite you at night. I rips them away. Seems the ankle a much-loved watering hole for all of God's nasty little creatures knows of it.

The trees about us now towered and loomed so big they stopped the sun. Everything about Louisiana is different, though, Morton. There is spiders the size of your hand, snapping turtles heavy as a man, even frogs is bigger. Sometimes I think it's pretty, other times I think it's hell's pond. It's where my father worked digging canals when he first come to America. Two of his brothers died of malaria doing it. They stopped using slaves because they were worth money, but there was always Irish coming off the boats looking for work back then. He saw a man getting robbed one day and he ran the thief down, a Negro. My father got the offer of a job by our master, who'd seen it all. He was there buying a mulatto woman to bring back to Texas. So my father traded his spade for a whip, for not many white boys can run down a Negro, not that it did me any good. I just got his skin mostly, not his feet, hee-hee.

*****

I ask Abe, "How was your father killed?"

"By a rock to the head, Morton. By a slave who had been stealing pigs. It caused mayhem amongst three neighboring plantations. So a pig got left out one night tied to a stick and painted blue. When they found my father he had blue paint on him and his skull pushed in. It by the river so it reckoned he'd seen the pig thief washing paint off there. It was during the war, you see. The pigs were for the soldiers back then. Because Jeff Davis said they needed meat to march on. So there wasn't much meat for the slaves."

164

*****

After a couple of minutes, me and Luke, we come to a bayou. Two water oaks either side of the bayou look like they're shaking hands over the water. Spanish moss coming down from their arms looks like teeth, and the water below is like a looking glass that's turning it all into a giant mouth. Inside the mouth sitting on a stump where the tongue ought to be is a barefooted boy fishing, watching a cork floating in the water.

The boy so still a blue dragonfly had landed on his rod, its wings, shining like broken glass, slowly rising up and down. We ask the boy where we are, but he just drops his low lip and shrugs his shoulders, like he don't speak English. I don't know if he'll help us till he smiles and jumps down, leaving the rod next to the stump. He beckons us to follow him on a mud trail into the trees. We follow the straw hat he is holding to his head. Luke all this time is moving well enough with the danger. We come across a trapper's gallows with pelts drying on it. On the ground, near to it, a rat has its head inside a mud turtle's shell that he's lifting, right up off the ground, like a giant helmet. Luke says, "It's so big we could throw a saddle on it and ride off, the two of us." It's not quite that big, but its tail as thick across as a nickel, no lie.

The rat takes its head out of the shell to scratch at the wet, spiky-like-a- mink, fur on his head. It sniffs the air, knowing we there, then stares at us with defying black eyes before scurrying away.

After a time, in the distance we see smoke rising. There is the smell of meat cooking and the sound of singing and laughing, and we see the log huts of a village where a feast is going on. Before we get there we come to where food is being prepared. There is a half-barrel with frogs in it and another filled with soft shell turtles. A woman wearing a bloody apron with her hair tied back in a bun is sitting on a stool cutting legs off frogs, like a seamstress snipping threads.

A giant alligator snapping turtle is lying on a wooden fruit box, near to her, with dying rolling eyes and blood dripping from its beak. A pitiless boy keeps poking its head with a stick. It tries to fight back but is too slow about snapping to stop the boy's fun.

The boy we're following brings us on to the center of the village where a fire is blazing. People are dancing and a toothless laughing man is tapping his foot as he leans into this fat Cajun with sideburns playing a squeeze box.

We stop to get our breath and get an unfriendly look from the man. Luke tucks the gun into his britches.

"There's the man I sold the horses to, Luke--that's your horse, but where's mine at?" I turn to the Cajun. "Sir, I want the horses back."

He tells me he can't, but that he'd give us Luke's horse back and another one. "For ten more dollar."

I ask, "Where's the money you owe me at?"

"I have not got it yet."

It a hardly likely story, but my face all long and I'm wet, too, so I can't drive a bargain home and he knows it. So I try an' be nice instead.

"This is for your child, sir." I put the pig down beside a little girl near to him. "We needs two horses bad. I don't got no more money." He walks away to think, and while he do, the little pig starts rolling in the mud. A hag with wrinkled arms comes over with a hickory stick, its end shaped like a hip joint. She raises it high over her head, bringing the ball-like end down on the pig's head. I guess the Cajuns was hungry.

I want to tell the man about his brother, but Luke says, "Don't. I can't parley French too bueno." He's thinking *If we say something we might whip up his anger* and no telling where it would go.

I touch the man on the arm. "Where's other horse at?"

He don't want to say, then he nods towards the fire. What I thought is only sticks is legs, too. It's my horse burning away on top of it. Lord, I'm wondering how they even got it up there.

The man sees I ain't happy. He points to another horse. "Take him, he's strong. He just don't look so good."

But it looks good to me. I grab his hand at the deal. For the horse is a fine, big chestnut stallion with a shine on his coat you could've shaved yourself in. I think maybe his heart is trying to swindle his head and he feels bad, for maybe I wouldn't have sold the other horse for eating. Not everyone will want to do that.

Soon we are riding, eating as we do. The Cajun had given us food, too. I say, "How's your horse?"

"Tastier than buzzard."

"No, the one you're riding?"

"Well," he says, licking greasy fingers and smacking his lips, "they're both agreeable. How is yours?"

"Oh, strong like he said. If a man has one fine thing in life, should be a good horse."

"You got the pick, all right," says Luke. And as he do it's like he hex me or something because my horse it walks straight into a bush. I get off, and I go to the horse's head and wave at its eyes. It don't blink.

"When the Cajun say it don't look so good, you think he mean it's blind?" But Luke ain't listening, he's caught up in his mind again, or so it seems. He's looking at something behind me.

"Don't go anywhere," he whispers.

"How can I?" Luke doesn't answer. Then I know what it is he's looking at. I look into my horse's smoky blue eyes and I get an idea. "Act like you don't see them." I tie my horse loosely to a tree. "Walk on with me and your horse. When I say it, I'll jump on yours."

We walk fifty yards or more. Then I turn and act panicky, like I've only just seen them. I get on Luke's horse, up behind him. They're about a hundred yards away--the Cruikshanks, that is. They run forward shooting. They get on my horse and thunder after us into woods, onto a long dirt trail that gets narrow and then goes right, between two hollow trees. Then we come to a straight through a tunnel of trees. Their hooves getting louder, the sound of them runs ahead of us. They fire, but I don't get hit and I'm covering Luke. They fire again. I start counting between shots, like you do between lightning and thunder. With another shot I'm thinking *I'm dead*. We come to a river. Luke turns the horse tight over a small wood bridge. I hear the Cruikshanks getting another bath and their horse screaming as they crash into the water. Luke turns our horse, and with pistol drawn, he goes back, stopping on the bridge.

Simon sits still in the shallow river, his skinny face red, like the skeleton of a drowned man come back to life. His hat and gun are gone. Peter is standing with his gun still in its holster.

Luke says, "Boys, why are you following us? The judge set us free."

167

Simon says, "We seen your picture and--"

"Well, it's fake. There's no bounty on me. The Johnsons made it so someone would shoot me. We're going to vamoose. You best leave us be now, you hear. I could shoot you right there. Who'd know? If your bones got found in these woods no questions would get asked."

Simon knew he wasn't lying. Luke was a coward for sure, but he still a Texan.

Simon stands up, his shirt sticking to his ribs like shedding skin. "All right, we'll leave you be. It's just they're bitter about their brother getting shot. They reckon it's your fault mostly. Though maybe they want to get you killed and us in trouble both." His skull smiles even though his eyes are hurting.

I say to them, "I think that's where the dog lies."

They just stare back at me, not understanding. Peter says, "They said they weren't sore, but they lied."

"So there is no hard feelings, sirs. You keep that horse." I say. "He may not look so good, but he's strong as an ox."

We ride away.

A little after the bridge, a lichen-covered sign at a crossroads says, *New Orleans twenty-five miles*. Another sign covered with mold and at the bottom it said *Rouge*. We reckoned it must say *Baton* at the top. There was horses coming from New Orleans way, so I reckoned the road wasn't flooded at all. Luke and me, we took the road and hoped we was headed towards Baton Rouge.

I don't know what they said after we left, or if giving them a blind horse was wise. Maybe if we'd given them the seeing horse instead things would have worked out a whole lot better, least for the horses anyhow. I guess Peter would've been asking were they really going to leave us be and Simon would've said: *When a Cruikshank gives his word that is that. Though might tell the Johnsons where they're going. I didn't promise nothing about spreading the good news.* For that is what they surely did.

# 16 ROUGE

WE MOVE along a woody trail to Baton Rouge through flies, seeds, and Delta dust blowing about every which way under a sticky hot September sun. A cooler breath kindly blowing every little while, too, just to let us know it'd soon be paying us a longer visit.

Everything looked so green after Texas, green as wet moss, though a few leaves on swamp maples were starting to blush. Soon the sky would be filled with birds, though not yet. The horse we riding on kept stopping to eat grass, with Luke nearly falling off whenever it did. "This horse sure is stupid."

"Thought there's no stupid horses, Luke."

"Maybe he's not, but I wish he'd stick to regular meals." Luke jumps off. "Let him have his fill. I've to go into the forest anyway--nature is calling."

I get down as Luke starts to look for a trail into the trees.

"I don't hear nothing," I say.

The trees are quiet except for a distant woodpecker tapping and wind rattling through dried leaves above.

Either too much noise or none at all always gets me noticing, for if there is something in the woods the other critters don't like, they are nearly always decided on being all noisy or all quiet on the matter. Like they'd voted on it and agreed.

"Well, what is it, Abe, what's wrong? Why don't you like the look of those trees?" He smiles then slaps his forehead. "Flies are eating me alive ... God damn them."

I do not answer his question, though I guess my face must show his words to be true. Flies are near us, staying still in one spot, they'd been following us for miles. Their eyes like overturned bowls shining shifting colors of greens and reds, and yellows. Like watching autumn trees swaying over still water you're walking by. They a proper nuisance them flies, between them and beg bugs, we had picked up in the bat cave, or the jail, we must have lost a quart of blood between us in the past few weeks, no lie. Best not even think about them. "I think the trees are taller in Louisiana than Texas, Luke, what do you think?"

"Sure, the cypresses are maybe. What's wrong?"

"It's nothing."

"Why, Abe? What're you thinking is in the forest? More ghosts?" he says, mocking.

"Don't be silly." I say, as he walking away, "They wouldn't be out yet."

He turns. "There's no ghosts out at any time, my feathered friend."

"What do feathered friend mean?" I ask, 'cause I don't like the sound of it now.

He acts like he don't hear me and looks up at the sun shining through leaves. I keep staring, till he feels it. "It don't mean anything." He laughs and strolls into the woods. When he hasn't gone but very far, he shouts out, "Oh, Lawd," in a mocking Negro voice. I ignore him because he's only being himself-- annoying, that is. I see dandelion seeds in my horse's mane and I pick them out as I wait for him. In front of me this green hummingbird is calling door to door to these bright blue flowers. Its feathers shining like polished green mirrors.

I forget about Luke, and the horse, as I'm watching the bird, listening to the woodpecker tapping and the wind blowing through the leaves and smelling the change in season.

There is a log near to me covered all over in thick fern like moss as tight as a corpse wrapped in a sheet. I go sit on it. Branches break where Luke has gone in. I turn towards the sound but hear nothing more, so I pay it no mind. The hummingbird turns to look at me, tilting its head to the side like it's curious. It's only a few feet away. I keep watching how its wings are there, but how I can't see them. I hear Luke yell. I'm thinking *He's just trying to mock me again.* I hear something running through the woods coming towards me clattering, breaking branches. I stay still as a possum, not looking, for I ain't interested in any more of his foolishness. He runs by me. From where he came branches are still breaking. He ain't mocking at all now. I jump up.

Luke stands beside me and holds up a big stick, waiting for whatever it is to come. Then it does. It's a black bear. It comes running out of the woods. Maybe it got wind of the horse we'd been eating and its juices that had fallen onto our clothes. Its arms flailing with nails mean as bowie knives. Its pearly white fangs big as boar tusks. Luke throws the stick at it, yelling, "Get outta here ... Go on now."

"Shoot it--it don't understand you, Luke."

The horse gets scared and rears its front legs up high. The bear stands up, too. It's severe looking with sloppy gums. It roars, and the horse run off. Luke grabs for the gun, it fires in his pants, he falls backwards. The bear comes down and runs back into the woods. Luke's face goes grim. He lays his head back and closes his eyes. Slowly he puts his hand down into his pants and feels around, looking truly serious. Through the hole where the bullet has gone a finger wiggles out. He laughs. I sigh. "Put the gun in your jacket, Luke. It safer there." And he does.

We walk into the woods looking for the horse. There is silence there, too. I'm thinking *Something's not right again*, but we go on. Then the screaming starts--screaming from the horse, that is--and I know something terrible is happening. But it gets even worse because the screaming stops.

They danger-filled, woods, but you don't expect when it's men that makes them so. For when we find our horse it's hanging in the air with a rope going from its neck up to a fork in a branch and down to a trunk used as a weight. "That's cruel, murderous even. Climb up and get the saddle, Abe. We may need it."

I don't argue. It would've been too tiring, and he had managed to scare the bear away, even though he did bring it on us to begin with. I start to walk towards the horse, but stop when I see a leg is twitching. "It's dead," Luke says, which is true enough, but I'm wary to go on. The rope above is twisting, sounding like a creaking stair. I hear no sound for a few seconds till air comes out of the horse's ass. Its bowels opens up and drops their load onto the ground. The bladder opens next, raining down. I jumps back when the shit starts coming, and it all but misses me.

It smells as bad as it looks disgusting--the horse's face, that is. The way its tongue hanging out and its eyes is looking at you and the way they ain't, and how its long teeth look like they're grinning in a crazy way. Luke is laughing so loud I think if the horseshit had done hit me, he'd be laughing all the more. I swears it then, I wanted to punch him. But I bit my tongue, because I was stuck with this fool. For if I fell out with him now, returned home over a month late with no reason or money for doing so, I'd have had to face my wife and her momma and give account about all that. How could I, without them thinking *You the fool for hitching yourself to him on a fool's journey?*

I am so angry, but I just suck in my lips, close them tight, and say nothing. After a time Luke notices, and he stops grinning and annoying me so. He sits on the trunk. We hear animals on further in the distance, and I smell goat from when the wind would blow that way. Alongside us, either side of the hanging horse, is a fence made out of branches with spikes at the top. The horse has been corralled into a place and sprung a bear trap, I guess. We are quiet for a while. Luke keeps looking at the horse, his eyes and mouth wide open.

"Abe, do you ever think something is out to kill you?"

"You mean like white folks?"

"No." He looks at me. "I mean something real powerful that's everywhere, just trying to strike you down."

"Don't know, Luke. How do you even know this even a bad thing?"

"It doesn't need explaining, Abe. It certainly is a bad thing. I'm sure if the horse could talk, out of his mouth ... he'd agree with me on that." He stands up and put his hands in his pockets to pull up his pants, which were sagging.

"Luke, if you hadn't have got a bad leg you'd have been sent off to war instead of down near to Mexico. I bet when you hurt your leg you is thinking *It a bad thing*. But maybe it saved your life."

"How so?"

"Because you're the sort that gets shot in a war."

He thinks about that, then crinkles his nose like he's been stung again. "I'm 'the sort that gets shot in a war'! What's that supposed to mean? I wasn't barely old enough to fight in the war, not even in '65."

"It means nothing, Luke, like 'feathered friend.' Don't mean nothing."

He pouts his lips and nods a little, knowing I've bested him. "To be truthful, 'feathered friend' means you've been tarred and feathered, because you've done something wrong or you're wrong about something, though I just like saying it, too, sometimes."

He smiles.

I say, "To be truthful, you being 'the sort that'd get shot in a war' kind of means the same thing."

"Why d'you think I got injured before the war?"

"Because you said Fleming Condell ran forward to claim the mortal blow--of the cow you shot. You was probably slow because you'd a limp. Though on that I'm only guessing it."

"Well you guessed right, sort of. I was injured before I went down near to Mexico."

We left and went on, leaving the saddle on the horse because Luke thought all that had happened was a sign, though I'm not sure I agreed.

We stayed in an old barn that night where you could see stars winking through holes in the tin roof. Luke, pointing to his favorite bunch of stars, the one called Orion, said. "People call it the Hunter." Though it didn't look like one to me. It looked more like a butterfly.

Next day we made only ten miles walking, as we were too used to the saddle. It was two days after the blind horse and a day after the bear that we came across the abandoned plantation. There were two stone piers and on the gates was the name Ryderson.

On each pier was carved a man riding a horse. One of the riders had his head broken off. It was still early and foggy with the dew still wet. A line of web stretching between two iron bars had drops looking like pearls on a necklace.

The gates were chained shut, but folks seemed to have borrowed some of the bars from the gates as there was a gap in them. We went through carefully as there were thistles growing there, and we walked up the avenue lined with sassafras trees.

Briars were growing up through the bones of the fallen house and it all gone, except for two chimneys made outta little yellow bricks. Beside them grew red hollyhocks that had their seed wheels on and their flowers looking all ragged, like a hen with too much attention from rooster.

Peppermint grew near the hocks ... It so soothing to the belly. And an ivy vine creeped up a third of a chimney then spread out and up; the poison kind. All green looking, like the mint, but it burns instead of soothes ... could Luke tell the difference? Should I warn him and risk ridicule, in case he knew already, or let nature be free to do as it pleases? On a chimney, a fireplace with a church arch is crisscrossed with so many dewy webs its hearth looks like a chandelier.

In front of the house fallen to the ground were stone columns. Luke kicked one of them. "Greek revival," he says. "That's Greeks for you--always ends in tragedy." A bird fly into a hole in one of the chimneys. Luke, as he looking up at them, says, "Sherman's tombstones."

"Did Sherman come down this far?"

"I don't rightly know, but that's what they call 'em: Sherman's tombstones." Laying under a chimney was a metal claw-foot bath with a bullet hole near the top. It full with rainwater dripping down from bricks. You could see a chimney clearly reflecting in the water like it stretching up to the sky. Baby skeeters kept twisting about in the water like injured snakes. I take off a boot and a wool sock and put a locust thorn into a blister on my heel. While I'm doing all that, Luke keeps looking up at the chimneys. "Sure high times while they lasted, boys. Yeeeeehaw," he says, yelling in a peculiar Southern way and laughing, too. I didn't know if they his words or if he only mocking or remembering someone else's.

The whole place were ghostly looking. Like the folks living there died when the house burned down. But it don't give me shivers now, not like what happened soon after that did and still does. I only mentions it because that is how my thoughts is coming. We walked on. It were a mile or so later that we came upon the strange farm.

I think we took a wrong turn someplace, for we came onto a road with two trails before which were unsigned.

The farm were mostly scorched earth, but with a big field of corn in amongst all the scorched fields and it near harvesting time. I can still see the wind running its fingers through the corn. Through a hole in the clouds the sun kept looking out like a solemn eye. Then the clouds closed over the sun and it got darker, though it still hours before sundown.

Ahead of us a narrow brown dirt road winds like a snake through the field of yellow corn, so that we can't see but thirty feet in front of us and you couldn't know what be round each turn. There is for sure quail for I hear them and I whistle and they call back to me, but as we turn a corner they see us and fly away. As we going along we come across a pumpkin-headed scarecrow in a dress. The pumpkin is rotted, but the dress is washed anew. It's not much of a scarecrow, as crows are sitting on its arms. I keep thinking to myself, *How mighty peculiar it all looks*, and by that I mean, *how everything do*.

Beside the dirt path is a bare tree, and on it sits a blue jay with no tail.

Out loud I say: "One for sorrow, two for joy, three for a girl, and four for a boy--"

"What you saying there, Abe?"

"Nothing, just a rhyme my father used say, that he hear back in Ireland, about a bird called a magpie. It's this black and white crow. We didn't have 'em in Texas, but the blue jays always reminded him of them."

"It looks nothing like a crow."

I think I hear another blue jay, but when I look, I see it's only a mockingbird.

We walk on and come to the end of the yellow corn. Beyond it the fields stretch out to where land joins with sky and the dirt path snakes onwards further still, till it can be seen no more.

175

Close by is a rundown white farmhouse--or at least half of it is--shingles is missing, but only on part of the roof; the rest is in good repair.

The surrounds are a mess of weeds, and some of the trees that should be bearing fruit are dead-looking. At the bottom of the trees, gnarled roots come out of the ground, looking like old men's hands that have the arthritis. And again all around, where there are no furrows to be seen or sods that be busted, far as the eye sees is scorched earth. I think to myself, *Is it lying fallow or just neglect?*

I see one field half-plowed, but not that year--stuck in a furrow, and with poisoning weeds growing about it, is an unhitched plow.

In front of the house is a garden, and beside it is a small, square patch of green. It's a neat little herb garden where a tall woman is picking herbs. We watch her singing to herself, singing, Rock-a-bye Baby. She sounds almost like a child. After a little while she must feel our eyes, for just as she is coming to down will come baby cradle and all she turns. When she sees us a fear comes upon her, though I can hardly see her face for she has on a bonnet, has it on tight.

Even so, she's peculiar looking and I know she's scared, for her singing stops, her hand curls up like a bird claw, and her shoulders bunch up like when you pick up a plucked turkey by its wings. She holds a bunch of herbs to her breast, like it's a baby child, and runs into the house.

Scared or not, we're hungry, and not out to cause her any mischief. Even if she don't want to give us nothing, I wouldn't have judged her none.

Outside her porch walks a big white goose ... She surely has food.

"She looks afraid, Luke. Maybe we oughta leave her be."

"Hell no. I'm famished, I could eat the ass off a low flying duck. She's bound to have victuals."

"All right, let's ask her then." We walk on and I start singing: "I am going away to the great farmhouse! O, yea! O, yea! Ooooooo!"

Luke stops. "That song you was just singing there, it's the saddest song I ever heard."

I stop and look back. "How comes?"

"Well, there was this buck slave of ours named Henry. Every fall he used chop wood outside my window--that's where the wood shed was. He'd sing that song in a low base voice all day long from six in the morning till six at night. I surely hated it."

"Luke."

"Yeah."

"Don't call Negroes bucks. We ain't rabbits."

"Well, I do believe you're being a hypocrite there, for you said the Injuns, if they caught me, would call me a hare, implying I'm a coward, for a hare is nothing but a big jackrabbit."

"Then I is sorry."

"It's all right, Abe. When you've been called as many names as I have one more don't matter." He looks sad so I turn away.

"All right ... Anyways, Luke, I'm hungry. Let's go see if she's got anything."

"All right, let's."

The house is small, made outta logs with lime pointing, and a little porch with four posts holding up a roof is at its front. A small, trodden-down dirt path leads up to its front door. Five or six tobacco plants are growing either side of it with light-colored leaves like Virginia tobacco, not the dark heavy clay color of Louisiana. The leaves dry as paper and the stems bent and twisted by the wind, making them look like old scarecrows.

Yellow and orange sunflowers hum with bumblebees to the left of the porch steps.

The humming stops, or seems to, as I hear the loud sound of someone pissing coming from inside the house. It's like someone is holding a jug up high and filling a cat's water bowl on the floor.

I'm thinking, *That ain't right.*

I look at Luke with a that-ain't-right look on my face, but Luke, he don't notice. I mean neither my look nor the pissing. Maybe he thinks such thinking ain't polite, she being a woman and maybe even a lady, but that noise is so loud and it bothers me so. I even look at a horse nearby to see is he the one, but he ain't doing nothing, other than shaking his skin trying to shoo away flies. But the pissing is into a chamber pot, that much I know, because the sound it echoes.

177

Now my wife Bolinda she never sounds that loud, even though she only uses it when she thinks I'm asleep. But when I use it, I wake her up and she lets me know about it. She'd say, "ABRAHAM, I can HEAH you again. Lift the pot up off the FLAW so it don't be making that noise."

We knock at the door and stand waiting to be let in. The door already open a mite and there is a rope on the latch, though it wouldn't have been hard to push it open. We hear, "Pssst pssst." A finger squeezes out through the crack in the door and beckons Luke. He walks right up to the door and looks in through the crack at the woman, who is dolled up.

Her name is Edith Cromwell, and her first words to us are, "Sir, can you vouch for the Negro? I'm here all on my lonesome."

"Sure can, ma'am. He saved my life."

She must think I'm deaf, stupid, or something, for I hear her loud as a bell. I'm thinking, *She's not right in her head*, or maybe it's fear because that'll make anyone act stupid.

"I hears you, ma'am. You is safe as a house, leastways from me anyhow." I laugh and clap Luke on the shoulder.

"You see? As much a gentleman as any Negro I've ever met."

Most any nice thing Luke would say he'd always chop it down just as it got to standing.

The door swings open with a sound like an old cat who is pretending he likes you. We go inside. It is bigger than I thought it'd be. Inside the walls are painted with green milk paint--you can smell it, that and fresh baked bread. A dresser is there against a wall with china plates standing up in it and they just for looking at. Lace curtains are on the windows with little spots of black mold. The rest of it looks like a humble tidy house with a woman's touch. Edith lights an oil lamp because it is so dull. Soon all three of us are sitting at a dinner table with a fine china service on it, eating cornbread and lime flavored chicken and pork tongue stew. I was lucky, I got a whole tongue in my bowl, but to me it is too spicy; as hot as hell and taking me there. Sooner still, Luke starts turning up the charm to as high a glow you can. "These herbs from your garden?" he says. You see, there's this glass jar on the table with herbs in it.

"Yes, sir. You care for them?" she says, tittering like a girl half her age.

She looks about thirty-five, with long lips and a long neck.

"Yes ma'am, I do care. Is this rosemary?" says Luke, holding the herbs up to his nose.

"That's dill," Edith says.

Luke makes a little O with his lips and smiles. "I hear dill is wonderful for the complexion--by your face I can tell this is true."

She looks down shyly and Luke go on. "Where's your husband, ma'am? I assume a lovely belle like you is married."

Edith titters. "Have more wine." She says and she pours plum wine out of a jug. "My husband is no longer with me. We fled Georgia during the war, lost all our possessions."

Then her face goes wistful. "Even after all those years, Ollie never adjusted to poverty ... He hung himself last spring."

Her long lips start quiverin'. She looks at me like I remind her of some of them possessions, and she twirls a lock of hair that droops from under her bonnet, like she's thinking back on some pretty piece of lace, or a slave, that fate made slip from her big ol' hands.

"Why, I see no poverty here, ma'am. Look-see here at this fine china tea service," Luke says.

I'm drinking no wine, just tea, as I don't think she trusts me, and I guess my wits are still with me, even though I'm not thinking about anything in particular. But then I look at Edith's wrists and how big they are, and from her wrists up how big her arms is and then to her throat. Like I say, I'm not thinking about anything in particular. Edith takes a gulp of wine, and her Adam's apple bobs up and down like a cork on a busy fishing line.

Then it comes to me: Lord, save my soul ... Edith is a man. But to Luke she's all woman.

To answer Luke, Edith says, "It's all that remains. Excuse me, I've another herb I can ... show you."

Holding in tears, the "widow" stands up and hurries outside.

"She's about to get over her grieving. More vino, ma'am? Oh yes, please, sir," says Luke, doing Edith's voice and doing it well. Edith's glass clinks against a jug as Luke pours it full to the brim, and then his own too, measure for measure, and he has an awful leery look about him as he doing it.

"What's wrong with you, Luke. Can't you tell? We oughta go."

"You crazy? She's the first willing woman I've met since Aracela."

He's acting like I'm a killjoy, but, no sir, I ain't. There's a reason how comes you get to know someone before you get to know someone. For if you spend enough time with them, if they a man dressing up as a woman, that's the sort of thing you'll find out.

Edith returns with a sprig of herb.

Luke puts some bread down on the table in front of me. "Abe, you run along and feed the chickens with the leftovers. Go on now, off you go."

I look at him, but he turns away. He ain't going to listen. Well, if he don't think I've sense and wants treat me like I'm only good for a step-and-fetch, that's what he's going to get.

"Yessir," I say. "Omago leave the white folks be and feed dem chickens, gonna go feeds dem good." I pick up the piece of cornbread, walk outside, and sit on the porch. Chickens come up to me, all curious, but I run them away because cuss them chickens, they can pick the earth for all I care--my belly weren't full in an age.

I could smell a horrible stink, but I knew not from where it coming from, and a breeze came and it seemed to go so I paid it no more mind. I eat some cornbread. I see on the porch there is a drunken bumblebee lying on his back beside me, its legs with golden pollen sacks slowly flailing in the air. As I watch him I stop eating and start singing again: "I'm going away to the great farmhouse O yea, O yea, Oooooooooo."

As I'm singing, the goose tries to grab the last piece of bread from my hand. I chase it off and it making an awful goosey clamor about it as I do, but when I thinks back on it, Morton, I wish I'd let that goose have that piece of bread ... when I remembers what happened to it soon after.

I sit back on the porch, resenting the way Luke had spoke to me. But really that were only an excuse; he'd have used any to get to his new beloved, so I try not taking it to heart. I'm thinking, *It's funny and all, sure, but I'd be ashamed if I did something like that*, if I ever got drunk enough. I have to shield him from it. He's not my friend, true, but he ain't my enemy neither, and we'd had plenty of scrapes together. So I creep round the house hoping for ideas. There's a holly bush in front of a window. I lift back a branch and look inside. Below me the remains of a chicken are hacked up on a board with a meat chopper driven into the wood. Beside the board long silvery cutting knives are neatly lined up, who uses silver to cut up a chicken? Towards the back I see a black stove with a simmering pot and beside it, at head height, cow horns are nailed to the wall, a bloody apron hanging from one of them. Nothing in the kitchen ... I move on ten feet or so to the next window. Inside a blue butterfly flutters crazily against the glass. Its wings frayed and pale and flapping all their brilliance onto the glass making a tiny galaxy.

I look around and stop. I see a picture of Edith, dressed in regular men's clothes, smiling, with his arm round a small, plump woman. She is like an apple, as much as a woman can be, with what looks like rosy cheeks and a sweet face. The real Edith, I'm guessing, during happier times for both of them. But seeing that photograph really makes me fret, for everything is all the more real to me now.

I back away from the house. In the garden I see a large wooden gravestone chiseled out with:

EDITH
CROMWELL
1838 – 1874
Only the Lord
knows why

Yes, indeed, truer words never spoken. I walk to the door and look inside. Luke is sitting beside Edith on a little couch with Spanish moss stuffing coming out of a hole in the front. Luke is trying to look interested in some sewing work, Edith is showing him. Their eyes are looking at each other's, and Lord help that fool, but his eyes is full of lust now. He folds his legs and his knees start touching Edith's. They're chewing the rag, not canoodling yet, but soon to be. Edith's lips start to pout like fat leeches and they inch towards Luke.

I bursts in. "I fed them chickens, they is all fed. Sorry, ma'am, but what you say your name is again?" I've a friendly smile on my face, so Edith won't get suspicious and will keep on thinking I'm just some happy fool who loves feeding chickens.

"Why, have you ants in your pants?" Luke says. I say nothing to that.

"Edith ... Edith Cromwell."

"But the gravestone outside says Edith Cromwell," I say, still smiling. "Ain't that funny and peculiar."

A look comes over Edith's face, like someone has stepped on his grave, or at least noticed he shouldn't rightly have one to be stepped on, he being alive and all. Luke stares at me unkindly, even though I'm all the while trying to save him and no easy employment that be.

Edith smiles. "Oh, that's my mother-in-law buried out there. That's what got me and Ollie talking to begin with--the name Edith, which I shared with his momma." Edith's eyes narrow. I've got me a fight on my hands, Morton.

"Edith is a beautiful name, I think," Luke says.

"Luke, can I have a word with you, outside for a minute, man-to-man?" I say.

Luke looks glad, like now he has a proper chance to give me a talking to. He wipes his winey mouth with the back of his hand, trying not to let Edith see. "Excuse me, ma'am, be right back."

He follows me outside, and I walk till Edith can't hear what I'm about to say. At the end of Edith's garden, where there stood an oak tree, I stops and turns to face him.

"Luke, you needs to listen now, you hear?"

"You going to start preaching?" He looks beyond me and gasps. I turn my head, too, towards the tree that had the jay in it, though it ain't there no more. I don't know what I'm seeing. It's two moving shapes who become men on horses. Then I see the sun come off the hair on a waistcoat made out of buffalo hide. Marvin and Daryl Johnson have just turned the corner, before the end of the cornfield. They haven't seen us yet because we're in front of the tree beyond the herb garden.

Luke pulls me to the ground. We huddle next to the oak where it's wild and scratchy, thick with briars and gooseberry bushes. "Good work, Abe. Just shout things out. You're so circumspect sometimes."

"I don't know what that means, Luke, and I didn't even know they was there."

The Johnson brothers stop at the farmhouse and dismount. Daryl sniffs the air. "Whoowee, what is that smell?"

"I don't smell nothing," says Marvin.

"There's a hog pen over there ... yonder tree."

"Where?"

"Three hundred feet yonder, Lord have mercy." Daryl nods towards a long strip of land rising up like a mound, like an island in a sea of tall grass. A boar was in a sty there. The boar shuffled a bit and seemed to be missing part of its front leg, then it flumped down on a bed of grass and lay there twitching its big ears under an apple tree.

Whether they were crab apples or regular-size apples I do not know, it so far away. Marvin walks up and taps on the door, and they get invited in.

Luke says, "How did they know we're here?"

"I don't know. Let's take their horses and get."

"You're no gentleman ... There's a defenseless lady in there all on her lonesome."

"Luke, Edith's no lady ... she a man."

Luke stares at me, then his face gets angry, and he starts to pull his gun out. It catches on a thread from the coat, the thread breaks, then he points the gun in my face and cocks it. "Sir, you have insulted a lady and my honor. I demand satisfaction."

I swat the gun away like a nuisance fly.

"Get that outta my face. I ain't interested in your cracker nonsense." I say. "I'm trying to help you now, you hear. What I said is the truth."

Luke puts his gun back inside his coat, but he's still angry. "That's crazy talk. You're a loco hombre, Negro. That is what you are, that is all you are."

I calms down. "Luke, could you draw me without seeing me?"

"Sure, I could."

"Could you draw Edith?"

"Sure, I got an inner eye for beauty."

"All right, what do her dress look like?"

"Floral and pretty."

"What her hands like?"

"Big, but she's working a farm by herself--you'd expect that, poor girl."

"Her throat, what's that like?" I say, but he ain't listening, he's caught up in his mind again.

A minute later he picks a purple orchid, from near his feet, and starts stripping petals from it like it got a heavy bearing on what he'll decide to do.

When the flower is shorn he says, "Well, all right then, let's just take their horses. I'm no good to her dead. I'm sure they won't harm her none." Then he turns to me. "Didn't you notice those big lovely eyes?"

"No, Luke, I too busy looking at them big ugly hands." He shakes his head at me and we sneaks up to the house.

184

The horses are tied to the handle of a double-headed ax buried in a stump of wood next to the porch. I go to lift up the reins, but a cicada starts making noise like all hell beside me. It's sticking to a post on the porch. "Why won't these filthy men clean their horses?" Luke says. I stop and look back. Luke is going through a saddlebag and has a bunch of wanted posters and a flask of whisky in his hands. His cheeks are puffed out as he's holding his breath.

The cicada starts going scee sceeeeeeeeee again.

"Luke," I say. He looks at me, his cheeks still puffed and getting redder. "What you doing? You don't have time for that."

The cicada stops and we hear the noise of footsteps.

We run either side of the tobacco plant alley, back to the briars behind the gooseberry bushes. There is the sound like the old cat again, and the cicada starts to make its noise as the door opens. Daryl Johnson walks out onto the porch, fidgeting. Like me, he's been sent on a fool's errand.

Daryl walks toward us scratching at his beard, it still sore looking and patchy in places, like with a baby crow, the way its feathers are sprouting in places when in other places it's still bald. He run a hand under his red nose and his sad, mangy dog's, eyes that look watery now. I think that's from the hay, though, and not like he knows what's about to happen. He stops near to us. His ball-like belly rising and falling slowly, like a bed sheet hanging in a gentle breeze, at the same time my heart is beating like the head of a woodpecker going at it. Daryl fumbles about with his trousers and takes a piss. When he done he turns and walks back to the porch.

Luke whispers, "Reckon the Widow Cromwell is might-y lonesome. How did you read the grave?"

"I can read."

"But the judge said--"

"And he happy saying it. I'd to swallow my pride. And if it's her mother-in-law buried over there, she born only 37 years ago. It don't take no Detective Al Pinkerton to figure it out, Luke. It right there on the gravestone."

"Abe, that's made of wood, not stone." He starts to laugh like he has hiccups. We say nothing for a time, then Luke starts to sketch on the back of one of the wanted posters he took.

When he's done he's looking sad. "Abe, if anything happens to me I want you to take this to the Secretary of the Treasury in Washington." He hands me the picture. It looks sort of like him and sort of like George Washington.

"Where is his ears?" I say.

Luke grabs the picture back. "Shit, I forgot 'em."

"I suppose they is there under them grapes."

"Grapes, what grapes? There's no grapes."

"What's them round things then?"

"Curls. It's a wig he's wearing."

"How comes his hair ain't gray if he's wearing a wig?"

"Because it's *young* George, not *old* George. Don't you know nothing about dead presidents? It can be any color wig you like if you're president."

"What's that?" I point to the picture.

"It's a tail."

"Like a Chinaman tail?"

"No, it's like a rattail. A Chinaman tail is like a horsetail."

"I think that looks silly."

"Well, Abe, this may sound rude, but you are a vagabond Negro cook who currently resides in a briar patch in God-knows-where, Louisiana. I don't think our Founding Father needs your advice on how to wear his hair, now, does he? There is a bow in the rattail that pretties it up considerable."

"You living in a briar patch, too."

"Well, I'm hoping for better things. This is temporary."

"I think he's wrong."

"Who, the President? He can't be wrong, that's why he's President."

"Sure, he can be wrong, Luke. He just a man--maybe smarter than most folks, but still ..." The cicada starts again. I looks back towards the house. A blood-red cardinal lands on the top of the grave and starts cleaning his beak there, like you would sharpen a knife on a stone, then fluffs its feathers out like it's happy.

"Pretty, ain't she," Luke says, gulping whisky. "Some people keep them in cages, but they should be let free."

"Luke, it's not a she. The lady cardinal is brown colored. It couldn't change that even if she were president of all the birds. That's a boy cardinal over there, I knows that for sure certain

*A blood-red cardinal lands on the top of the grave...*

The bird's feathers get tight, its head perks up, and it fly away. From the house comes the noise of shouting and plates breaking. I'm hoping they're not the nice ones, for they hard to come by. The door bangs open and jars loose a shower of white dust. An angry, tearful Marvin starts to drag Edith out. Marvin's buffalo skin waistcoat is gone, and he's wearing only long johns now. Edith grabs at the door-frame, but Marvin is too strong, and he pulls Edith down the porch by one leg, with her head banging on steps. She grabs a sunflower with her hand--I mean his--and holds it till it comes up from the roots. Marvin knocks over tobacco plants with his arm like a reaping sickle, trampling over them. He stops close to us and lets go of Edith's leg. He stands there staring at Edith, breathing in and out deep breaths. His pink long johns have white patches on them--bleached spots from I don't know what, maybe sweat, piss, or the sun. His sleeves are rolled up and show his strong, stocky forearms, with veins like cords of a net wrapped around hams. He's bald without his dirty brown hat, and the black centers of his light blue eyes look tiny now, like the middle of new frogs' eggs. His face is both shocked and sad. He points to Edith. "You ... you filthy pervert. Of all the foul, wrong things to do to a man. Daryl, you go git that rope, you git it quick."

It's all so strange now, like watching street performers not good enough for a stage, for Marvin's words come real slow. Though maybe his anger would only be out of him one word at a time, like when you're emptying a bag of flour with your hand on it, in case the whole lot comes out at once in a dusty cloud.

Daryl goes to his horse and grabs a rope as Marvin rips off Edith's bonnet and wig. I turn to Luke to see how he's reacting to the unveiling, but he's not beside me no longer, no sir. He's standing, and he starts floating towards the Johnsons, like a ghost, not even thinking of his own anger or near escape from Edith's deceptive wiles. "What you fixing to do, boys?" Luke says. There's no sound now except the throaty caws of crows from the other side of the cornfield.

"I'm fixing to fix this pervert," Marvin spits on the ground and looks disgusted, and not because of the sight of Luke, no sir, though maybe. No, he's been kissing the widow. That's the truth of it, and slow on the getting as Luke is, I think he knows it, too.

189

Luke says, "Easy on now, boys. He lost his wife last year, he has a confusion upon him."

"I'm confused about nothing. His neck is for stretching and yours, too," says Marvin, pointing at Luke then clenching his fist, with murder and tears in his eyes and no will in him to carry any cross of shame on top of what he's already got.

Luke goes for his gun, but as he does his hand catches in threads from inside the Jew's coat, like they're a handful of nooses from Haman's gallows, and his hand is stuck. Edith breaks free of Marvin and runs into the house. Luke's hand comes free. But Daryl is pulling out his gun, too, giving Luke no time to aim. He fires and fires till he empties his gun and we hear clicks. Marvin and Daryl, not only are they still standing, they haven't even been hit, not once, either one of them. But the goose is lying dead in a heap.

Marvin looks at me, and he can see I've no gun. He laughs in a cruel, nasty way, walks over to his horse, takes a gun out of his saddle, and grins. I hadn't noticed it before--and I usually do--but his teeth are bad, with bad black gums. No brushing with soot or salt for him. Daryl has his gun out, too. He goes and hits Luke over the head, puts the rope on Luke's neck, drags him to the tree, and throws the rope over a branch that looks made for hanging, and he pulls the rope tight. "Git your ass over here." I turn and see Marvin is pointing his gun at me." I walk over to him. "Git on the ground," he says, and I kneel beside him and close my eyes. I say a final prayer to the Lord, asking him to look after Bolinda and my stepson.

I know we're being punished for the Jew's coat, or the sins of our fathers. But still, even though I'm about to die I'm grateful to the Lord I've never been a slave and haven't had too hard of a life of it, all things been thought upon. I even grateful Marvin didn't call me nigger just before I die, and even though he about to kill me, and I'm thinking *I'll never see light again in this world*, I open my eyes one last time and look at Luke. He's gasping like a trout, as Daryl has pulled him up to his toes. Then his feet start to leave the red earth and his face is red, too, like a birthing baby, but his eyes are looking at something.

I even think I see Luke smile as I hear a sound like the old cat again.

The Johnsons follow where Luke's eyes are looking to. It's the farmhouse door. Standing there, like Lazarus, is Edith's husband - risen from the dead. He has on dungarees, the rouge is mostly gone from his face, and, praise the Lord, he's holding a shotgun with two barrels. He lifts it high, aims, BANG! From the corner of my eye Marvin is standing there one second, then he's just gone. I hear him bounce against a tree and slide to the ground.

"Dang! Her husband's back," were Daryl's last words. He could've run, but BANG! The shotgun must have been loaded with more than birdshot with what happened to his head, and his fingers got torn from the rope he holding.

Luke falls to the ground still choking. Mister Cromwell clicks open the shotgun, to take out the two, still-smoking, spent shells, and drops them to the ground. He starts to reload, and I start to cry, for I'm thinking, *How comes he's doing that?* Lord, you can't kill a man twice ... And a bad thought comes over my head. I'm thinking, *He must have a taste for killing more folks.* My voice is shaking, but I just say it anyhow. "Goodbye, sir. We best move along."

"Name's Oliver. You can call me Ollie if you wants to." He speaking with a different voice now--it's deeper.

"All right then, Oliver," I say, "we best be going, and uh ... say goodbye to your wife for us, sir. You tell her from us now she makes a lovely tea, she surely do."

His eyes stare at me a moment, then look away. "I ain't that crazy. Take their horses if you like. They won't need them." He left the gun standing against the porch. Then he undo the Johnsons' reins, pulls the ax out of the stump, and walks towards the hanging tree, stopping when he sees his dead goose. He looks at it a while, but he's thinking about new things. He walks to the hanging tree and starts chopping it down, at the roots. With no words spoke we take their horses.

As we start to ride away, the sound of the ax getting strangely clearer as we do. After a bit we stop and look back. Ollie smiles and waves to us. As I turn and look ahead again I see Luke. He's a sight, with his face covered in blood and brains from one of the brothers, though which one it was I don't know. I guess it don't matter.

# 17 STONEWORKERS

W E LEFT the Cromwell farm and rode our way along a dirt trail through rural Louisiana, hoping to get to Baton Rouge, or wherever we could catch a train. It began to rain heavy soon after, driving down on us like nails. You could have opened your mouth and drank, it coming down so. Luke used it to wash his face. We left the horses out in the rain and waited under a tree for it to pass, even though the rain was no respecter of the trees' leaves. After a quiet time, Luke says in Daryl's voice, "Dang, the husband is back," then in his own voice, "Stupid as a paper spoon, right till the end."

"When did you know?"

"I'm not sure, though certainly when the wig came off, and thank you for your warnings, Abe. Yep ... it's been one hell of a journey." Luke stays quiet for a while, just staring and thinking as the tapping rain makes a puddle on the top of his hat. I put my hands together under a steady drip and drink from my handmade cup. "We'll have money soon. I'll let my wife scream at me a little, and then I'll whip out that money, throw it on the kitchen table, and see how that suits her."

We look at the tiny rivers on the ground flowing through the red mud a while, then Luke says, "Abe, where do you think your momma is?"

"Don't know."

"What she look like?"

"Like me--little darker, perhaps."

"What religion she have?"

"Baptist! How comes you asking me all this?"

"Well, I could do a poster of her. You could place them in Baptist churches. Maybe get you to pose for me. I got that idea just now. Yep ... because Mr. Cromwell and his wife, they look awful similar." His eyes get big and wide like he pretending to be stupid.

"Yeah, they sure do," I said, and we sure laughed about that, hee-hee, even though I knew it were wrong to. The rain stopped and on we rode. We hoped the rain would take the stink away from the horses, but it seemed to bring it on. Soap was needed. At a bridge we came upon these colored boys laughing and leaping from it into a slow river. When I saw them I knew I was surely missing home. From the bridge I saw a flooded bayou, a spoonbill standing there on its bank. Beyond the bayou was the mile-wide misty river. Noisy birds flying over the water looked small as flies. A giant setting sun, big as an orange held out in my hand, shimmered down to sleep, its shine stretching out long and pink over the river's flows. As I sat there on my horse, watching the spoonbill shake its head from side to side, sifting the waters, something inside of me began hoping for good things. We waited there saying nothing. The boys left, then the sun disappeared altogether. The waters became bloody for a time, then darkness came and it was night.

Next day we came across three dark-skinned Negroes, a middle-aged woman and two young men, who were loading dressed squares of limestone onto a cart at the bottom of a hill. The stone was shot through with pearly shells from the time when they was made. They were on a muddy road and had to make a few runs to get their load over the top. The woman was a stoneworker wearing blue jeans and a white shirt. I got down and asked did she need a hand because she was loading, too, and so I helped her and moved a big stone. It surprised her I could.

"You like some food then, is it?" she says, and not unkindly. She talks like a normal woman, but sounds like one who had her head down a barrel she fetching something from.

I say, "No, ma'am, but if you got any, I wouldn't say no."

I smile and she tells one of her boys to fetch bread, and he do. She rips the loaf in two, gives me half, and half to Luke ... Her arms so strong. I could have done with a whole loaf, but half is better than nothing. She looks at my saddle then. The Johnson brothers had carved their names in both of them, in deep cuts.

"That's a J there, ain't it?" she says, all proud.

"Yeah, it is. It says 'JOHNSON', ma'am." I runs my finger under the letters of a name, for I can tell she can't read.

"Is that so." She put her hands on her hips and says, "So why yo' horses so dirty, Mister Johnson, yo' old master's too?"

And she look at me like I'm poorly at my chores, for the horses' bellies caked in dried mud.

"Oh, he ain't my master old or new. I was never a slave, ma'am. My name is Brown, not Johnson."

She looks at me then at Luke. "Oh, pardon me, I never met a full-grown nigger man that weren't a slave before." She quiet for a second, then she laughs. Her teeth have a big gap in the front, and when she laughs it comes up from her belly, making it jiggle. Her boys start laughing, even Luke laughs, too, like I'm uppity, like I'm foolish.

I'm going to call her a gap-toothed bitch right there and then, but a gentle voice inside of me says, *Hush, Abe, hush.*

I stay quiet for a time. I still have anger in me but act like I don't. I roll up my sleeves and pick up a big stone, first resting it on my thighs before lifting it higher. As I'm grunting trying to get it onto the cart, the woman says to me, "What's that mark you got on yo' wrist there?"

"That ... Oh, it's just a snakebite from when I were a baby child."

Her eyes move up to my face. "You wouldn't happen to be Abraham Brown, is you?"

The stone resting on my thighs drops to the mud, with a plop. It misses my feet, but splashes red clay all over me, the woman's face, and all over one of her boys and his butternut-colored jeans.

I start to cry.

I go and put my arms around her and say, "Momma." I hug her. Tears start flowing from my eyes and I start praising the Lord, but she's not doing much hugging back, nor praising neither. I let go of her.

She's still laughing and so are her boys. "Momma! I ain't yo' momma, but I met a woman in Pensacola, when I putting granite on a warehouse there. She a cook who talks on and on about her sons, wondering what happens to them, how one he bitten by a snake on the wrist. We both from Texas, and we talks lots and lots and she six inches taller than me and half as skinny, so Lord, how on earth could you think that I yo' momma?"

And she laughs even more than she do before.

"Yeah, and she don't got no gap in her teeth neither," I say.

She stops laughing and wiping mud from her face, which she was doing.

"A gap in my teeth--what you say that for?"

"Don't mean nothing by it, ma'am. It's because you got kind eyes like my momma's. Didn't notice the gap before because I were looking at your eyes," which is mostly true.

Her frown go to a smile and she tells me she don't know where she lives or nothing, just where the building was at. So after that she got on her cart, which is hitched to a team of big-eared mules, and her boys get on the back.

Before she go on, I ask her what she's building now.

"It's a tower for a Dutchman," she says, and off she goes with the two young men, staring at me from back of the cart, with no words said from either one of them.

One of the cart wheels was buckled and groaning for grease. The two young men just kept staring back at me their feet dangling over the edge. One of them slumps back on his elbows. We watch the cart till it goes over the hill and we turn and go.

Later, we came across train tracks, we followed them, and caught a train not far from Mississippi. We really pressed for time and had to free our horses as it Saturday and there was no more trains till Tuesday. We took the saddles, though, as they was good, and we on our way to Washington, riding in a peeling green boxcar with swinging sides of salted beef and boxes of railroad spikes. We'd to pay with the Cajun's gun, for the honor, to a small colored porter.

The porter a sad looking skinny man with a little head and a big nose. I remember him smiling as he shut an eye, aiming the gun at a side of prime beef swaying back and forth, like a hobo's bag on a stick. "You can stay here," he says, "but you got to keep quiet and say I didn't put you here, if you gets caught."

So we agreed to what he asked because it better than riding with hogs, and off he go back to his red caboose with the gun.

Then we go to Jackson, Meridian, Mobile, Montgomery, Atlanta, Chattanooga, Knoxville, Abingdon, Big Lick, Richmond, and after asking for help all along the way, and selling our saddles, we came all the way into D.C., where I hoped the only peeling green I'd see would be cash money.

*****

The train that Abe and myself are on stops about ten miles outside Macon, Georgia, for over an hour, for no reason I am told. Listening to Abe, Reconstruction seemed like a better time. Maybe past problems, however bloody, tragic, or impoverished, always seem easier to bear than the ones we have now, for the spyglass we look back at them through is panoramic and contains their solutions. Outside our window is a billboard showing a happy American family, complete with dog and toothy smiles, all sitting inside an automobile. A caption reads, "World's highest standard of living" and below it reads, "There is no way like the American way." The paper is torn and rotten at the bottom, and I can't tell for certain what is being advertised. No business had the money to put up a new poster for many months it seems.

I ask Abe can he see it. He scrunches his old eyes and opens his mouth. "A little, just a car ... couple of heads. The country is in a terrible mess, Morton. The President don't know what he's doing, I reckon."

"Neither did Ulysses Grant," I say, "and things worked out ... or at least they did for Rutherford B. Hayes after him."

"How did it work out again?"

"Well, all the locusts disappeared. There were swarms over a thousand miles long back in Grant's time, with trillions of locusts, enough to cover Egypt, causing hundreds of millions in damage. They all disappeared over the course of a few decades."

"How did that happen?" Abe puts on his glasses again.

"No one knows for sure," I said, adding as earnestly as I could. "Maybe it's because that's when all the Jews started arriving, in their hundreds and thousands, and they chased them all away."

"Yeah, that's right. People are so ignorant nowadays. I bet the only people who'd know something like that would be a few old coots like me and you, hee-hee--"

"God punished the Egyptians with locusts, but He punished the Israelites with bees, from Assyria. It's in Isaiah 7.18."

"I never knew the Lord used bees."

"He has quite an arsenal at his disposal. He can use flies, darkness, frogs, Babylonians."

"You think God punished Luke because he was bad?"

"Maybe He was punishing both of you."

"I didn't get stung, and I ain't bad."

"Perhaps. Then there was gold! In 1876, there was a billion dollars worth of it in the Dakotas, nearly half the size of the national debt. That's why Custer was out that way. He was making the gold safe."

"I remember. I bet those natives didn't want to have nothing to do with that. Ain't it sad what happened them at Wounded Knee, though. They weren't treated right at all."

"Custer's men getting their revenge."

"It's like the ghost of the Civil War stick his hand up out of the ground to call down more blood, saying, 'Didn't get quite enough the first time'."

"That was one greedy ghost, Abe."

Abe looks at me, his face still scrunched. "He surely was, Morty, … surely was."

# 18  SALVATION

ONCE WE got to Washington D.C. I part ways with Luke, after agreeing to meet a few days later. I got a ride about twenty miles south toward where I live, but had to walk the last ten miles, eating sweet blackberries and whatever else I could along the way. Nuts were out on the bitch trees and their leaves were turning from green to copper and yellow.

When I got home it looks the same, as when I left, except a branch was broken on the dogwood tree where my chickens roost, hanging on by a thread of bark, it dangled down into a moving sea of yellow. Tansy was a-flower, and Black-eyed Susans were swaying back and forth staring at me. Newborn chicks running in among them all, scratching for food.

I had expected to return to my nest to find thorns, but instead of thorns it was more like roses. Only they were flat, like flowers pressed in a book, for a pregnant woman had been rolling around on them. That would be my Bolinda, who was almost five months gone. I'd been away nearly three months and she didn't know she was with child when I left, what with the clamor of it all and she not seeing the womanly signs.

In eleven years of marriage she never bore me a child, though I did have a stepson, Jacob, Bolinda's nephew. Her sister died giving birth and he given to us to raise. To me the boy was always good, or bad, at putting lies by me, and in truth I didn't get along with him back then.

Bolinda welcomed me back, she even nice about it. I was weak and skinny and afraid she would start nagging me about my wasteful ways. Though because of her condition she glad to see me. Though maybe Bolinda took pity on me after what her momma Lizzie said. When I'm only back, sitting at my kitchen table, remembering what the walls looks like, Lizzie comes into the kitchen and her first words are: "You yellow devil, you long-legged mulatto devil, done left his pregnant wife for a floozy." I say nothing. I just stare down at her bow legs not really meaning to. "You looking at my legs again, ain't you? You going to call me a bow-legged old bitch again, ain't you? And after what you done to her." She throws her hand towards Bolinda, who comes over beside me and puts her hands over my mouth and joins her fingers there.

I push Bolinda's hands away and I keep my lips shut tight. Both women are waiting, but they can wait till forever. I'm not saying nothing.

Bolinda put her hands on her hips and says, "Momma, hush. Can't you see he done some hard traveling. He's lost a lot of weight. Leave him be, Momma, just leave him be." And after that night Lizzie wasn't near as criticizing as ever before. When Lizzie walked away Bolinda said, "I'm glad you is home, Abe." It's easy letting a whole lot of things go by with Bolinda, when I think of ways she might have been. She had her daddy's legs, too, straight, long, and good for running because that's what his did. But that was years before and another story besides.

A few days later I met Luke. He told me when he had gone to collect his prize money from the Secretary of the Treasury, to design the centenary silver dollar, that he was a charming, prosperous looking man who had a smile just a tad too pleasant to be genuine.

The Secretary's office had a marble head of George Washington that stood in front of a window and a picture of President Grant hung on a wall.

When Luke went there he wasn't alone with the Secretary, for another man was sitting in front of the window, blocking out the sun. Luke says, "I thought this was a sure certain thing, Mister Secretary, with five hundred dollars sitting here waiting on me?"

"No, Luke, that's only the prize you're competing for. Normally it's five finalists, but you made such an impression on Senator Harris you made the final two. How is your father and brother, by the way?"

"Good, sir. Didn't know you know them."

"I don't, but I've heard so much about them and their bull-wire. This is the other finalist, Luke."

The man was from England. He reaches over a hand and says, "Noman Wamsden. How do you do?"

"Luke Sprague."

"Can I ask, bull-wire, what is it?"

"You can ask," says Luke. "It's like barbed wire, except a little different, far as the patents office is concerned anyhow." Luke told me the man spoke in an uppity fashion and wore a moustache waxed up either end like prongs on the devil's fork, as if that showed he had bad character. "What kind of a name is Noman? Mister, where I come from a man gives a son a name like Buck or Luke or Jake or Zachary, not Noman. What kind of man can you amount to if people think you ain't one at all?"

"Luke, his name is Norman Ramsden. He has a speech--"

"Impediment," says Norman, "like your foot seems to impede you, though better a foot or tongue than a heart or a soul."

"My soul is fine last I checked, my heart also." Luke stares at Norman, like a Texan would, and when Norman only smiles back at him Luke says to the Secretary, "I object, Your honor," like he thought, having won his court victory, he could now rely on lawyerly means to win his way.

The Secretary took the wind out of this high aim of Luke's by asking him, and I don't doubt politely, what he was objecting to. "This man is from England." Luke says. "If George Washington knew he was drawing his picture his wig might fall off."

Norman moves his chair a little, scraping it across the floor, so as not to block out George Washington. He makes a bridge under his mouth with the tips of his fingers, his eyes narrowing at Luke. "I don't see any feathers on the back of your neck."

"You calling me coward?" says Luke.

"No, I'm talking about the headdress of the true American, the Red Indian. I'm sure Sprague is an English name. Like me, you're from British stock."

"Like you? I don't like you and I'm not going to," said Luke.

"Forgive his outburst. He's a Texan. Some of us still think we're fighting in the Alamo," said the Secretary.

"What's that?" Norman asks, so the Secretary starts telling him about the wars between Mexico and Texas.

Luke interrupts. "The Alamo is as famous as David and Goliath. He knows damn well what it is. He's acting stupid to provoke me."

"How was it like David and Goliath?" Norman frowns.

Luke breathes in deep and pushes out his elbows like he's trying to take up the room. "*Because* ... there were lots of Mexicans, they'd us outnumbered."

"Whatever the Alamo was like, it's not like David and Goliath. Mexicans are small--I've seen one," says Norman. He taps the Secretary's desk and laughs.

"I never said it was like David and Goliath, *I said* it was famous as such. Hell, mister, you know nothing."

The Secretary asks to see their work. Norman shows him a picture of two dogs fighting, over sausages, and a boy looking on at them with his hands held up to his mouth, which is shaped like an O. Norman says, "It's comic, but the sadness on the face of the boy shows a depth, I think."

Luke snorts. "Dogs waving their nuts about in the air shows depth ... Is that so?" And he sounds catty when he telling me about it. Norman shows them more pictures, telling them he has military generals and peoples from history, and he mentions this man called Nelson. When Luke sees the picture he says, "His arm is missing." Like he's thinking he's caught Norman out, but only showing how ignorant he is, when Norman tells him that this Nelson lost an arm in battle. Not that I knew that either, but I wouldn't have acted like I did. I'm humble that way. Luke says, "All I know of history is the British got ran out of here a hundred years ago."

"Since the North and South are trying to mend fences," said Norman, "your old gripe against the English seems silly."

Luke reckoned he said that just to spite him, because of bull-wire, for he heard him talking with the Secretary before, about fences, and saw how Luke maybe wasn't too happy about his brother's blessings. But to me that's plumb crazy. Luke had nothing to show when the Secretary asked to see his work, so he draws a picture of Norman right there in the office, giving him a big nose, a devil's moustache, and a sham smile. "Maybe you'd be better suited drawing for nickel cowboy stories instead." Says Norman.

Luke didn't care for that and talked to me about it like it was a comment with no charity that came from nowhere, for a nickel ain't worth much next to a dollar, which is why they was there. But the Secretary had faith in Luke, for he had painted a good portrait of Senator Harris the year before. The Secretary called in the engraver next, who they had to do a picture for so he could put it on a sample coin. Then Norman told the Secretary he was staying at the Washington Arms Hotel, he left, and the meeting was over.

A day later I brought Bolinda and Jacob to meet Luke. Bolinda was all right with me, like I said, but mostly it's because I told her how Luke was going to give us lots of money. She was doubtful, but anyhow we all met in a cafe.

Luke had gone to a Salvation Army store and looked like a dude, part-ways between a Mississippi gambler and a tramp wearing jumble.

I reckon all the politicians from the sticks, when they traveled to the capital, must have took their old wares, what made them look like dandies and hicks, and dumped them at the Salvation Army now that they had gov'ment dollars to buy fancy threads like they ought to, like they'd wear in France or England. Luke's hat was a tall one, made of red silk, his new coat was the color of old mustard, and his waistcoat was what a field in Ireland might look like, if that country is green as people say it is.

Luke talked and talked. "That other man's work is hopeless, I mean no match for mine. I don't know what'll happen, but I'll figure something out, I promise. I've got credit at my hotel, but how long will that last? No 500 dollars yet, but I'm still going to get it and pay you what I owe you. So ... Bolinda, is it, and your son here?"

Luke pats Jacob on the skull and smiles. "Abe never stopped harping on about you two. Had to say, 'Stop it, Abe, enough about your wife and son now, stop chewing on my ears like a goat, talking on about your family'."

I look at my wife, who is still a beautiful woman, but she looks weary, even more so after listening to the problems and promises of former young Master Sprague. "You is right, Abraham, he talks too much. You gone three months with no momma or brother found--"

"But, Bolinda--"

"No, you listen here, Abe Brown, with all our savings spent on some wild goose chase and all you got to show is this man and his stories. Lord up above, help us."

"But Bolinda, it weren't a wild--"

"I got work to do, Mister Luke Sprague, or whatever you calls yourself. You owe us money, and I'll believe your words when I sees it. Come along, Jacob." Bolinda starts to go.

"Wait, Bolinda." I say. "Hear this man out. I think the hand of God in all this because he drew that picture of my momma, and I think that's going to help find her."

"It's true," Luke says with his eyes big and helpful looking.

Bolinda put a hand on her right hip, bent her arm out like a wing, and starts moving her head from side to side like a goose do when it walks, but her eyes don't move from me. "Heah him out--Abe Brown, is that what you jest said? Ain't that all I been doing for near on an hour is heah him out? And I'm sure about nothing. Jacob, you understand what this man is saying?"

Jacob says, "No."

"That a seven-year-old boy, Bolinda. What's he going to know?"

"Don't talk bad words over him." She put an arm around Jacob and says, "Abraham Brown, pictures of mommas don't buy no clothes and they don't buy chillen no books."

"You'll get your money, ma'am, but before you do I brought Abe a gift."

Luke had brought an old carpetbag along with him. He lifts it up off the floor onto the table and opens it out, and he pulls out the Jew's coat and smiles.

"I don't want that, Luke. You can keep that."

"What's wrong with it?" says Bolinda. "Looks like a fine coat to me and winter is coming."

"That coat is bad luck an' he only giving it to me because he don't want to give us nothing else." I had spoke the truth without meaning to, but Bolinda didn't fault me on it, or maybe she just didn't want to believe it.

"I could keep it for Jacob," she says, "for when he's older." She picks it up rests it on her big belly and looks at the inside, where it's ripped. "I'll fix up the lining, but you better get that money off this man, Abe Brown."

"All right, all right," I say and that get her to leave. Coat or not, Luke he'd done humiliated me again, or worse he'd swindled me, though I'm the fool for expecting otherwise. Luke just sat there smiling. I looked around the cafe, which was full of Negroes, and Luke's voice when he spoke next sounded so loud, slow, and Southern to me.

"Abe, whyyyyyy were you telling herrrr you'll be giving her piles of money? You were counting gold coins that still nuggets stuck in the ground and there yet plenty digging to do."

I whisper, "Luke, you said you'd get me money. I need it for my chillen." My hands are held up to make my point, but he turns away.

"Can't you stop talking on about your wife and chillen for five minutes now?"

"Five minutes--how about three months?"

"Have you considered in your mind how I might be feeling, Abraham?" He looks at me and points to his head. "I could've gotten dozens of commissions out of all of this and be set up like some French man in a bakery. Instead, I might end up back in Texas drawing banditos, Lord up above help me."

"But ... but I never mentions chillen to you before, Luke. I didn't even know I has them. But I got one, sort of, and there's one, maybe two, that's coming. I just want to buy new books and all them other things Bolinda's talking about."

"There you go again, Abe, talking about your problems when you ought to be helping me with mine. So I, likewise, and in turn, can help you with yours. Those babies won't be reading for a long time. Things will turn better for you by then, I'm sure of it. So fret none, my feathered friend. I've got me a plan."

I heard him say that before in a Mexican desert and it near cost me an eye. I thought he'd changed, but he still the same Luke I'd met seven weeks or so before.

Luke told me someone had insulted Texas and needed taking down a button hole or two, and that in the doing of this we'd have a royal flush with no other players in the game. Which makes not a lick of sense because who else is putting in chips if you're playing cards by yourself?

Next day Luke and me are in an alley looking across a street at the front of the Washington Arms Hotel. A man dressed in tweed with a pointy moustache walks out the front door and smiles up at the sun. Luke says, "That's him. Go over and slap him. Don't be too gentle, and if you can hurt his right hand a little it would be no bad thing." The man starts walking, but stops to give money to this begga' who ain't even beggin'.

I say, "He don't look like no bad man to me. I want my money, Luke. You can go kick him in the backside with your gimpy leg for all I care."

And I walk away knowing that man is in no danger, no, none at all.

I meet Luke a few days later outside his boarding house on H Street, which is a good name for it as there is lots of boards on the low windows. The owner, a Belgian with an American accent, had said the boards was there since the last hurricane. Luke believed that, he being from Texas where they get them, too, though I know that's a lie for I live where you don't hardly get them at all, which is no distance away, least not for a strong wind.

Luke had gone to see the Secretary, who had praised his new clothes. Maybe Luke could look all right with them; he seemed to think he looked respectable now. They kind of suited him and his eyes, the way they would be serious one moment and laughing the next, like on a snake oil salesman who is selling a cure-all for all the funny problems in life and the ones that ain't so funny.

The Secretary, as he admiring the clothes, says, "You make my black, white, and brown getup decidedly dreary, Luke."

"I'm only managing on credit, luck, and charm, sir. It won't last long."

"What can I do for you?"

"Sir, I can't say what America stands for, but it cannot be for giving some bastard choice government commissions."

"I gave him my word, Luke, but Senator Harris says you're a good old boy. I might be able to give you a slight advantage."

"Senator Harris is a hoot and a gentleman, sir."

"Senator Harris is a rogue and the ugliest son of a bitch I've ever seen. He'd better hope women never get the vote."

"We all do, sir."

"I know," says the Secretary, who then invited Luke to supper. The next time I met Luke he told me how his evening go. What I'll tell you is part what he said and part how I think it had gone.

He had went to the Secretary's mansion, in a fine neighborhood, knocked on the door, and a white-haired black servant opened it. Luke pushed by him and dumped his oversized mustard coat and big red hat on the servant, who had to let the door slam shut to catch them. The ceiling was so high it hurt Luke's neck just to look up at it.

A boy of eight with a freckled nose walks up to Luke. He's wearing a suit and a top hat that's too big for him and a shirt with a too tight collar. "Sir, you want to come outside and see my cat?"

"That would be quite a diversion, young man. But you are in luck: there is nothing I like more." The boy leads Luke down a corridor to a heavy oak door that has a pointed arch at the top. The boy turns a large key and swings the door back to show the blackness of night. "I can't see anything," Luke says.

"I'll get a lamp."

Luke steps into the dark and hears a hellish snarl. A chain suddenly snaps tight and a light wind caresses his face. The boy sneaks around Luke with a lamp held high. There are two angry emerald green eyes looking back from a shiny black bag of sinew and muscle that's as coiled as a pushed down spring.

"It's Andrew," says the boy. "I call him Andy sometimes."

"Little fellow, that is an adult panther, not a cat. Calling him Andy makes him no more cuddlesome."

"He's a baby, he's still growing."

The animal moves for Luke, who raises his arm, and the chain snaps tight again. "That chain is far too weak, young man. Some of those links look bent and the link at his neck looks far too big. I think it's angering him."

"My sister Rachel says, 'He might escape into Washington, which would be no bad thing so long as he eats the right people'. Sometimes I throw bread in the yard and watch from my window. He's really good at sneaking up on pigeons. He kills cats, too ... Slow ones."

"You have a sister ... Is she pretty?"

"Sir, even if she was, I wouldn't say, but I can tell you--"

"Thomas ..." A shadow appears at the door. It's the Secretary. "Thomas, stop absconding with guests. Not everyone is interested in your cat. This way, Luke." The Secretary beckons Luke and leads him and Thomas back towards the front door.

From a side room off the hall comes the wife of the Secretary. She's young and pretty, with kind, wide-spaced eyes, tied up blonde curls, and a cream-colored lace dress, which if she was ever an abolitionist, she could have hid ten slaves under it and walked them to freedom. The Secretary says, "Luke, glad you could come by. This is my beautiful, charming wife, Rebecca." She curtsies. "And you've met my son, Thomas."

"Hello, ma'am." Luke looks at the boy. "Indeed I have--after Thomas Jefferson, no doubt?"

"Everyone says that."

"Thomas, watch your manners," says his momma.

"He was showing him Andrew."

"O Lord, Thomas, not everyone is interested in pets. This way, if you please, Mister Sprague."

"Luke will do fine, ma'am."

He follows her bouncing curls on into a large dining room with a plastered ceiling that has flower designs in the corners and in the center. Pictures on the walls show folks wearing wigs with red cheeks, some of them smiling, some of them stern, and a chandelier hangs over the table that so big, if it fell during mealtime it would have killed the whole family.

A young woman walks in. Rebecca says, "This is our daughter, Caroline. We have another daughter, too. She is out riding." In the back of the house a door slams. "That will be her."

A tall young woman with long, flowing brown hair walks in wearing riding boots. Rebecca says, "Rachel, this is Mr. Luke Sprague." Rachel puts out her hand. Luke takes it, but he doesn't look her in the eyes.

"Pleased to meet you, Mr. Sprague. How do you do?"

"Good, good." Luke still won't look at Rachel. She ain't a pretty gal, and her momma Rebecca is taken aback at how he's acting--both parents are.

"What happened your leg, mister?" Thomas asks Luke, thinking the silence ain't pleasing to his momma.

"Well, I had a dog. I thought I knew him well. But he bit me in the leg so I kicked him straight to hell." Luke slaps his thigh and laughs. Rebecca frowns at this, but the Secretary laughs out loud. He's from Texas, too. That's not important, but maybe I didn't mention it before.

Later, the family and Luke are sitting, eating a meal. Rebecca says, "How was your journey up from Texas, Luke?"

"An adventure, ma'am. I'd two lots of bounty hunters on my tail and a former runaway slave as my guide. He was wanted for horse stealing and murder."

"They don't take kindly to horse thieves in Texas," says the Secretary, as the old black servant removes plates.

"You are correct, sir. They do not. He taught me a song, too." He sings, "Can you see them buzzards? Yes, ma'am. Can you see them flopping? Yes, ma'am." Luke clicks his fingers to see will the servant sing along. "Do you know it, old timer?" The servant pulls his head back away from the snapping and just keeps doing his job.

"Can't says that I do, sir." He walks away with the dirty plates, wondering who the jackass is.

The Secretary calls to him, "Oscar."

Oscar turns. "Yes, sir."

"Bring up another bottle of wine for our guest here--and go for the cobwebs."

"Ain't no cobwebs in your cellar, sir," says Oscar, who probably don't want to go down there because he's wearing his good serving cloths, a fine blue jacket and a crisp white shirt.

"I mean just bring up something old, not as old as you, maybe half as old as my wife, or a little older."

The Secretary winks at his wife, then says, "You aren't wanted by the law, Luke, are you?"

"No sir, I've no record."

"Why? Haven't they caught you yet?" says Rachel.

Rebecca laughs at her daughter's witty comment. It's her way of trying to get Luke to pay her daughter some mind.

But Luke is straight as though he's pallbearer to a coffin. He don't want to get this girl's interest up. He sort of crosses his eyes so he can look straight at her without looking straight at her, if you understand me. "No, ma'am," he says. "Drawing wanted posters for the law is risky business, especially in Texas. It's because I've got talent evil men conspired to have me arrested, or worse, shot like a common dog."

Then Luke starts to gulp back wine and stare at Caroline, who is blonde, fifteen, and pretty, with a chest that's starting to trouble the stitching on the front of her dress.

"Momma, he's looking at me with his eyes."

"He don't have nothing else to do it with, darling."

"Oh, pardon me, young lady. I was admiring your necklace. What is it? Emerald?"

"No, that's the color of your waistcoat. It's chrysolite."

Luke smiles, trying to look interested and intelligent.

"It's to remind Caroline of the Lord--it's the seventh gemstone in the New Jerusalem," says Rebecca.

"Oh, of course it is."

"I can take it off and show it to you if you want a closer look," says the girl, sounding a little ornery.

"No need. Looks comfortable where it is."

"Caroline, your manners. I hear your drawings are miraculous, Luke," says Rebecca, smiling at her daughter Rachel.

Luke's face goes suddenly wan as he's thinking that these ladies are up to something. "They're all right. I wouldn't say miraculous, though ... I mean, I'm not Jesus."

They're all uncomfortable now, till Thomas speaks up. "Are you married, Mr. Sprague?"

"Thomas! Do not ask our guest such a personal thing," says his momma, so wary it makes Luke suspicious.

"But you and Rachel were talking," Thomas says.

The Secretary interrupts his son.

"It's time for myself and Mr. Sprague to talk. Would you care for a post-prandial brandy, Luke?"

"Brandy, why yes, I would. Ladies, Thomas, it sure was an honor."

Thomas smiles, relishing the praise.

The women go to one room while the Secretary goes to a study, leaving the door open. Luke walks up to the boy. "You ask a lot of questions, Thomas. That's good. Means you'll never be accused of being boring." He taps Thomas's hat, causing it to fall over his eyes.

Thomas lifts it up. "Thank you, sir. How did you get a crippled leg? Really?"

"I told you, a dog."

"That's a big old lie."

"You calling me a liar?" Luke thinks of something to say that'll stick with the boy. "I got this leg from kicking a man who kept pestering me with stupid questions, Tommy." Luke sticks his angry eyeballs up close to the boy's. The Secretary calls Luke, who stands up and straightens his waistcoat.

Thomas watches him limp towards the study, and he's a little wiser now, for not all adults are sweet as his momma. The Secretary shuts the door and hands Luke a brandy. "Take a seat, Luke." They both sit. The Secretary shrugs and starts to drum the cushioned armrests of his chair. He stares at Luke and grins. "That is the greenest waistcoat I've ever seen, Luke."

"Indeed, sir."

The Secretary gives Luke a false smile. He's beating about the bush. Finally his face gets serious. "Luke, I have a daughter, and I want a man, a skilled man, to do her justice ... What do you think?"

Luke swirls his brandy a moment, then looks the Secretary in the eye. "Sir, you have a wonderful family, a beautiful home, and a lovely wife. Your daughter is clearly very special. I am flattered and indeed honored, sir, however, I cannot marry her. You see--"

"Marry her! Where did you ever get such a piss-headed idea like that? I want you to do a portrait of her and give her all the advantages a great artist can."

"You ... want me to paint her?"

"Yes, what did you think?"

"I don't know."

"Something like your Senator Harris portrait."

"It's a year since I did that, sir. Presently, I'm aiming for truth and realism in my art."

"Realism ... Truth ... Don't give me that moral bullcrap. Just do something to make my daughter look better than she does. Rebecca and I love her dearly. Just do it, for the love of Christ." While he's talking, the Secretary slowly walks to the door, opens it, and slaps Thomas, who is listening in. He sees Oscar returning with a bottle of wine. "Not now, Oscar, we're onto brandies. DON'T OPEN IT." The Secretary shuts the door. Oscar looks down at the cork that he's got in one hand, and the open bottle that's in the other. Inside the study, the Secretary sits down facing Luke again. "You'd be doing a good thing here, Luke. All the other so-called artists have disappointed me with their false promises and their flimflamming."

"I'll think on it, Mister Secretary. I need to chew this over with someone first."

"Chew away."

A few days on, me and Luke are sitting in a cafe across from each other. I'm sucking the flesh off pork ribs, Luke is cutting off tiny pieces from his and eating them like a lady squirrel would a nut. He starts to wipe his mouth with the back of his hand, but takes out a handkerchief instead. I say, "Do it, Luke. There's no reason how comes you wouldn't."

"I promised that Irishman I'd never draw like that again."

"What she look like? Is she really that plain and ugly?"

"Well, no, she's not plain or ugly, she's just peculiar looking. She rides horses a lot and kind of looks like one. Her teeth are long and ... you know, I can't even see her in my mind's eye without thinking about horses now."

I laugh, even though I know it was wrong.

"It's true," Luke says. "I feel like bringing along a bag of oats next time I go there."

"What sort of girl is she?"

"I don't know ... Her parents love her."

"Do it, Luke. Make her feel good. Ain't nothing wrong with that."

# 19 PORTRAIT OF A LADY

A FEW days later Luke and Norman were brought into a big empty room where the Secretary worked, and the Secretary left them there with paints and brushes and everything, along with his daughter Rachel. Luke became a different person, gazing into Rachel's soul, rather than her face.

Norman struggled. He kept looking in Luke's direction for inspiration, but none came.

Later, the Secretary came back rubbing his hands and smiling. "Gentlemen, I'm taking this lady to lunch to meet an admirer. Can you finish on your own?" They say that they can.

Norman was frustrated. He put down his brush, walks over to Luke, and says, "It's clear why you were chosen. I was wrong to mock you. Good luck. I'm bowing out. I cannot compete with such genuine God-given talent."

Norman holds out his hand and Luke shakes it, saying, "Well, sir, I must say you're a gentlemen and no mistaking." I know all this, Morton, because Luke told me so. Don't mean it's the truth, but it's what he told me, so it's probably nearer to it than not, though when is anyone called 'Luke' ever so polite?

Later, as Luke put the finishing touches on his painting, the Secretary and Rachel enter the room to look at it. The painting is not of a pretty girl, but it looks like her and it looks all right. Rachel bursts into tears. She lowers her head and looks away, then slowly she takes another peek.

The Secretary isn't sure whether she's heartbroken or overcome. He prepares for the worst and puts a loving arm around her.

She breaks away and goes to stand in front of Luke. He's scared he's either going to get a slap or a hug and don't know which will be worse.

After a moment she hugs him and says through tears, "Thank you, Mr. Sprague. Thank you."

He starts to pull away, but then he hugs her. "You're welcome, child. There, there."

The Secretary gives them a moment then says, "Rachel, sweetheart, excuse us." He leaves her in the room and leads Luke down the corridor of a gov'ment building. "Luke," he says as they stop in front of a door, "I've news for you." He ain't smiling now.

"Good or bad?"

The Secretary smiles, but it's with pity. He opens the door and they walk into an office. They see a head floating over a newspaper.

Senator Harris is sitting on a blood-red velvet chair behind a gilded, marble-topped desk. He's about forty, or fifty, with a face like a cartoon--big nose, droopy smiling eyes, and stiff high gray hair brushed back from his forehead. He looks up. "Hello, Luke. Good to see you, boy."

He folds the paper and puts it on his desk.

Luke shakes his hand. "No, Senator Harris, good to see you, sir."

"Is your father keeping well?"

"He is, sir, last I heard, selling his bull-wire. What's the news, gentlemen?"

"That's good to hear. Luke, there won't be a commemorative coin. President Grant thinks it's not the right time." A sad-looking Grant looks down from a picture on the wall, seeming to agree with this.

"We're trying to improve things with the British. Don't really want to go playing up on old feuds when we've an economy to rebuild." The Senator slides a bill across the table. "Here's twenty dollars for painting the Secretary's daughter." Then he holds up a coin, looking at it as he rolls it between his thumb and long finger like a very flat cigar. "Luke, this is the coin you designed ... Pretty, but may I point out to you a small mistake?" Luke's eyes look shocked, like them of a duck that's been whacked on the head. "There is only one l in 'celebrating'."

The Senator smiles at Luke, without judging him to be an ignorant jackass. He flips the coin towards Luke, who catches it, his face forlorn.

Few days on I'm back in the cafe with Luke. I'm looking at the coin in my hand. I say, "Where's my thirty percent at?"

"Well, I'm giving you a hundred percent of what I got. Like I said, they stopped thinking it was a good idea. Too busy cozying up to the British. Unpatriotic is what it is, and all I get is a coin that's a monument to my stupidity. I spelt a word wrong."

"Is it 'celebrating'?"

"How did you know?"

"I'm guessing because 'celery' only got one l. So this coin here is useless."

"You want to give it back?"

Luke reaches for it, but I pull it back. "No, it's worth something. It's silver ... You paint his daughter?" He nods up and down. "What you get paid for that?" I say.

"Twenty dollars."

"You going to fork some of that over? I should get least a jackass note."

"Abe, I owed that to my hotel. It wasn't part of our deal, which was me giving you a portion of a prize." He smiles. "I had to go to the doctors for quinine, too. I thought I got malarial from the swamps, but turns out it's just a bad cold." He takes out a yellow kerchief from his green waistcoat and blows his nose.

I hold the table tight with both hands, I all angry now, for I didn't give a rat's ass for his problems. "You lied to me."

"No, you were my partner in a deal, and it came undone. There's no prize, Abe." He holds up his hands, twiddling his fingers, showing me how empty they is.

"The painting must have been a wedding present."

"For whom?"

I pick up a newspaper that on the cover showed Boss Tweed, the Tammany Hall crook, had escaped from jail. Inside was a notice I'd seen earlier. I read it. "'Secretary of the Treasury, James Adams and his wife, Rebecca, are proud to announce the engage--'" Luke snatches the paper from my hand.

"'Engagement ... of his daughter, Rachel Mary Adams, to Texas Senator, James T. Harris.' Reckon I'll get an invite to that old shindig" ... He looks at me then and says softly, "Abe."

"Yeah, Luke."

"What do you think I should do with my life now?"

"What do I think?"

"Yeah."

"I think I don't care. I'm just glad I won't be hearing about your gimpy leg no more."

"Come on, amigo to compadre, what you think I should do?" I don't answer, and I guess it looks like I'm not going to. He starts glaring at me now, looking angry, but he clenches his jaws, trying to hide it. "If it's too much for you to give me some friendly old Negro pearls of wisdom, then I should not have bothered."

He's trying to make me feel guilty, and he's trying to flatter me, too. It's like he pressing me down the way a slave would be, back before freedom came, and he thinking he's the sun and I just the world traveling round him and his sweet-smelling plans. But even though I know it, part of me felt beholden to him, too. So I could either get angry or just let him browbeat me, and that ain't no choice, for that's like half a dozen bad eggs or six ones that's rotten. "Luke," I say, "I ain't yo' slave. Feels like you thinks I is sometimes, and even more than that, too."

He huffs a little. "Well, I am sorry."

I look at him, and I think he means it, though I know he'd soon enough forget he ever said it. But I got to thinking, *maybe I shouldn't be stingy with advice,* for as my father used say, "Kind words never broke anyone's teeth."

I say, "You should draw for them newspapers. You've a gift for making people look bad. Some of them politicians needs that."

He points to my newspaper. "There's one of Senator Harris."

"They didn't have to make him look that bad."

"No, that is really how he looks. Well, Abe, good luck." He looks about the room and out a window. "Hope you find your family someday."

"I've got my family, Luke, and if this is all you is giving me ..." He looks back as I hold up the coin. "Then there's something I want you to do."

# 20 MY WORD IS MY BOND

A FEW DAYS on, Luke came out to my house in Port Tobacco, Maryland. It's thirty miles south of D.C. He was there to draw a picture of me, Bolinda, and my stepson Jacob. As he setting up, he dropped a pencil on the floor and it rolled all the way to the door. "What's wrong with your floor?" he says.

"Don't know. Boards is buckling I suppose."

"No supposing about it."

He soon began. Of course, when he started, he drawing too fast. I'd to say, "Slow down, Luke, no hurry, no rush."

Later, when he done, Bolinda and me walk over to look at it. Them the scariest steps I took the whole time I with him. Worse than being bound, lynched, burned, Captain Wilson, bounty-hunting brothers, Buffalo Soldiers, branches, butchering, bugs, Billy, braves, blancos, borders, buzzards, banditos, beasts, buckshot, bats, Buddy, bees, bird-shit, beatings, bitches, being broke, Brits, breezes, boats, big waves, bile, bayous, bloodsuckers, bears, briars, blood and brains, and all the clamor we'd been through, crashing over us like foamy waves rolling over rocks on a beach ... But I likes what I see.

For in that picture I'm handsome, we all the right color, and I'm a husband and father back in the bosom of my family where I belong. I look at Bolinda and she likes it, too, even though she pregnant in it. Luke asked her, before he start, did she want to look skinny in it, but she shook her head and told him, "Draw me as I is." He made her eyes kind looking, like they is, and her teeth white and pretty, like they is, too.

For I never met a woman with prettier teeth than my Bolinda. Jacob liked it, even Bolinda's momma Lizzie, who in the back cooking, for my house also a cafe, she liked it and all. I fed Luke one last time, then we go outside. I could see Luke wasn't limping much at all now. "Where your limp go to?"

"It went away." He says, "I've never been much of a walker. All the running about must've stretched out my leg." He jumps up on this old one-eyed horse his innkeeper had loaned to him. Then Luke took off his hat and starts fixing his hair--it getting long--before putting his hat back on again. John Wilkes Booth rode a one-eyed horse. I wonder if it the same one and who would it think was the vainest man he ever carried?

"So, Luke, what are you for now?"

He squints his eyes, as though his adventures have banged him hard as steel. Maybe they have, though not near as much as he looked like he was thinking. "Well, your advice on satirical sketching is good. I have made inquiries at several newspapers, and they are receptive. However, I cannot forget the French woman I met in New Orleans."

"You could never find her again."

He smiles. "You are wrong, Abraham. I'll just ask someone of a similar background and they'll point me to someone else, and so on and so forth, and before you know it, I'll be at her very door."

"So you think you is in love?"

"Well, I don't know. It's just everything I have felt for women before now just seems ... mean."

"Sounds like it to me. So then what'll you do?"

"I'll return with her back to D.C. I was not impressed with New Orleans. Sure, it's pretty, but it is danger filled, and the sanitation is appalling, though on its limitations you are already both well--and practically--informed." He snorts and laughs.

"You talking funny, Luke. I don't mean I wants to laugh, I just think it's peculiar and strange. If you want to know the truth it's even kind of bizarre."

"Hadn't noticed. Thank you for telling me I'm being high and mighty. Wise company will do that to me. I've found recently I'll sometimes use three big words where one small one would've sufficed before." He looks away as though I'm tiring him.

I say, "Well, ain't nothing like words to stop people talking."

We say nothing for a while, till it starts getting uncomfortable.

Then Luke says, "Well, I best be gone looking for my belle. I'll bid you adieu, Abe Brown, and simply say our time together has not always been unpleasant."

He pulls his reins tight, like he's fixing to leave.

"Lord, go on, I'm not keeping you, and a ... safe traveling, Luke. Wherever you go."

He grins. "What's it like living at the back of a swamp?"

He's squinting at the still water beyond my house. The sun is shining through cloudy sky from behind him onto my face. "It's home, I guess. The land cheap to buy." I heard a croak and turned back to look at my house. A branch of a tree is swaying up and down a raven having just landed on it. A few brown chestnut leaves fell off and floated down to the water. A breath of wind blew one of them along it, like a tiny skiff, the other leaf starts to sink. The raven croaks *harrrrrhhh*. It opens its beak and starts nodded back and forth like a cat choking on a chicken bone. The raven's eyes flash oyster shell white as it blinked. All the fluffed up feathers under its throat suddenly got flat. Knowing we were there, it starts flapping through twigs croakin' *harr harr harr* and bustled away on the wind. The still swamp was shining like liquid lead. Two bare trees were reflecting in the water, making their branches look like roots, or nets cast over the water, or spider's webs even. I still were vexed with him, though not at that moment, and I thought it best to say nothing.

"I hear ravens are a harbinger." He says.

I scrunch up my face. "Huh?"

"A sign ... In some places they're considered lucky," he smiles at me with pity.

"Where?" I ask, but he doesn't answer me and nudges his horse's belly.

222

"Well, Abe, may the termites never call on you." Those were the last words he ever said to me. My house made of wood and on posts for when the swamp would flood. It a nice thing to say, I think. Luke headed off towards D.C., by the back road, going through a birch stand that so bare and white they must be praying for snow to cover them all. And that's it, Morton, I never seen him no more.

*****

"MACON, MACON. Next stop MACON." Yells the porter walking down our coach.

"Abe, you sound bitter towards Luke, even now. Why?"

"Termites did call, a big part of a chestnut tree fell onto my house, and so many things happen to me over the years that I could have used that money for."

"Sounds like you spent it a few times over."

"I'd have been happy spending it once, Morty." Old Abe slowly stands up and looks out the window, his face trying to register familiarity with passing landmarks.

I ask him did he ever find his mother or brother.

I wrote to a Baptist church in Pensacola. Sent the preacher there the picture Luke had drawn for me. I sent letters back and forth to him, as momma couldn't read and my wife wouldn't let me go traveling again. Then, one day, a woman comes into the cafe. As I'm serving her at a table she grabs my hand where the snakebite is. "If you ain't my Abraham, then I don't know who is."

She had traveled all the way by herself. I say nothing, just stare at her. I don't cry, or hug her, or nothing.

"Don't I get a hug?" she says. She got one. She surprised the stoneworker woman, the one who brought us back together again. Momma said, "That woman Madeleine Carter always complaining on about her sons, saying they no use as cutters, she didn't know what would become of them. That they didn't know how enjoying it was to be hammering stone all day, that you could hammer under a tree and didn't have to be out in a field, picking cotton, under a fiery sun.

"That's why I mention you to her, Abraham. There she was with two fine boys and me with two gone. Their father must have been a stick because their momma built like a stone house, and if they not strong enough for lifting stone, their father had to have been a stick, plain and simple." But she said it straight--with my momma Klea it always hard telling when she serious or only playing--then she bursts out laughing.

She looked much older than when I'd seen her last, but still had joy in her eyes, till the light went from them altogether about ten years on. I never saw my brother Jackson again, though maybe I will someday. I ain't dead yet. My momma come to live with us and that changed things between me and Jacob. One day I'm chopping wood and I hear the boy break a window. I get angry, so I wait to let Bolinda go talk to him. She comes outside and asks me to do it.

"No, I'm up to my plums with work, woman."

"Well, I up to my eyes the three months you gone, Abraham Brown. Being up to your plums don't sound half as busy." And she walks away laughing.

So I go to his room. He had been hammering his window shut.

"What you doing, Jacob," I say. "Huh?"

He starts crying and tells me my momma told him, "If you ever lie to me again, I'll turn into a bird, fly in that window one night while you a-sleeping, an' peck the eyes out of your head."

I laughs when I seen how scared he was, how he only just a little boy.

I hug him and say, "She's just lying, too, little man. Don't be afraid." After that we get on all right mostly. In anger, I cut down the rest of the chestnut tree that had fell onto my house. But when the buds started blossoming on branches next year my daughters Nettie and Sarah were born, and that stump it sent out shoots, it gave me hope. Sometimes things was good, sometimes they was bad, mostly they was bad. Jacob was given the Jew's coat. He grew up before our very eyes and it fit him like it were his own skin. I tell you, that boy became a blessing to us all.


I asked old Abe, "Whatever happened to Luke?"

"He become an artist. I seen his sketches in the Washington Star over the years. Though I haven't read for many years, for my sight got so poorly. My wife told me many a times to stop asking about him because she thought I were angry about the money he owed me, which I ain't no longer. But she'd think I was if I asked about him. He'd changed his name to Roger Bond many years before. I don't know why anyone would want to do that."

"Well, I should have known. Roger Bond, why he's a raconteur and lecturer. I compete with him, or did, about twenty years ago."

"You must be lying, Morton. I don't believe you."

"No, it's true. I was insulting him only today, not that anyone would have known. The speech I gave in Savannah was nearly twenty years old. I'd never used it before, and it was just sitting in a folder in my study for years. I know Bond had a French wife, Marie, who I suppose is the lady Luke met in New Orleans, for I have met her. She was a widow. Her former husband was a merchant, a prominent democrat, who was tipped to become mayor one day. He was found dead, in a bathtub, in a Bourbon Street hotel. No foul play was suspected, though he disgraced her, leaving her in penury, or without a picayune, as Luke would have said."

"Is that so?" Abe said. "A foreign wife ... That would suit him, I think. She could admire his art without having to mind what he saying so much."

"One evening I was at a roast. They were serving duck, and after the--"

"Oh, I loves roast duck. Lord, you got me hungry now ... but please, go on."

"No, a roast is where you act like you're giving a toast to a person, but really you're making fun of them. It's all good-natured. Anyway, I was sitting across from Roger Bond, as I knew Luke then. He said his wife brought him dinner once:

'There you go ... Voila, it's a canary.'

'A canary,' he said. 'Why, that's the biggest canary I've ever seen. It's as big as a chicken--and darling, we do NOT eat canaries in America.'

'It isn't a canary, silly, it's a canard.' Canard is French for duck, you see. He thought it was the funniest thing ever."

"That is sort of funny ... I guess," Abe says.

"I never really knew what to make of his humor. He said once, in front of a German friend and me, when I told them of a criticism I had made in person to the President, that yes, I deserved to have narrenfreiheit, which means the 'jester's privilege' or 'fool's freedom' to be exact. I took it for an insult, but he said it wasn't.

"That his mother was German and she always allowed him a short time each day to be a fool; then he could say and ask whatever he liked. She died when he was quite young, I believe."

"Something were sad in him, Morton. I never asks him about it. Though sounds like he found happiness."

"Yes, I hope so, I really do. I don't recall him having the crow's feet you mention. Though perhaps they were just lines from being nervous and the company of his lovely wife smoothed them out." Abe shrugs in agreement--or is it indifference. I say, "By the way, my German is not so good, but the German for coward, if I recall rightly, is hassenfuss, which means hare-feet. Which is probably why he was so insulted at your comments on him being called hare-foot, should he be captured, by red men, and renamed."

Abe slaps a thigh. "Oh, that's funny. I only calls jackrabbits hares because my father used to, when we hunting them."

"Did you know how Luke was crippled?"

"No, Mort, I don't."

"I heard him say he partook in a duel during the war. He was no more than a boy at the time, and after discharging and wounding the hem of a coat belonging to his opponent's second, and nothing more, he had a revelation that dueling was an act of supreme folly. But still he stood his ground and he got shot."

"Luke, he had a wound on his leg, all right. I seen it. But the bullet, it come out the front of his leg, I'm sure about that."

"Guess he turned to run?"

"Yeah, well, that could be where the dog lies there."

"Why didn't you ask Luke yourself how he got his limp, with that wound staring up at you?"

"I don't like asking folks their business, Mort, 'specially white folks, and because it'd be like cooking a real big ham and you the only one left to eat it all."

"Whatever do you mean?"

"I'm just thinking you ask that man about one problem, which would be a slice of ham, you could end up with a whole ham. And yeah, that's kind of selfish, I know, but also it's too much ham, if you sees what I'm saying. I guess in life you want to be kind to folks, but it's nice to know the amount of slices you getting, too, hee-hee."

"That coin could be worth a lot of money."

"I know. Never thought much about selling it before--and I'd lost it for many years. It's just my daughter Nettie is losing her home. They're going to foreclose on her. Her husband Robbie Jones lost his job, as parcel post clerk, couple months back. They nearly owns that house, too. They just need nine hundred and thirty-seven dollars. If I could get that I'd be a happy man. Don't want her ending up in a Hooverville." She don't know why Jesus is punishing her and why the whole country is cursed. I tell her he came to save, not to judge, but I tell you I don't know what to say to her anymore."

I call the coffee seller over and ask does he remember the man I was with when I boarded. He does. Then I ask could he kindly go get him for me in the white cars. Soon Davis appears.

"Davis," I say, "this is Mr. Abraham Brown."

"Hello," says a mystified looking Davis.

I asked Davis to give the coffee seller a quarter and to give Mr. Brown twelve hundred dollars. Davis hesitated, out of loyalty, I suppose, as though he was wondering had I suddenly become senile. The sum was well over half the amount from the Georgia portion of my lecture tour. "You heard me, Davis." I said it impatiently, conscious we'd soon be pulling into Macon.

"You think this coin is worth that much?"

"I'm sure it's probably worth a lot more, Abe. It's not for the coin. The money is for your story. I want to write it. If my book, *Fastest Draw*, does well, you won't have to look for a buyer for your coin, a buyer will look for you. I hope you don't object to the title."

Abe stares at the bundle of notes on the table.

"I don't know what to say, or if I can accept this."

"Yes, you will, but before you do there is something I will say."

"Go on."

"Well, I might lose the twelve hundred dollars if I don't sell your story, but that's not a big concern. What worries me is that you might see it in a bookstore, or, more likely, hear tell of it and think I've shortchanged you."

"No, twelve hundred dollars is just fine. Here's the coin."

"No, Abe, you keep the coin."

"Why, thank you, sir."

"No, sir, thank you." Abe picks up the money. He licks his lips and looks at me to see if it's all right to count it. I nod.

When he finishes, I ask, "Do you know how the coin had a wrong spelling on it?"

"Don't know for certain, but I'm guessing it was Luke's fault. He told me he went to see the engraver, a Mr. Parkes, this serious man who wore glasses far down his long nose. When he looked at Luke's work, his face was surprised, for he asked Luke did he check it properly. Of course, Luke would have said he had, not wanting to be second guessed. But that man the type who would plow a straight line, neither going to the right or the left, even if there was a rock in the way without someone moving the rock for him. Luke, maybe he didn't take enough care with his spellings, for he used to working on drawings where mistakes are easily rectified; engraving, that's different."

Outside the window, the lights multiply in number as we leave rural Georgia and pull into the station at Macon. Davis walks off to the restroom, and Abe stands up, looking out the window again as the train lets out its steam.

"I wonder, why did Luke change his name?"

"Maybe because people were out to get him. But I'm Abraham Brown, always was, always will be."

"I suppose that would be it."

"Thanks for listening and letting me be an old n-n—narren ... narrator, and uh, excuse me, but what you say your name is again? Morton what? You told it to me and I forget it. You must be like a Frederick Douglass or somebody if you gives lectures because you talk all proper, like you is reading from a book ."

"No ... Fred is long dead, though I did meet him twice. My name is Morton Sweetman. Can't say it always has been ... and you may be a narrator, Abe, but you are no fool."

228

"Oh, don't you worry, I ain't running myself down. I just say that because I likes to rhyme. You must be white. I thought when I first see you, *Damn! He's light skinned*, hee-hee. I should have known you lied about being part Negro because you talk funny. Ain't it strange, the very day I meet the finest white gentlemen ever is the day I get talking about Luke Sprague. That stingy bastard. I don't know how comes you is in the Negro coaches, must have been God sent you here. Yes, God did. Goodbye. I won't forget your name now, Mr. Morton Sweetman." He clasps my hand and pumps it up and down.

"You know, Abe, you might meet Luke again one day."

"I don't think so. I don't plan on going to hell, and Luke, he sure ain't in heaven. Though I shouldn't say that--that's for the Lord to decide."

"Didn't know he was dead."

"Yeah, he is. My wife told me he died about five years ago and not to talk about him ever again, just leave him be."

"I don't think Luke is in hell. Maybe he's in purgatory."

"Don't believe in that. Anyway, bless you, sir. Yes, bless you. You got my family out of a hole."

"Thank you for the coffee, Abe," I say, raising my cup.

"You're welcome. Stay safe in Atlanta, if that's where you is going." It was. The train comes to an abrupt stop. Abe walks away singing "Miss Caroline Girl," passing Davis as he does, and dismounts the train.

Davis sits down where Abe had just been. He looks at me about to speak but waits as we hear the porter loudly saying, "COFFEE, MA'AM, COFFEE, SIR, SANDWICHES, ahem," as he walks by us towards the Pullman car.

"Who was that man?" says Davis.

"Someone from a thousand years ago."

Davis was silent for a while then, he said, whispering, "It's not so bad in here really, is it? But shall we move back to the white carriages now? I believe it's the law down here, sir."

I lay my head back and shut my eyes. "No, Davis, I'm going to have a nap here. Wake me up when we get to Atlanta, but you stay awake and keep an eye out, you hear." And in my best Scottish voice, I say with a smile, "Yes, you stay awake and you keep an eye out for all those dangerous Negroes."

# EPILOGUE

B EFORE WE part company you may recall, at the start of
this story, I was giving a talk at the Savannah Theatre House.
I didn't include my lecture then for, as the junior narrator in this
story, I did not want to appear as anything otherwise. But now
that it will not cause any undue diversion, I shall end as I began
and include part of it. I stand on the stage looking out at the
audience and the millinery maelstrom of their moving hats for a
while. The noise fades until all I hear are a few coughs. I bang my
cane down on the polished floor and speak, with my stage
Southern drawl. "I am not a great man. Maybe this is sad news to
you, and given that I have been previously so sure of my own
personal greatness, I can assure you it is quite upsetting to me. If
you are great, please have pity on me. I know now that love is a
kind lie. If you meet me on the street I won't keep you long. I
promise to break away quickly, for such is my lack of greatness I
can no longer make demands on people's company or time.

"But before the wine of kindness is drunk, please, before you
put on airs, or press your lips together with a commiseratin'
smile, make sure you are great, or at least aimed in its direction.

"Otherwise ... I will find it hard to endure you. For if you lack greatness, but believe you have it, I cannot help but feel somewhat grander than you are. For you see, I'm natch-rally competitive, and your dee-lusion is something I'll be unable to simply overlook. Oh, sure, I'll be polite for a while and perhaps purse my lips together and suppress a smile, and I'll slightly knot my forehead to prevent my eyebrows from rising--they act like barriers at railroad crossings, don't you know, and rise independently of each other when so ever I spot someone who thinks they are great. Likewise, they lower to prevent the passing of those with an unfounded opinion in this regard." I navigate my way down steps to where the bigwigs sit, in the front row, passing by them like a stern schoolteacher. I lower my raised right eyebrow at them. Then I quickly stop to turn back and lower my left one. A few laughs start to infect the audience. There is a nice tension--I'm hoping for an outbreak with no quarantine. I walk down the central aisle. They are now at my mercy. I hope.

"Please, make sure also that your greatness is something we can both agree on. For instance, if you have inherited a large sum of money and a great name, why, this has about as much greatness as, say, a well-placed bucket under a fruit-laden apple tree that is shook with vigor." I wait for silence then remove an apple from a pocket, and I take a bite from it. In the front row I have spotted a man, a playboy and scion of a wealthy newspaper magnate. I act as though he has taken an interest in my apple. I take another from my jacket pocket, hold it over him, and drop it. He catches it and stands up, bows, and takes a bite from it. The audience laugh, and I motion him to sit down quickly and he does.

I continue.

"And, if one of those apples was in the 'Garden of Eden' and became evidence in the condemnation of man and womankind to a life of pain in toil and childbirth or was taken and placed on the head of William Tell's son, well, that apple would not be great at all, only a witness to something great. For mere knowledge gained through learnin' or chance doesn't show greatness no more than the eyewitness account of a fool to a momentous occasion.

"When I told my nearest and dearest of my lack in this regard it was a relief, like a murderer who finally confesses to man and God his heinous crime. Any punishment is worth the removal of that burden. Maybe I had put on the garment of greatness like a fat knight puts on a corseting suit of armor, but now I'd rather enter my battles naked as the day I was born. I might be sliced in two by a sword, but hope my assailant would realize something of his own cowardice in this.

"Maybe a lack of greatness should be introduced to the world in small amounts, don't you think? I mean, what man wooing a young woman would quite truthfully volunteer his dullness and lack of originality, when a third of a lifetime of anecdotes and jokes should be fuel enough to kindle the fire of romance without the need for incite or wit. The lack of which could be introduced and tolerated when more mundane, but essential, qualities, such as kindness to children, reveal themselves? Now, why have I come to these conclusions? Well, I shall tell you. I have visited the lectures of some peers of mine, a few of whom take themselves a might too seriously for my liking. Yes, one in particular, I have heard his sketches and in them seen something of myself. It appears a curse at first, but to meet a jackass whose behavior so closely resembles your own so as to cause your countenance to blush is a gift. For what can be gleaned only from years of high company can be learned as quickly by looking in a mirror. So thank you, Lord, for fools and all they teach you without so much as trying."

If you enjoyed *Fastest Draw,* please take one minute to go to **amazon.com** to give it stars. If you have a few minutes you can write a review. *Many thanks.*

# ACKNOWLEDGEMENTS

CONTAINS SPOILERS. Thanks to my Mother Catherine for encouragement, my father Larry, and brother Laurence, for writing advice, my editor in Austin, Karl Monger, for his high praise and sterling work, and to Rachel Veiders, Rosanne Cornbrooks Catalano, and Heidi Ratner for additional editing, Will Griffith for his valuable input and Katie Ostmeier for her kind enthusiasm. Thanks also to the African American cab driver who told me the story of a catfish so big in Lake Wylie, South Carolina, that a diver had refused to return to the water after seeing it. Thanks to teachers John West and John Doyle for encouraging my writing, and Sumner A Russman from Oklahoma, for encouraging my artistry. Thanks to Paul Power, Grainne Byrne, Maureen O'Mahoney, and Sheila Fahey for their support.

Several drawings are based on photos from the nineteenth century, any negative characteristics ascribed to designated characters is done with no intention to cause offense to the memory of the dead.

All characters and events in *Fastest Draw* are fictitious. Though *Six years with the Texas Rangers*, a memoir, contains a story about a gun being taken from a mulatto chef, by Buffalo Soldiers.

*The Federal Writers Project* mentions a story of Klan using false bellies to pour water into to scare freed slaves; the suggestion any Texas Rangers did this is from my imagination only. Other books I found useful include: *The Beleaguered City the Vicksburg Campaign* by Shelby Foote. *The Last Stand, Custar, Sitting Bull and the battle of the Little Big Horn.* By Nathaniel Philbrick. The stories about *The Christian Bear*, and *The Blind Cajun Horse* are not my own, their origins are unknown to me. I borrowed an insult from Frederick Douglass.

# ABOUT THE AUTHOR

GARY POWER was born in Ireland in 1971. He grew up in Dublin and now lives in Galway. He has lived and worked throughout the United States, and Latin America. The screenplay for *Fastest Draw*, his first novel, was recommended for the shortlist of the *Dublin International Film festival, DIFF*. An early draft of the novel came fifth in the *2013 American Gems Literary Contest*.

*Fastest Draw* is illustrated with drawings by the author.

Praise for the Screenplay: A joy to read, funny, original, vivid in its character, story and its sense of place and time. *DIFF*

Made in the USA
Monee, IL
12 April 2020